ONE SPIN ON THE MERRY-GO-ROUND

Seán Duignan

One Spin on the Merry-Go-Round

Seán Duignan

BLACKWATER PRESS

Editor
Susannah Gee

Design & Layout
Paula Byrne

ISBN
0 86121 732 2

© – Seán Duignan

Produced in Ireland by
Blackwater Press
c/o Folens Publishers
8 Broomhill Business Park
Tallaght, Dublin 24.

All rights reserved. No part of this publication may be reproduced, stored in a retrieval system, or transmitted in any form or by any means, electronic, mechanical, photocopying, recording, or otherwise, without the prior written permission of the publisher.

This book is sold subject to the conditions that it shall not, by way of trade or otherwise, be lent, re-sold, hired out or otherwise circulated without the Publishers' prior consent in any form of binding or cover other than that in which it is published and without a similar condition including this condition being imposed on the subsequent purchaser.

While considerable effort has been made to locate all holders of copyright photographs used in this text, we have failed to contact some of these. Should they wish to contact Blackwater Press, we will be glad to come to some arrangement.

For my wife Marie who tells me she is never wrong.

Contents

Preface ix

1. 'You'll be Sorreee' 1
2. 'Internment in Ireland for 14-Year-Old Girls' 10
3. 'Oh My God, I'm Heartily Sorry' 19
4. Flying Down To Rio 30
5. 'Don't Tell Me Lies . . . Don't Tell Lies On Me' 38
6. 'The Message is Albert is the Bad Guy' 49
7. 'Labour Will Strike a Hard Bargain' 57
8. 'Bingo — Eight Billion Smackeroos!' 67
9. 'All Bluster, Bluff and Booze' 77
10. 'Tonight Means the Beginning of the End of this Government' 85
11. 'The Hume–Adams Report Does Not Exist' 96
12. 'Tell the Pol Corrs I'm Vindicated' 107
13. 'You're Supposed to be My Pal, John Major' 118
14. 'The Priest Changes Everything' 129
15. 'Sinn Féin Will Pay a Price for Going to Capitol Hill' 136
16. 'The IRA Have Nowhere Else to Run' 144
17. 'I am President of the High Court, i.e. Goodbyeee' 153
18. 'I Am What I Am . . . A Risk Taker' 159
19. Bruton Finally Banjaxed. . . Bruton to be Taoiseach 167

Preface

The following is based on diaries, in addition to numerous notebooks, which I kept during almost three years working as Government Press Secretary under Taoiseach Albert Reynolds. It is not in any sense an attempt to record the history of the two Reynolds' administrations. It seeks merely to give an anecdotal flavour of what it was like 'inside the tent', particularly during crisis periods. The diary extracts are exactly as written, usually at high speed, complete with sometimes false premises, fallible predictions and what seemed like such good ideas at the time. The only changes, purely for identification/clarification purposes, are in parentheses. I am grateful to colleagues Ed Mulhall, Gerry Barry and Liam Kelly for suggested changes and improvements to the first draft.

1

'You'll be Sorreee'

IT BEGAN with Harry, and it ended with Harry. For such an amiable fellow, he attracts trouble like a lightning conductor draws electricity. But I liked him to the end. We first met on the day I presented myself for duty at the Department of An Taoiseach. 'I'm Harry Whelehan,' he beamed. 'They'll tell you this job gets easier . . . . it doesn't.'

Within 24 hours, I was watching him genially assuring Albert Reynolds that there had been no other choice but to take the course which forced a pregnant 14-year-old back home from Britain to prevent her having an abortion. 'You've got to think political, Harry,' Reynolds kept saying, almost pleadingly, to which his Attorney General patiently responded with what he insisted were the legal facts of life. 'There it is, I'm afraid, Taoiseach.' As Charlie McCreevy observed after the collapse of the Fianna Fáil–Labour government: 'Harry didn't have a political bone in his body.'

The last time I saw Harry before the end was on that ghastly November night at Áras an Uachtaráin when a glacial President Mary Robinson appointed him President of the High Court. As we dismally lined up prior to the ceremony, Justice Minister Máire Geoghegan Quinn swept across the ornate ante-chamber and confronted him: 'Harry Whelehan,' she said in a fierce stage whisper, 'I'm saying this to your face. When I'm out in the snow, on the election trail in Galway, and people on the doorsteps ask me "What about Harry Whelehan?" I'm going to reply "To hell with Harry Whelehan".'

In jest, of course — gallows humour, surely? — but one look at their faces disabused me of any such possibility. Not for the first time, I thought of my predecessor PJ Mara's sardonic warning when he heard I was to succeed him: 'Not for you, Diggy, oul' son. You should've stood with Anne Doyle. You'll be sorreee . . . .'

On Monday, 10 February, 1992 my home telephone rang. It was Tom Savage. 'How would you like to get off the picket line, Diggy?' My stomach turned over. I knew instinctively what was about to come, because I also knew Savage to be Reynolds' communications adviser.

I had been out on strike in an RTE dispute which coincided with the latest Fianna Fáil heave against the then Taoiseach Charles Haughey. In fact, Haughey had just been toppled by a faction promoting Reynolds who himself had earlier been fired by Haughey. Now, the so-called Longford Slasher, scything through the ranks of his erstwhile ministerial colleagues, was also demanding the head of their pal, PJ, and I was being made an offer I would find hard to refuse.

Only a few nights previously, I had been among a small group of PJ's friends who enjoyed an abandoned *buail amach* in the hallowed Constitution Room of the Shelbourne Hotel to mark his departure as Government Press Secretary. It had not remotely occurred to me that I might be his successor.

Looking back, I still wonder that I did it. It wasn't as if I was unaware of what it would involve. I had seen these fellows under pressure. More than a decade as RTE's 'pol corr' (political correspondent), operating in Leinster House with first-hand experience of the trials and tribulations of successive Government Press Secretaries, had left me with few illusions.

I had particular experience of the demands on such as Frank Dunlop, Peter Prendergast, Liam Hourican and, of course, the ineffable PJ. They all appeared to me to have wound up in a lousy job, working all the hours on the clock, as well as being endlessly on call. Mind you, PJ seemed able to combine business and pleasure, but then *ní fheicimid a leithéid aris.*

Apart from all of that, I liked working with presenters Anne Doyle and Eileen Dunne, and the rest of the *Six-One News* team. Despite the strike, I was a contented RTE employee. Above all, I realised it was not very bright of someone in his mid-fifties to switch to such a precarious occupation. Now, if I were ten years younger . . . .

In fact, I had been offered the job ten years earlier. Charlie Haughey, upon becoming Taoiseach, had sent for me to come to his office where he asked me to come aboard. I admired Haughey and was extremely flattered. However I was scared (quite sensibly in retrospect) apart from having been advised by the majority of my colleagues, most of them admittedly not admirers of Haughey, that I should take long steps in the opposite direction.

Haughey went on to appoint PJ to the job, a wise decision which yielded many mutual benefits apart from giving birth to the Boss/Mara legend of fond Dermot Morgan memory. Ever since, however, I had wondered whether I should have given it the proverbial lash at the time. Now, once more, the job was on offer. I knew I would never be asked again.

Will I . . . won't I? I was strongly influenced by my friend, Liam Kelly, who observed: 'What the hell. You get one spin on the merry-go-round. Go for it.' I suppose, too, curiosity had a lot to do with it. I felt I already had a reasonable insight into what makes politicians tick, not just in terms of public persona or how they handle the media, but also on how they conduct themselves when they lighten up, let down their defences and swop gossip and indiscreet tittle-tattle over a drink. All that I knew but was there more?

For example, how did they really operate away from back-slappers and begrudgers alike? How did they carry on in lodge when the political storm clouds gathered and the hard choices had to be made? Who were the tough guys, the panic merchants and the gutless wonders when the heat in the kitchen went over 90?

I recalled one of history's few 'fly on the wall' verifications of what it's actually like at the centre of power, the Watergate Tapes Exposé, the Mary Rose Woods tape-recordings of what went on in the White House in 1973 as President Richard Nixon desperately clung to office.

Trapped forever on these tapes is a hapless functionary who somehow managed to get through to the Oval Office where Nixon, Haldeman, Erlichman *et al* were agonising over their latest Watergate disaster. He burst upon the startled plotters with an apocalyptic pronouncement: 'Mr President, the lira has fallen'. To which, after a deadly pause, Nixon quite reasonably bellowed: 'I don't give a fuck about the lira'! *Alarums. Exeunt omnes.*

I knew in my bones it must be the same in every other inner sanctum when it hit the fan; outwardly, everybody composed, concerned, correct and caring; below the surface, a paroxysm (or paralysis) of paranoid panic. 'All the more reason,' said my wife Marie, 'to give the lot of them a wide berth.' Marie tells me she is never wrong.

I went (with Tom Savage) to meet Albert Reynolds in his attractively rambling apartment in Ballsbridge. On the way, it struck me that, apart from two or three interviews in the *Six-One* studio, we had only a few fleeting previous encounters. My first impression, reinforced on numerous subsequent occasions, was that the phones never stopped ringing and the teacups never stopped being re-filled. I also learned a valuable lesson.

As with a number of Taoisigh before him, Albert Reynolds was strongly influenced by the woman (in this case the women) in his life. True, he had valued *consiglieri* in sons Philip, MD of the family pet food business, and Albert Jnr ('Abbie'), a merchant banker in Chicago, but it was Kathleen Reynolds and her daughters; Miriam (although she lived in Scotland), Leone, Cathy, Emer and Andrea, who were the real political *famiglia*.

Later, when he was under attack for his injudicious 'There's women for you now . . . .' remark in the Dáil, I vainly tried to get across the extent to which he relied on these women for advice, and especially criticism, on almost every conceivable aspect of politics and government. 'What's the point,' he shrugged at the time: 'I'll never be politically correct. For example, if it's reported that I call them my real kitchen cabinet, the sisterhood will jump all over me. Forget it.'

In any event, at that first meeting, perhaps because of my West of Ireland upbringing, I liked what I saw, but then I have always been fatally attracted to the cavalier (buccaneer?) approach as against the uptight morally indignant tendency. True, Reynolds didn't drink — I forgave him that — but I found his breezy blend of small town mateyness and 'up she flew' optimism appealing. Here was one of my own western breed who made no apologies for his background or the kind of grafting he had to do to climb to the top. Keep 'er goin', Patsy, and fuck the begrudgers.

On that same day, I had read Fintan O'Toole in *The Irish Times* on Reynolds being chosen to lead Fianna Fáil: 'In doing so, Fianna Fáil is making a very big mistake. . . . When Mary Robinson said: "Come dance with me in Ireland" and the people accepted the invitation, knowing what would fill a ballroom on a wet Tuesday night in Rooskey was not part of the equation.'

As if reading my mind, Reynolds remarked that his opponents, including certain pointy-headed political analysts, would attack his rural upbringing, the 'ballroom of romance' basis of his success and his membership of what Charles Haughey had already dismissed as 'the country and western wing' of Fianna Fáil.

I immediately made the mistake of reminding him of his celebrated warbling of *Put Your Sweet Lips A Little Closer To The Phone*, complete with cowboy stetson, etc. on Mike Murphy's TV Show, adding ingratiatingly that it did him no harm at all. There was an uncomfortable silence and then Reynolds grated: 'It was awful.'

The common conversational ground was quickly established — anything pertaining to whatever was being published about whomever in politics — and it immediately emerged that Reynolds was at least as *au fait* as I was with the political aspects of the media 'game', also that he knew far more journalists on a one-to-one basis than the fellow he was offering to employ as press secretary.

I tentatively raised the sensation which had helped catapult him to power, the recent claim by former Justice Minister Sean Doherty that Charles Haughey knew far more than he had ever admitted about a 1982 scandal involving telephone taps placed on two leading political journalists, Geraldine Kennedy and Bruce Arnold. Indeed, after all those years, Doherty was now insisting that, as Justice Minister, he had actually kept then Taoiseach Haughey abreast of developments by regularly providing him with transcripts of the recorded conversations. Not even Charles Haughey could weather that. The man they couldn't hang had swung, and Albert Reynolds — Albertus Magnus to Sean Doherty, even as Ray Burke dubbed him Albert Anastasia — was crowned the new Boss.

Reynolds' response to my probing was terse. He was insistent that he had nothing to do with the Doherty revelations. He couldn't, he said, speak for others who might have opposed Haughey, but he had no prior inkling that Doherty was going to precipitate Charlie's downfall. Neither of us ever broached the subject again. The conversation ended with handshakes and murmurs of 'welcome aboard'. It dawned on me that, although I had never actually accepted the job offer, my presence in Albert Reynolds' living room was regarded as tantamount to sealing the deal.

I went home and discussed it with Marie who eventually shrugged and told me to make up my own mind. I sat thinking about it for another few minutes and then took the plunge. Scared that if I delayed further I might change my mind, I drew a deep breath, and like the Sundance Kid, took a tottering run at it and jumped. The shock when I hit the cold water was numbing.

On Monday, February 17, 1992 I began work. Edging up a marble staircase, I almost bumped into an official (Assistant Secretary, Wally

Kirwan, as it transpired) who apologised for having to rush away but, as he explained, there was a flap over something called the 'X' case. Unperturbed — bliss it was in that dawn to be alive and ignorant — I proceeded to the office of a woman who wiped the obsequious smile off my face. Fixing me with a ball-bearing stare, emphasising each word, she announced: "The Mara era is over!" She reminded me of Lotte Lenya in *From Russia With Love*. I glanced surreptitiously downwards to see if there might be a stiletto sticking out of the toe-cap of her boot.

'The Mara era is over,' she repeated. 'Your expenses will be kept strictly within new limits. There will be no return to the old system.' Well, fair play to you PJ. You must have led them a merry dance, only they were ready and waiting for the next poor hoor, i.e. raring to scare the bejasus out of poor Diggy. You will come to heel, imbecile, or feel the toe with the stiletto.

I went to meet the Secretary to the Department of An Taoiseach, the legendary Padraig O hUiginn, who studied me with wry amusement. When I mumbled that I wasn't sure whether I was up to the job, he off-handedly observed that being press secretary wasn't all that vital. And that, because I was by now in a blue funk, was the straw I clutched like a drowning man. Perhaps this press secretary thing might not, after all, be such a bad number.

O hUiginn, of course, was right — up to a point. I was not picked to be a 'player' in the administration; I would never attend cabinet discussions nor would I be classed an adviser to the Taoiseach. I remained content to relay his utterances to a ravenous media and try to counter their incessant pawing and gnawing at our version of events. God knows, that kept me busy enough without seeking to draw down additional hassle on my head. I therefore started out trying to operate broadly on the basis of what I perceived to be the O hUiginn analysis, as a kind of attendant lord, one who would do to swell a snap briefing, start a news conference or two but never presume to advise Prince Albert.

For the first week or so, I thought I was performing splendidly but then I got another phone call from Tom Savage. 'Look Diggy,' he began, 'Albert's a little worried about the way you're doing the job.' Suffering shit! 'Now, it's no big hassle,' hastened Tom, 'it's just that he doesn't hear from you enough.' 'But,' I protested, 'I'm at his beck and call whenever he wants me.' 'No, that's no good. You don't wait for Albert to call you. You call him.' 'But I can't be bothering Albert Reynolds without sufficient reason. I mean, he's a busy man. He's the Taoiseach, for jazesake.' 'Believe me, you won't be bothering him, Diggy. You've got to keep chasing him. You're his link to the outside world, or at least to the hacks, so he'll get very nervous if he doesn't see you around.'

Lesson number two. I had been long enough around politicians to appreciate the massive importance they attached to the media. However, it was not until I actually found myself inside the tent that I felt the full seismic force of this awesome phenomenon. The reality is that where politicians are concerned — not just Albert Reynolds but all politicians — the media is a constant all-consuming obsession. I begin keeping a diary:

18 February, 1992

> 'N.B. They're all media mad here. This obsession with everything to do with the media cannot be over-emphasised — repeat — cannot be over-emphasised!'

So, while peripheral at one level, I rapidly found myself being pushed towards the centre at another. It soon transpired that in the course of any given day I would spend at least as much time as any minister or adviser with Albert Reynolds. The job, as it developed, entailed ever increasing daily contact between Taoiseach and press secretary in a multiplicity of ways, whether directly or by telephone, whether in his office or mine — he developed a habit of dropping into my room when passing — and whether accompanying him on trips to Abbeyleix or Australia.

On that first day, I got a fresh insight into how the blood sport is played in the form of a Taoiseach's office description of the great chainsaw massacre as recounted to me by certain awed members of his new staff. I had seen all the media reports about how (on the eve of my arrival) Albert Reynolds fired or demoted more than half the existing Cabinet, including several who were household names — Gerry Collins, Michael O'Kennedy, Ray Burke, Mary O'Rourke, Rory O'Hanlon, Vincent Brady, Noel Davern, Brendan Daly — and how he then proceeded to get rid of another nine out of twelve serving junior Ministers, including such up-and-comers as Dermot Ahern and John O'Donoghue.

I was fascinated by how he went about it. Before leaving for Áras an Uachtaráin to receive his seal of office, he informed staff he wanted to see most of the above upon his return. He was reminded that by then he would have not much more than a half hour to spare before leading his new ministerial team into the Dáil. That, he assured everybody, would give him plenty of time.

Private Secretary, Donagh Morgan, conscious of the time element, reasoned that (whatever their fate) the Ministers would have to be dealt with *en bloc*, but some sixth sense told him to double check, so he went back into the Taoiseach's office. 'You'll see the Ministers all together then, Taoiseach?' 'Oh, no. One at a time, please.'

It was all over in less than a quarter of an hour. None of the victims was given much more than a minute. Only two argued the toss, Health Minister Mary O'Rourke and Chief Whip Dermot Ahern who demanded to know how he had transgressed to merit such a fate. 'You didn't,' said Reynolds. 'You just backed the wrong horse.'

I remember thinking at the time that those who live by the sword are liable to die by the sword. Now, having lived through the Reynolds era, I am convinced that he himself fully appreciated that, and even included it in his calculations.

Sean Duignan, Spindoctor

There are at least four entries in my diary detailing incidents of the Reynolds' 'death obsession'. This is typical:

October 1993

> 'He (Reynolds) was clearly pleased when I told him Des O'Malley was stepping down as PD leader. He said: "That's how it goes. O'Malley is gone. Someday, it'll be my turn. Sooner or later, it's your turn." I mumbled something about all of us strutting our brief hour, then shuffling off the stage, etc. "Without a backward glance, Diggy," he said, "without a backward glance." He's just saying that. He can't mean it.'

Subsequently, he talked briefly to me of the day of the short shrifts — 'a revolving office door would have come in useful' — and of how most of the sacked Ministers simply shrugged fatalistically when informed of their fate. A cruel trade. But he never told me the rationale behind the carnage, although he occasionally referred to the problems posed for his predecessor, CJ Haughey, when he retained arch rival George Colley as Tánaiste in his first cabinet, even after Colley publicly challenged his authority. Was that why he forebore to bind up the wounds, opting instead for a root and branch purge?

Early on, he told me: 'The main thing to remember about being in this job is that you're here to make decisions, and that involves taking risks. . . . You cannot get all the decisions right, but you'll have no hope at all if you try to play it safe, and duck taking them. . . . You've got to be prepared to take the responsibility and also, if you get it wrong, to take the consequences.' I was soon to learn that Albert Reynolds consistently played for high stakes, was prepared to back his hunch to the limit, and preferred to bet on the nose rather than each way. This made for a precarious existence; it left little margin for error, and, when the chips were down, no margin at all for the unexpected. Playing that system, you win big — or you lose big.

2

'INTERNMENT IN IRELAND FOR 14-YEAR-OLD GIRLS'

FROM DAY one, the rooftop helicopter pad was the only feature of Government Buildings I really fancied, apart from the drinks cabinet in my office. Admittedly, the restored baroque Edwardian pile with its great cobbled courtyard, grand ceremonial staircase, Evie Hone's stained glass *My Four Green Fields* gave graphic expression to Charles Haughey's monarchic vision.

I stood beside CJH during a ceremony in Canberra's megalithic Parliament Building in the late '80s when he enthused: 'This is a parliament building for the 21st Century. It takes vision and courage to spend money for posterity. You make up your mind, then you just go ahead and do it.'

However, it was the grey neo-Facist interior of the refurbished Merrion Street prefecture which I found off-putting, despite the relieving effect of ethnic artefacts strewn about the place. The great central corridor leading to the Taoiseach's office was almost a hundred yards long (Duce!) prompting McCreevy, trudging its length to be ticked off for some Social Welfare indiscretion or other, to describe it as 'the longest plank in the world'.

Ah, but the heliport! The media persisted on focusing on the government jet parked at Baldonnel, failing utterly to home in on the magic carpet which, if not under their noses, was no great distance above their heads.

Stately, plump Buck Taoiseach rises from his desk, saunters to the adjacent ascenseur, glides upwards to the dome pad (surrounded by army sharpshooters) before drifting with his dutiful press secretary out under the threshing blades to the bluebird that lifts them up, up and away above it all. From flying a desk to a dream machine, less than one minute. Even more rhapsodic is the return to base, skimming in low over the plains of Kildare and swirling dizzily down the Dublin roofscape before easing (to the strains of the Blue Danube?) onto the pad, thence to be instantly beamed back down to the Taoiseach's office. Next!

Mind you, as the bad days multiplied, the roof ritual brought Kafkaesque hallucinations. Sometimes I was a bodyguard anxiously scanning the skies as we shepherded Salvador Allende from his besieged presidential palace. More often, I was part of Nicolae Ceauçescu's doomed entourage lifting off as the tanks wheeled around the fountain in the courtyard below. Invariably, as last aboard, my job was to stamp on the fingers of any pesky underling trying to cling to the undercarriage. At the end of the day, of course, it didn't work out that way — not quite! — but that helipad (plus the booze cabinet) is still what I miss most of all.

Two secretaries awaited me in my new office. I later discovered that Sinead Sullivan and Jane Rock had me instantly sized up — not office trained — and were confident that, having looked after and coped with PJ, I was not going to present problems of any great moment. Professionally protective, they cosseted me through the next year. At the merest mention of expenses, they burst into the Department theme song: *The Mara Era Is Over*.

Then there was Bart. I had known Bart Cronin of Gneeveguilla, Co. Kerry, for many years, first as Aer Lingus press officer in the days when flying was still a source of wonderment, and latterly as press handler for a succession of Government departments. Over the next turbulent year, I came to trust and rely on him more than anyone else.

For a start, Bart was an experienced Reynolds man. They had worked closely together when Reynolds was Minister for Finance. Indeed, Bart was quite prepared to take the great man on when he thought it was for his own good — 'not that he pays much attention to me' — and, upon becoming Taoiseach, Reynolds sensibly appointed him Head of the Government Information Service.

Behind an artless homespun exterior — all North Kerry people are seriously brilliant and mad — lurked the most perceptive and compassionate of men. A fluent Irish speaker, Bart's vocabulary swung exhilaratingly between the poetic and the profane. He could write like an angel and swear like a beef boner. He was a good friend and a wise counsellor in the Merrion Street jungle.

21 February, 1992

> 'PJ told Albert he would work on for a few weeks — transition — to help ease me into the job. I was extremely relieved and thankful. Albert seemed agreeable, but later he made it clear to me he wants PJ gone as soon as possible. Clearly no love lost between that pair. What did they do to each other? These guys play rough.'

On that same day, PJ told me not to forget that, although there had been a change of Taoiseach, there had not been a change of government, i.e. that Fianna Fáil were still sharing power with the Progressive Democrats and that the Department also housed an Assistant Government Press Secretary, Stephen O'Byrnes of the PDs, who had an office on the ground floor.

There had been considerable tension between the two government parties prior to the Reynolds take-over, and everyone knew that strained relations between Charles Haughey and PD leader Desmond O'Malley had been exacerbated by sensational developments in the long-simmering controversy over extensive fraud in the beef industry. There had been allegations of massive government export credit insurance favouritism towards beef baron Larry Goodman — he and Haughey were accused of having close personal links — and the country was already in the throes of a marathon, not to say enormously costly, judicial inquiry into the scandal.

The problem was that Albert Reynolds, as former Minister for Industry and Commerce, was also implicated, and O'Malley had publicly condemned his role in the affair. Reynolds, for his part, spoke dismissively of O'Malley and the PDs, pointedly referring to the Fianna Fáil/PD coalition as a 'temporary little arrangement'.

Still, I decided, I had better make some gesture, if only via a courtesy phone call, to the man who was, after all, my PD opposite number. I was quickly disabused of that notion. Both PJ and Bart told me that, since the formation of the government, contact between the government press secretaries had — 'by mutual consent' — been kept to a minimum. So, rightly or wrongly, I stayed clear of O'Byrnes. Nor did he seek to contact me.

Reynolds did subsequently make one innocuous reference to O'Byrnes in my presence, but clearly wasn't concerned whether or not I established any kind of relationship with him. I had enough nous to realise this boded ill for the administration, and I was soon in agreement with Bart's description of Reynolds and O'Malley: 'Two wrestlers circling one another.'

I could see that Tom Savage was influential — did he push me for Press Secretary? — and he occupied the office closest to the Taoiseach's quarters. Their relationship was to grow markedly cooler after the traumatic November '92 general election campaign, and I felt the coolness was more on Savage's part than the Taoiseach's. True, the two did work closely together afterwards, notably on the final doomed attempt to surmount the Whelehan appointment fiasco, but I felt the old camaraderie was never fully restored.

Meantime, I was intensely curious about the more august denizens of the Department divided as they were between a crack cadre of civil servants — the top echelon occupied imposing offices down the length of the imperial corridor — and an indeterminate class comprised of so-called 'politicals' who ranged from hired advisers to what were loosely described as specialists.

At this time, several of the specialists seemed to be leading a mole-like existence in the gloomy basement. Mostly stragglers from the *ancien* Haughey *regime*, they were either trying to look inconspicuous or defiantly awaiting the inevitable. Among them was writer Anthony Cronin who, it was whispered, would now be surplus to requirements. I was somewhat shocked, as an admirer of Cronin's work, but two veteran Department officials — 'we counted them in and we counted them out' — offered to mark my card on what they maintained was par for the course.

'Look at it this way,' said one. 'You cannot put the purging of old guard appointees down simply to revenge; its the only way room can be made for the new lot.' At that time, they were too polite to mention that, sooner or later, the same fate awaited me. That changed after we got to know one another, when the message, albeit without malice, was: 'Yiz are all just passing through.'

Months later, in the wake of the disastrous November '92 general election, I huffily mentioned to the same duo that I could sense the entire Department staff take a collective step back from us as the bad election news flooded in. They merely laughed: 'So you noticed.'

Early on, I was told a certain tension existed between the Taoiseach and Padraig O hUiginn. As that view involved an appreciation of the status quo ante, I couldn't really gauge whether it was true or not. I did notice that O hUiginn was uncommonly formal and somewhat subdued in Reynolds' company.

Naturally, I was aware of the special relationship that had existed between Charles Haughey and O hUiginn. It was so close that when Garret FitzGerald came back to power in 1982, he effectively sidelined O hUiginn during his period in government. Then, when Haughey regained office in '87, O hUiginn smoothly resumed his role as the most powerful public servant in the land. Against that background, it was inevitable that the man who had ousted Haughey to become Taoiseach should now regard the incumbent Secretary of his Department with a certain caution. That seemed a pity to me as, like so many others, I had long ago succumbed to O hUiginn's irresistible blend of Cork ascendancy, urbanity and humour.

Of course, I needn't have bothered. O hUiginn, close to retirement, and the start of a whole new career, could afford to operate with a certain 'old dog for the hard road' insouciance. He might not any longer have the same open door to the Taoiseach's office, but he remained indispensable. Indeed, far from being sidelined, he was to have a key influence on Albert Reynolds' fortunes after the November general election.

Dermot Nally, Secretary to the Government, was also close to retirement. As monkish as O hUiginn was worldly, he was known to have been particularly rated by Garret FitzGerald. Highly respected within the Department, he was often praised to me as the public servant's public servant, i.e. the pro's pro. I came to admire Nally's closely argued if typically unemotional contributions in a succession of crisis situations. Therefore, I was not surprised when, upon his retirement, the Taoiseach persuaded him to play a vital behind the scenes role in the then embryonic peace initiative.

He rarely crossed my path after that, although I will not forget encountering him when literally on my way out the door on the day Albert Reynolds resigned as Taoiseach. He said nothing, just grasped my hand, then shook his head in the same reproving way as my old schoolmaster, and walked on.

Of all the luminaries surrounding Reynolds, the one I most wanted to meet was the notoriously reclusive Martin Mansergh who had always seemed to me a most unlikely Soldier of Destiny. A key adviser to Haughey on Northern Ireland, most observers felt that he too would be discarded by Albert Reynolds. But, in one of his most astute moves,

Reynolds decided that Mansergh remained essential to the Northern Ireland game plan.

Fianna Fáil positively delighted in their very own Protestant Republican complete with distinguished Anglo–Irish pedigree and Oxford honours. They might joke about him being a cross between Dr Strangelove and Dr Mengele — 'Mansergh pronounced as in panzer' — but they would brook no criticism of him by outsiders. Reynolds shared this enthusiasm, clearly regarding Mansergh as his most valuable adviser. I soon noticed that, although they might not always see eye to eye on issues such as the economy or whatever, they seemed to think almost as one on Northern Ireland.

Initially, Mansergh kept his distance but I continued working on him and he eventually came around. As with so many savants, he was almost painfully shy at one level and brutally candid at another, but, once he trusted you, he could be extraordinarily forthcoming.

Two things struck me about him over the next two and half years. Although cast primarily as a theorist, he was also one of the most practical persons I ever met. Whatever the problem or calamity, he never wasted time bemoaning fate or seeking to apportion blame. Instead, he would immediately set about identifying counter measures to try to nullify the setback or, if possible, actually turn it to advantage.

Secondly, he was every whit as republican as portrayed by admirers and critics alike, although his insistence that he was unalterably constitutional made not a whit of difference to his detractors. They still painted him as a kind of Provisional IRA pawn. I remember him on one occasion lucidly, and without a trace of bitterness — he might have been talking of someone else — explaining to me how that reasoning was fundamentally erroneous.

An interesting aspect of his ultimate vindication was that, after the fall of Albert Reynolds, Taoiseach-designate John Bruton sought to persuade him to cross the political divide in order to act as his adviser on the North. They had a lengthy and fruitful discussion on the offer but Mansergh, after briefing the FG leader at length on the peace process, finally declined. As I observed at the time, he was not *that* constitutional.

As a lot of my time was spent in the Taoiseach's outer office, awaiting the pleasure of the all powerful one, much of it passed in the company of private secretaries (a generic term as I never could differentiate between their grades) such as Donagh Morgan, Colm Butler, Brenda Boylan and Declan Ingoldsby who was related to Eithne Fitzgerald.

I knew they were hand-picked for their intelligence, diligence, etc., but they were still game for a laugh, perhaps because, God knows, if you didn't at least occasionally see the funny side, you'd burst out crying. In fact, had Morgan not been obviously destined for a distinguished public service career — he headed the powerful and controversial Programme Managers during the Reynolds era — he would have given his cousin, Dermot Morgan, a fair show biz run as an impersonator. He helped keep me sane (and still able to laugh) through some extremely hairy episodes.

I soon observed that the inner political circle was headed by Padraig Flynn, Charlie McCreevy, Michael Smith and Máire Geoghegan Quinn. Other Reynolds parliamentary party intimates were Sean Fallon, Brian Cowen, Noel Dempsey, Noel Treacy, Joe Jacob and Eddie Bohan. These formed the nucleus of the Fianna Fáil 'country and western alliance' which powered the Reynolds engine. But the group dynamic was generated by one person, Albert Reynolds. There was no brains trust, kitchen cabinet or team of national handlers *per se*. Neither was there any eminence grise who could be certain to influence Reynolds thinking on issues as they arose. Not even Mansergh could claim that role.

Padraig ('Pee') Flynn was the nearest to such a mentor. Once one of Charles Haughey's most trusted lieutenants, he had dramatically switched loyalty to Albert Reynolds and been unceremoniously dispatched to the backbenches by Haughey for his pains. Now, as he put it himself, he was 'mighty' again, and he knew exactly what he wanted for his reward.

At the time of his *volte face*, I interviewed Flynn on *Six-One News* asking: 'How could you have done that to Charles Haughey?' He left me none the wiser, but I was later told he had been decisively influenced by a close adviser who warned him that he would never be leader of Fianna Fáil, and that it was time to align himself with whomever he considered the likely successor to Haughey.

Whatever the true story, Flynn enjoyed practically unlimited access to Albert Reynolds, regularly lunching alone with him in the Taoiseach's private dining room. I believe his subsequent departure for Europe removed the one member of the cabinet who might have defused the Whelehan affair. Having said that, I witnessed Reynolds rejecting his advice on at least one other vital issue.

'INTERNMENT IN IRELAND FOR 14-YEAR-OLD GIRLS'

Flynn and Geoghegan Quinn, the two West of Ireland ministers, were close both politically and temperamentally. They shared the services of media consultant Terry Prone (married to Tom Savage) who exerted a near hypnotic influence on Flynn, in particular. The problem was that Flynn and Geoghegan Quinn also shared the same objective — an EU Commissionership of which there was only one on offer — and 'Pee' was always going to get the Reynolds nod on that when it came to the crunch.

Geoghegan Quinn, in my view, was ahead of her time in Fianna Fáil. She manifestly had more ability than many of her colleagues. She enjoyed the backing of Reynolds who freely acknowledged that she was among the foremost of those who had risked their careers for him. But she also signally failed to build her own independent power base in the parliamentary party.

Whether this was because Fianna Fáil is irredeemably misogynist or because Geoghegan Quinn was too domineering or aloof for most backbenchers has generated considerable debate. There are still those close to Reynolds who believe that, had he survived a few more years as Taoiseach, she would then have been well positioned for the succession. But timing is everything in politics, and the departure of Reynolds came at a particularly inauspicious moment for the redoubtable Galway woman.

As for McCreevy, it was immediately apparent that Reynolds, the non–drinking, non–smoking, churchgoing conservative, had a soft spot for the Kildare swashbuckler. As Margaret Thatcher had a weakness for goatish Tories of the Cecil Parkinson variety, Reynolds found it hard to resist McCreevy's cheeky combination of charm, acuity and unpredictability, particularly since the Reynolds clan were also big fans. That notwithstanding, he still regarded McCreevy's 'right wing' tendencies with his Social Welfare portfolio as politically (whatever about fiscally) incorrect.

There was Michael Smith whom Reynolds liked, but also saw as a bit of a loose cannon. In the early days, I found Smith prickly — he may not have trusted me — but he then went out of his way to be pleasant when things were finally falling apart. David Andrews — the acceptable face of Fianna Fáil — could do no wrong with his oddly attractive blend of hauteur and self-effacement; Brian Cowen, alternately bantering and belligerent, was adored by Reynolds who spoke of him as 'a future leader of Fianna Fáil'; Michael Woods, earnest and conscientious, couldn't wait to get Social Welfare back out of McCreevy's clutches.

And, then, there was Bertie. I never did figure out the true nature of the relationship between Ahern and Reynolds. On the surface, the northside 'Dub' and the Longford leader seemed reasonably at ease with each other. But Bertie never held (and I believe never sought) membership of the inner circle. There was a certain 'them and us' tension between the Reynolds camp and what was known as the Bertie Set around whom many of the Haugheyite 'dispossessed' had regrouped. Neither side had forgotten that Ahern had been publicly prepared to challenge Albert for the FF leadership before belatedly backing off. And thereby hung a hotly disputed tale.

While Ahern's hat was still in the ring, according to his close associates, Reynolds activists launched a 'dirty tricks' manoeuvre aimed at exploiting the fact that Bertie and his wife Miriam had separated, and that he had entered into another relationship. One newspaper quoted Reynolds as having said something to the effect that the people wanted to know where the Taoiseach lived. Subsequently, Reynolds repeatedly maintained to me that he had never said that — he named a cabinet colleague as the culprit — but the incident clearly rankled and was not forgotten. Reynolds, for his part, talked darkly of his FF enemies trying to spy on him from a white Hiace van over the same period. Personally, I have no reason to believe that Ahern acted other than impeccably throughout Reynolds' period in power.

Meantime, Reynolds had started out with the doubtful distinction of being the first Taoiseach ever to be confronted with a major breaking crisis on his first day in office. My own arrival in the Department, on the following day (17 Feb.) had coincided with a High Court judgment upholding Harry Whelehan's move to prevent the young rape victim — known only as 'X' because of her tender years — from travelling to England for an abortion.

Forty-eight hours later, a glance at the front page of *The Irish Times* brought home the enormity of what was involved. A Martyn Turner cartoon showed a map of Ireland with a little girl clutching a teddy bear standing in the centre of the Republic which was ringed with barbed wire. The caption read: '17th February, 1992. The introduction of internment in Ireland. . . for 14-year-old girls.'

3

'OH MY GOD, I'M HEARTILY SORRY'

Article 40.3.3:

> 'The State acknowledges the right to
> life of the unborn and, with due regard to the equal
> right to life of the mother, guarantees in its laws to
> respect, and, as far as practicable, by its laws to
> defend and vindicate that right.'

IN SEPTEMBER 1983, after a bitterly divisive referendum campaign, the Republic's electorate — by a 2 to 1 majority — approved the above amendment to the nation's Constitution.

The government of the day pressed the referendum despite the fact that abortion was already illegal in the state, that the vast majority of the people were totally opposed to abortion, and that there was no likelihood that it would be introduced in the foreseeable future. Of course, hundreds of Irish women still made their way to Britain each year for abortions, so the 'X' case girl was merely one more in a dismal procession. And, but for Harry, she would have become just another statistic under the prevailing nod and wink system.

The trouble with Harry was that he refused to go along with the system. He saw his job, as he later told me, as briefing the government on legal realities irrespective of political implications or consequences, and that he had a constitutional role independent of government. So, when presented with the 'X' problem, as with any other case, he operated by the book.

The politicians, whether in government or opposition, could not understand Harr y taking this view, because when it comes right down to it, Irish politicians of whatever stripe, including the great moralisers, approach these kind of issues in enthusiastic conformity with Charles Haughey's much derided dictum that there are Irish solutions to Irish problems. So, on both sides of the House, they muttered that Harry and his people should have sought advice, i.e. deferred action until it was too late — 'let the file fall behind a radiator' — or at least dawdled until the deed was done, so as to keep them out of the whole embarrassing mess, while the young rape victim underwent an abortion somewhere outside the jurisdiction.

24 February, 1992

> 'Nobody wild about Harry around here. Practically every member of Dáil Éireann is castigating him for not having turned a blind eye. They won't admit it publicly, but that's what they mutter in corners. That is how they want the chief law officer of the State to operate, but not one of them will openly admit it.'

Initially, the problem was passed around. The girl's parents had reported to the Gardaí that she had been violated and that they were bringing her to England for an abortion. The Gardaí decided, in light of Article 40.3.3., that they had a duty to tell Eamon Barnes, the Director of Public Prosecutions. He, by the same token, felt obliged to convey this information to Harry who, in turn, might have been expected to pass it onto say Justice Minister Flynn. But Harry, wearing his independent hat, decided it was time for action. So he proceeded — without telling anyone in government as far as I could ascertain — to seek and obtain an interim High Court injunction to prevent the abortion, whereupon the girl and her parents compliantly returned home from England, mission unaccomplished.

The High Court then confirmed that, not only would the parents and child be prevented from procuring an abortion at home or abroad, but that they should be additionally restrained from leaving the jurisdiction for a period of nine months. I noted:

> 'They're all pointing the finger at Harry. Calling him a right wing Catholic and *Opus Dei* type. But he tells me he is not *Opus Dei* and I believe him. He just seems to me to be the kind of guy who calls it as he sees it in strict legal terms, i.e. a dangerous man. A guy like that can cause all kinds of mayhem. You gotta think political, Harry.'

The family appealed to the Supreme Court — the girl was threatening suicide — and the outcome was that Article 40.3.3., the Eighth Amendment to the Constitution, the object of which was to make abortion an absolute impossibility in the State, was sensationally revealed to be a possible conduit for its introduction. The Supreme Court decided, by a majority of four judges to one, that 40.3.3. actually allowed for abortion where there was a substantial risk to the life of the mother (this in apparent reference to the 'X' suicide threat) and lifted the injunction, despite adjudging that there was no absolute right to travel or to abortion information.

26 February, 1992: London

> 'Supreme Court decision phoned to me in motorcade on way into London. I phone Taoiseach in leading car with the news. We discuss it car-to-car speeding towards No. 10. Albert says something to the effect that this puts us right up to our necks in it, also that it means we'll now be attacked on all fronts.'

Another spectre was rearing its head. The previous Haughey-led FF/PD team had persuaded Ireland's EU partners to agree to the insertion of what amounted to an anti-abortion protocol in the terms of the vital Maastricht treaty, soon to be voted upon by the peoples of a number of EU member states, including Ireland. The intention was to make it a hundred percent certain that abortion could never be introduced into the State by framing the protocol in such a way as to provide additional protection against any future EU law. And so the wording specified that nothing in the Maastricht treaty should affect the application in Ireland of 40.3.3. To be sure to be sure!

Only now, given the Supreme Court findings, the protocol could actually facilitate the introduction of abortion to Ireland while simultaneously restricting Irish citizens' right to travel and information. And the nightmare was that this dual potential could also result in uniting both conservatives and liberals, for diametrically opposing reasons, to vote against the Maastricht Treaty.

Now what? Obviously, the protocol itself would have to be amended — embarrassing but, as Harry might say, "there it is" — so they came up with an *addendum* ordaining that the protocol could not limit travel between EU member states or the obtaining of information lawfully available in member states. With sighs of relief all round, this inspired saving formula was then submitted for approval to the EU Council of Ministers. And they, after due consideration, decided that the Irish could go and take a running jump for themselves. Our EU partners had finally had enough. Their answer was a resounding 'No!' 'Jesus, Harry, what have we been walked into?' moaned Noel Treacy.

From day one, Albert Reynolds took the brunt. He had carefully defined the agenda for his term as Taoiseach — 'Northern Ireland and the Economy' — and here we were already 'going down the fallopian tubes' like all the other politicians who had ever been sucked into the Irish abortion quagmire. Reynolds shook his head in bewilderment: 'What did I do to deserve this on my first day?'

To make matters worse, others were only too eager to get in on the act — clerics, doctors, lawyers, journalists, patriarchs, matriarchs, feminists, chauvinists, pro-lifers, right to choosers, pietists, chancers and what seemed like half the outside world.

'This barbarous law has taken Ireland back to the Dark Ages,' fumed Senator Chris Schacht on the floor of the Upper House in Canberra. France's Liberation maintained it put a question mark over Ireland's membership of the EU. A Dutch foreign office spokesman said they would be making a formal protest to Dublin. A Catholic newspaper in Belgium described Ireland as 'ultra conservative and priest-ridden'. In Germany, the *Frankfurter Rundsheau* summed up: 'This is no event from the previous century, or from the Romania of Nicolae Ceauçescu, or the Iran of the Ayatollahs. No, it is much worse. This unbelievable story comes from the EC–member Ireland in the year 1992.'

At home, *The Irish Times* concurred: 'What has been done to this Irish Republic? What kind of State has it become that in 1992, its full panoply of authority, its police, its law officers, its courts are mobilised to condemn a 14-year-old girl to the ordeal of pregnancy and childbirth after rape at the hands of a "depraved and evil man"? With what are we now to compare ourselves? Ceauçescu's Romania? The Ayatollahs' Iran? Algeria? There are similarities.'

Later, I was trying to slough off this image in a briefing session with James Clarity of the *The New York Times* when news broke of thousands of copies of *The Guardian* (of all newspapers!) being seized by Gardaí at Dublin Airport on the basis that it contained an abortion services advertisement. 'We're on a hiding to nothing Taoiseach,' I wailed. 'What am I going to say?' 'Say it as it is, that it's a damned set up,' he growled.

He was right, but that didn't help. The newspaper distributors, Easons, had been 'informed' in advance that a full-page abortion advertisement was going to appear. They decided, on legal advice, not to distribute the newspaper. A spokesman said: 'The law of the land, as it stands at the moment, is that there is a prohibition on the dissemination of abortion information.'

Before that, I had walked into the Taoiseach's office and then hurriedly retreated when I saw he was getting an abortion lecture from one Sinead O'Connor who had been ushered in by PJ. She emerged expressing satisfaction with what she had been told (more sighs of relief) but that only brought the wrath of a divided sisterhood down on our heads. Why should she ('we can't all be pop stars') be received by the Taoiseach on ('of all issues') abortion?

On the Maastricht protocol foul up, a stopgap called a Solemn Declaration was cobbled together in Brussels to compensate for the refusal to accept the Irish *addendum*. The text, in somewhat flowerier language, gave exactly the same travel and information assurances as contained in the *addendum*. The difference, however, was that the Declaration was purely aspirational. It could have no more than persuasive influence as distinct from the force of law. 'Words written on water,' observed the Bishop of Meath, Dr Michael Smith.

The enthusiasts kept coming at us from all angles, within as well as without government. The opposition parties provided the least difficulty, only occasionally seeking to exploit the government's predicament, although Dick Spring went so far as to leave Labour support for Maastricht in doubt until uncomfortably close to the 18 June referendum day.

Within the coalition, however, there was unconcealable friction. The PDs publicly took issue with practically every proposal put forward by Albert Reynolds for dealing with the problem. On one particular point, Reynolds' insistence that the Maastricht referendum be held before a vote on freedom of travel and information, Des O'Malley fought tooth and nail to have them taken in the opposite order. He enjoyed practically total media backing and, indeed, I talked to senior FF figures, including Minister of State, Seamus Brennan, and Chief Whip, Noel Dempsey, who thought his argument had some validity. It culminated in an 'eyeball to eyeball' cabinet confrontation with the Taoiseach effectively putting it to the PDs that they could like it or lump it, and that if it were to bring down the coalition, so be it. I wrote:

> 'Albert's bottom line seems to be "pull the rug, if you don't like it!" which is one helluva way to win your point in coalition.'

O'Malley ultimately blinked but signalled it might be different in other circumstances: 'We are the minority party in government. I cannot achieve everything in my career and my life, I would wish. It was not open to us now.' I thought it ominous too that Mary Harney said afterwards that the abortion row would not bring down the government.

She seemed to be insinuating that the break-up was on it's way, but on a different issue. *Beidh lá eile ag an bPaorach.*

'The PDs don't like it, Taoiseach', I ventured. 'Is that a fact?' he snapped. 'They don't have to like it, just so long as they go along with it.' *Beidh lá eile. . . ?*

Within Fianna Fáil, the opposition to the Reynolds formula was limited but equally passionate, though patently orchestrated by already alienated critics of Reynolds. The doughty chairman of the Pro-Life campaign, Senator Des Hanafin, veteran of many an anti-abortion campaign, marshalled party conservatives in a well organised rearguard action against concessions on abortion under any circumstances. Hanafin began by demanding another referendum to change 40.3.3. — this time we'll get it right! — tapping into a populist vein which had even Michael Smith going on about 'rolling back' the Supreme Court decision.

Hanafin also supported the push for a pre-Maastricht abortion referendum. He began picking up hit-and-run support from ministerial victims of the February purge including Gerry Collins, Michael O'Kennedy, Rory O'Hanlon, Vincent Brady, John O'Donoghue, Dermot Ahern, Michael J. Noonan, Sean Calleary, Michael Kitt and Terry Leyden. Other FFers offering supplementary assistance were Eamon O Cuiv, Mary Wallace, Seamus Cullimore, John O'Leary, Denis Lyons, Colm Hilliard, Tom McEllistrim and Don Lydon who maintained the Supreme Court had 'spat in the face of Christ'.

Finally, after Hanafin was cleverly manoeuvred by the opposition into voting against the Maastricht referendum bill in the Upper House, Reynolds went for his head. A parliamentary party motion to have the FF whip removed from him was overwhelmingly carried, although nine deputies abstained when Hanafin persuasively pleaded extenuating 'conscience' circumstances.

I asked the Taoiseach if he had considered allowing a free parliamentary vote on 'conscience' issues. He dismissed this as naive; a governing party's duty was to govern, not to equivocate, prevaricate, proscrastinate or, God forbid, capitulate. It was not the first or last time I listened to the Reynolds philosophy on the responsibility of power: 'Decisions, decisions, decisions and, hopefully, you get the majority of them right. The government governs.'

Meantime, the bishops were starting to impact with a concerted 'shove' which would culminate in a row with Reynolds at the same time as the combined 'progressive' forces, encouraged by the liberal media, were pouring scorn on practically every effort he made to secure a compromise.

The formidable Bishop of Limerick, Dr Jeremiah Newman, was first to the pulpit. Describing the Supreme Court judgment as 'abysmal', he accused politicians of twisting the issue in order to fool the people of Ireland. The Bishop of Clogher, Dr Joseph Duffy, warned the politicians to 'return the law to the way it was' before the Supreme Court judges handed down their verdict. The final straw, however, came on 14 April when the Catholic Bishops' Conference announced that they had noted with alarm that the right to life of the unborn 'does not appear to be on the Government's agenda at the present time'.

'Who the hell do they think they are?' erupted the Taoiseach. He began telephoning a number of churchmen including Bishop Brendan Comiskey and Bishop Joe Cassidy (for all I know, he may also have phoned Cardinal Cahal Daly) expressing his outrage. He particularly berated them for what he described as totally uninformed, not to say, grossly irresponsible language on such an explosive issue. Their responses were defensive and essentially placatory. It seemed several of their Lordships had not been present when the statement was drafted. It was, they now agreed, somewhat over the top. 'Well,' retorted Reynolds, 'I'm just not going to stand for it.' I remember thinking: 'You've met your Catholic match here, boys.' I had already been made sharply aware that, in the finest tradition of certain Taoisigh before him, Reynolds boasted an impeccable devotional track record. Garret FitzGerald might specialise in memorising chunks of world aviation timetables but Albert Reynolds kept a spiritual spot check on the times of Masses in churches throughout the country. Down in Rio, some weeks later, he actually delayed the start of a private Mass for ten minutes — after the priest had come onto the altar — while minders scoured the neighbourhood bars for his errant press secretary. A hitherto unsympathetic media rowed in behind the Taoiseach. Editorial sniping at Reynolds was one thing but belting him over the head with croziers, with the abortion baby in his arms, was dastardly. 'A direct smear,' thundered *The Irish Times*. 'From the wilder shores of SPUC or certain of its affiliates the charge might not be surprising. But from the bishops, who certainly know better, it is more than unworthy. It is calumnious.'

Calumnious, no less — the prayer wheels had turned full circle — and sure enough, a fortnight later, the Bishop of Galway, Dr Eamonn Casey, the hierarchy's most charismatic figure, resigned in disgrace. He bowed out after being forced to admit he had a lengthy affair with American Annie Murphy; he also acknowledged that he was the father of her son, Peter, and confirmed that he used more than £70,000 of Galway diocesan funds in payment to Ms Murphy. Reynolds was fascinated. 'Would you believe it, 'he marvelled, 'not so much that this kind of thing goes on, but that it's all coming out now.' 'That,' quoth McCreevy, more appositely, 'will soften their cough.'

It certainly seemed to have an at least temporarily arresting effect on the episcopal Princes of Maynooth. A week later, they issued a statement which we hailed straightfaced as 'a welcome recognition of the practical difficulties and complexities of the situation'. In other words, why couldn't you have said that from the beginning?

The bishops now publicly accepted that ratification of Maastricht did not equate with the introduction of abortion. Anti-abortionists need not fear casting a 'Yes' vote on Maastricht. There would be another day for referendums, including one on the substantive abortion issue, but not right now. *Ní h-é lá na gaoithe lá na scolb.*

It wasn't all plain sailing. The President of the Law Reform Commission, High Court Judge Rory O'Hanlon, an ardent supporter of the Pro-Life campaign, also a member of *Opus Dei*, announced he would favour abandoning Ireland's membership of the EU rather than have abortion introduced here. He was immediately summoned to meet with the Taoiseach and Harry. I waited outside and when O'Hanlon left, the Taoiseach said: 'Well, he now knows the score.'

It transpired that Reynolds had told the learned judge to go away and think about whether he wanted to keep out of such matters or step down from the Law Reform Commission. Mr Justice O'Hanlon duly thought about it and responded that he could not give an undertaking to stay out of the controversy. He was asked to tender his resignation from the Commission and declined to do so. He was then dismissed by the cabinet — he significantly remained a High Court Judge — and left the building warning: 'The people are behind me.'

For a time, it looked as if John Bruton might also be behind him. He criticised the sacking on the basis that it was inconsistent with the government's failure to deal with the chairman of Bord na Gaeilge, Proinsias Mac Aonghusa, who had earlier called on the voters of West Belfast to vote for Sinn Féin leader, Gerry Adams, in the British general election — that was still a sin then — but the FG leader eventually decided not to pursue that matter.

I stupidly became embroiled in an attempt to 'powerfully concentrate' the public mind on the issue. I let it be known that Harry had advised the government that, if Maastricht was approved in the referendum, his interpretation of the attached Solemn Declaration was that the Irish people would thereby have voted in favour of the right to travel. The Taoiseach then confirmed to an imposing Dublin Castle launch of the White Paper on Maastricht that, once the referendum was passed, Harry would not seek further court injunctions to stop women travelling abroad for abortions.

But, afterwards in the Dáil, he was questioned by John Bruton on the corollary — what if the people voted '**No**'? Then, said the Taoiseach, there would be a return to State injunctions against women seeking abortions abroad.

Gotcha! Infuriated liberals raged that Reynolds finally stood exposed, trying to terrorise the people — particularly the women of Ireland — into voting for Maastricht. 'You might not like to hear that,' he told shouting opposition TDs, 'but it is the reality.'

There you go again, Albert! They were moving in for the kill. What of his famous promise, when the 'X' case broke, that he 'would never preside over a police state'? I insisted to the pol corrs that this remained his position, that there was no contradiction, because the European Court of Justice would undoubtedly vindicate the right to travel and information, and we were only pointing out the technical constitutional reality. The editorial writers and analysts understandably remained unconvinced.

Earlier, I compounded the problem by pointing out to Maol Muire Tynan of *The Irish Times* that the 12 member states of the EU had until 31 December to ratify the treaty, so that even if the June referendum were defeated, there would be sufficient time to hold another referendum before the end of the year. Once more into the ordure. So, the *Irish Independent* demanded, does that mean people can contemplate voting 'No' in June on the basis that, if needs be, they can always change their minds anytime before the end of December? The Taoiseach stared at me: 'You're a real big help, Diggy.'

I was still mopping my brow when I arrived late for lunch with Jim Downey of the *Irish Independent*. Sometime into the second bottle of wine, regaling him with my latest misadventure, I delivered myself of another inspired *bon mot*. It was essential that the electorate be made aware of the dire national consequences of a '**No**' vote on Maastricht.

'How are you going to do that?' asked Downey. 'No problem,' I responded, 'we'll just strike terror into the hearts of the Irish people, won't we?' Downey, not surprisingly in retrospect, printed that.

'What the hell are you trying to do to me?' gasped the Taoiseach incredulously. 'Oh my God, I'm heartily sorry.' I mumbled something about joking, being off the record, quoted out of context, blah blah blah. But his look said it all — in this holy bloody mess, Diggy, I need a comedian for a press secretary like a hole in the head.

1 May

> 'Loose lips sink ships. I have a BIG mouth. It will be the death of me yet. *Binn béal ina thost. . . bí fucking curamach!!!'*

The Taoiseach tried what I called the Jack Charlton approach, i.e. this is the way it is because I say so, and if you don't like it, you can stuff it. Reynolds told the political correspondents he wasn't going to follow any more 'hares or red herrings'. In particular, he and the government would henceforth campaign only on the political, economic and social issues of Maastricht. No more abortion nonsense.

Unfortunately, most media people reacted by saying this showed the pressure was getting to Reynolds and that he ought to 'catch himself on'. When I told him this, he said: 'They'll see that I'm right. The people won't let abortion get muddled up with Maastricht. The Irish keep their money and their morals separate. They know precisely where their bread is buttered. Mark my words.'

The Progressive Democrats kept the pot boiling by publishing their 'alternative' wording on the right to travel and information which Reynolds regarded as tantamount to an attempt to sabotage Maastricht. I was fast becoming used to mutual FF/PD detestation.

On 2 June, the Danes dumped on Maastricht. Despite warnings of dire consequences for the Danish economy, they voted by 50 percent to 49 percent to reject the treaty. There was instant lamentation: do something Albert!

Throughout the day, he sat listening to arguments mainly favouring postponement of the 18 June plebiscite — Dick Spring was strongly of that view — as well as panic calls from Jacques Delors *et al* in Brussels.

Finally, just before midnight, he said to me: 'Tell the pol corrs it's still the 18th — full steam ahead.'

The Irish Times warned: 'The Danish referendum result is certain to give a great fillip to the anti-Maastricht campaign in Ireland in the run-up to the referendum.' 'Wrong', insisted Reynolds. 'The Danes may feel they can do this and get along fine. But we Irish know in our gut we cannot afford such a gesture. This simply means there will be an even bigger majority in favour. Let's go to Brazil.'

Sure enough, by the time we got back from the Earth Summit in Rio de Janiero three days before the referendum, the opinion polls showed that the electorate had recovered their nerve and that the national mind was now firmly focused. The vote was almost a formality — **Yes** 69 percent; **No** 31 percent — and Reynolds broke out the Dom Perignon as word came in from Jacques Delors of how grateful he was and how this was the 'happiest day' of his Presidency. Reynolds raised his (water) glass and said pointedly: 'Jacques will get every chance to show how grateful he is.'

He had just confirmed that a referendum on travel and abortion information would go ahead in the autumn, and Pro-Life activists were already claiming that, with Maastricht no longer a complicating factor, the voters would then put the government firmly in its place.

As we celebrated, a 42-year-old man was waiting to appear in Dublin District Court charged with unlawful carnal knowledge of the 'X' girl — I was told she had been quietly brought back to England for an abortion — yet a Kilkenny rapist had walked free after being given a good character reference during his arraignment. Womens' groups' expressions of horror and disbelief at this latest development were being perfunctorily acknowledged when the young woman involved suddenly transformed the situation.

Nineteen-year-old Lavinia Kerwick, refusing to remain within the traditional female victim's closet of anonymity, publicly vented her pain and outrage to such effect that thousands took to the streets on the basis that women in Ireland had enough of mutely enduring such savagery and now they were going to fight back — out in the open. Still, I complacently raised my glass to Noel Dempsey: 'Well, we're out of the woods. Dempsey said drily: 'Tell that to Dessie O'Malley.'

4

FLYING DOWN TO RIO

ALBERT REYNOLDS liked smoking, sweets, soft drinks, etc., all of which he had to forego when diagnosed as diabetic. That still left other enthusiasms such as travel and warm climes. 'You'll like Rio, Diggy,' he said. 'Wait until you see Copacabana Beach.'

The government Gulf Stream jet is comfortable but hardly splendiferous unless by the technical performance yardstick of its superb Air Corps crews. On long trips I spent most of the time up front with Reynolds swapping the latest gossip and trying to get him to reminisce on his old freewheeling dance hall days. He was a good storyteller, with apparently total recall, and some picaresque capers to relate.

4 June, 1992: Rio de Janeiro

> 'Never before such a gathering of world leaders in the one location. Albert strolled in amongst 120 of them for the official Earth Summit photograph this morning. A certain bearded one in olive uniform, with his country reportedly in economic free fall, dominated the whole thing. Beside Fidel Castro, they all (including George Bush) looked puny. *La historia me absolvera . . . !*'

It was in this setting that I first noticed a Reynolds characteristic which regularly manifested itself on such occasions. He approached even the most august world statesmen with a total lack of self consciousness. At one EU summit, I mentioned this to him, and he seemed puzzled: 'Talk to them, and they're all just trying to stay ahead of the posse. For example, they told me Mitterand doesn't speak English. When he wants something, he sure as hell does . . . at least to me.'

I made a point of observing him in such situations. Whether with Mitterand, Clinton, Keating, Kohl, Major, Gonzalez, Delors or whomever, he was relaxed — alert, interested, sometimes fascinated — but always relaxed. At EU level, he instinctively struck the right balance between affability and persuasiveness. We would joke about his style — 'I told Jacques to say to Helmut he'd need to be careful with yer man

Felipe' — but it was totally unfeigned. And this approach was to make a significant impression on the two leaders he had in his sights from the moment he became Taoiseach — John Major and Bill Clinton.

Back home, I could see there was more to existence than just Maastricht and the 'X' case. EU Agriculture Commissioner, Ray McSharry, whose term was due to expire at year's end, had everybody (not least Reynolds, Geoghegan Quinn and Flynn) guessing as to whether or not he wanted an extension for a few more years. The Workers' Party had split wide open — goodbye Leonid, Nicolae, Erich, Kim, Uncle Tom MacGiolla and all — and Proinsias de Rossa with most of the young guard formed New Agenda which (thinking better of it) they then changed to Democratic Left. In Britain, Prime Minister John Major upset all the general election odds to return triumphantly to Downing Street. Labour leader Neil Kinnock thereupon fell on his sword, and among the other casualties was Sinn Féin leader, Gerry Adams, who lost his West Belfast seat to the SDLP's Dr Joe Hendron.

Meantime, the Progressive Democrats had gone into their annual conference in Waterford with just 4 percent opinion poll support (Fianna Fáil were consistently above 50 percent about this time) and some FF Ministers assured me the PDs would do all in their power to avoid a 1992 election. But O'Malley had this to say when asked about his upcoming Beef Tribunal appearance: 'You cannot expect me to change my stance because one of the people involved now holds a particular office. The truth either stands or it doesn't, and the consequences are outside of my control.'

It was at the earlier Fianna Fáil Ard Fhéis in March that the full extent of mutual FF–PD loathing was brought home to me. The emphasis throughout the RDS festivities was on the need for a speedy return to one-party Fianna Fáil government. As for the PDs being the 'conscience of the government', Reynolds was having none of that. 'Fianna Fáil does not need another party to keep it on the right track, or act as its conscience.' Brian Cowen whipped delegates into enthusiastic assent, asking rhetorically 'What about the PDs?' and then providing the answer 'When in doubt, leave out.'

The reason for such bitter hostility was being openly proclaimed. Cowen put it in a nutshell for me: 'The PDs have already seen off a Fianna Fáil Taoiseach, Tánaiste and Minister for Defence. They are now trying to bring down Albert. Well, they can shag off.'

The row originated with the extraordinary FF/PD power deal of 12 July 1989, when sworn enemies Charles Haughey and Desmond O'Malley unblushingly bargained to share government 'in the national interest'. O'Malley was already on record that CJH was unfit to govern, and his right hand woman, Mary Harney, had said she would never vote for Haughey as Taoiseach. This did not prevent Haughey and O'Malley dividing the post-election spoils while Albert Reynolds and Padraig Flynn, who had opposed the deal, were brushed aside.

Subsequently, Haughey's FF critics were to claim that, apart from abandoning the party's core anti-coalition principle in order to remain in power, he had developed a simple recipe for keeping that government arrangement in place — give the PDs whatever they want.

In return for all that, according to this analysis, the PDs simply kept demanding Fianna Fáil heads. They had insisted on Brian Lenihan being sacked as Tánaiste while he was fighting a Presidential election campaign; they had forced Haughey to drop his nominee for Minister for Defence, Jim McDaid, and finally they sought and got the biggest FF head of all, that of Haughey himself, on foot of the Doherty revelations.

Now, the pro-Reynolds faction reckoned, the PDs were targeting Albert Reynolds for a similar fate; they had forced the setting up of the Beef Tribunal against fierce FF opposition; their objective in doing so was to get Haughey, and it was only when Haughey fell that they switched to Reynolds. Reynolds himself shared this conviction, saying to me: 'The PDs set up the tribunal to get Charlie. He went down before it really got underway. So, now, they've decided that I'm the next best thing.'

The PDs argued that Fianna Fáil were architects of their own misfortune, that O'Malley had been left with no choice but to react as he did on Lenihan, McDaid and Haughey, indeed, that the PDs were now the victims of a Fianna Fáil 'dirty tricks' operation. They claimed a cabinet decision on farmers' tax had been taken without their knowledge; that FF had tried to wrongfoot O'Malley by leaving him unprepared for a special Dáil debate on Greencore, and they maintained they were being smeared by FF with charges of political favouritism to known PD activists and supporters.

Political favouritism was an explosive issue given that it lay at the heart of O'Malley's allegations on the allocation of export credit insurance to beef exporters. Before the fateful June 1989 general election, with the assistance of PD Deputy Pat O'Malley, he had repeatedly charged in the Dáil that FF favouritism had been particularly directed towards the

Goodman beef empire. Significantly, despite finding himself sharing power with Charles Haughey after the election, O'Malley kept insisting that he had no intention of shirking a Beef Tribunal showdown with Haughey or anyone else in Fianna Fáil.

Bart Cronin warned me soon after we began working together: 'If you think the "X" case thing gets Albert wound up, wait until the Beef Tribunal starts motoring. That's what really gets to him.'

It stood to reason. The 'X' case and abortion were part of the unforeseeable happenstance of government, but the beef affair, with its direct bearing on Albert Reynolds' personal competence and integrity, was a constantly tormenting affront. He said to me: 'I can live with them questioning my competence. I will not abide an attack from whatever quarter on my personal integrity. I will fight that to the bitter end, even if it costs me this job.'

I could tell that he was in deadly earnest, even about the job. And he remained extraordinarily consistent in this 'integrity' regard. He applied it right across the board whether in relation to business, politics or the media. He would brook no argument on it and, to my consternation, had no compunction about having recourse to litigation in its pursuit.

This particularly incensed the media which, apart from now having to weigh the legal consequences of a hitherto unchallenged approach to successive Taoisigh, regarded such tactics by one of them as both unwarrantable and unworthy of the office. Ultimately, this media animus did Albert Reynolds a deal of harm.

I accompanied Tom Savage to a briefing with barrister Gerry Danaher in relation to the Taoiseach's upcoming appearance before the Beef Tribunal. Even allowing for recondite legal terminology, the sheer scale and complexity of the issues and transactions involved had me confused. As we left, I remember remarking to Savage: 'It's a hundred times more complicated than abortion.' 'I don't know about that,' he said, 'but it's certainly a hundred times more dangerous for Albert.'

From the outset, I felt the main threat to the Taoiseach came from the charges levelled against him by such as Des O'Malley and Labour Party leader Dick Spring, less in relation to his alleged mishandling of the export credit insurance scheme than to the far graver accusation of political favouritism to the Goodman group.

O'Malley had said that Haughey, Reynolds and other FF Ministers were 'extremely close personally' to Larry Goodman, and that Reynolds had shown political favouritism to the beef baron. Spring maintained that decisions by Reynolds which resulted in Goodman International gaining a virtual monopoly of available export credit insurance had been influenced by Reynolds' personal contacts with 'persons in the beef industry'. This meant O'Malley and Spring had both come as close as made no difference to impugning Reynolds' integrity, i.e. accusing him of dishonesty, and I was being constantly reminded that this was *verboten*.

The Spring accusation was not so worrying inasmuch as he was in opposition — the moving finger had yet to move on — but if O'Malley repeated the substance of his Dáil allegations at the Beef Tribunal it would bring down the government — all were agreed on that — although, of course, the corollary was that if he pulled his punches, the coalition could conceivably run its full term.

The general FF mood appeared macho — Reynolds was still riding high in the opinion polls — but there was an underlying air of uncertainty. Some FF ministers told me there would be a time to deal with O'Malley, but a showdown ought not be provoked over the Tribunal. Most FF backbenchers I met were apprehensive without being able to put a finger on what might be awry. It dawned on me that many of them feared there might be something to the allegations.

One FF veteran said to me: 'The difference between us and them is that we never go on with that 'holier than thou' bullshit. We fight hard, but you'll never find us accusing them of being crooks and thieves, yet they keep throwing that stuff at us. To tell the truth, when we're faced with one of these blasted allegations, the first thing we whisper to one another is: "Did we do it?"

22 June, 1992

> 'We should be coasting but Albert keeps flying off the handle about the Tribunal. He can deal quite calmly with any other crisis, but he is obsessed with the thing in the Castle. Some guys (journalists) are guaranteed to go right up his nose — Fintan O'Toole, Gene Kerrigan, Mike Milotte, Cathal MacCoille — he is convinced that O'Toole is out to bring him down, he probably would if he could, but I dread it when he picks up on something we can't do anything about. It's so shagging complicated.'

Bart, coming up towards retirement, felt the pressure too. The Taoiseach kept urging us to counter various claims and allegations detrimental to his position which emanated mainly from the small group of journalists specialising in the labyrinthine workings of the Tribunal. The problem was that our rebuttals were necessarily as convoluted as the imputations and rarely got published.

So I started to skive off on the basis that the pol corrs didn't really want to know — they did generally leave Tribunal developments to the Dublin Castle press corps — and I frequently passed the buck to Donal Cronin, an outstanding media specialist later to become a Reynolds' speechwriter. He was Tribunal press liaison officer for the State, although the PDs hotly contested the all embracing 'state' tag, and he performed the thankless task of dealing with a sceptical and often derisive media down at the Castle.

My main headache, not easy to convey to the Taoiseach, was an inability to sufficiently grasp the more arcane aspects of the sorry saga. This contrasted with Reynolds' own uncanny capacity for fathoming the essence of any report, analysis or submission pertaining to the case. As Bart put it: 'He can go on for ages about what might appear some abstruse points of detail, but they're all part of a jigsaw, and he knows every piece.'

Again, this underlined another aspect of Reynolds' capabilities which was misrepresented both by his critics and, in one significant regard, by himself. He was to be dogged by his own tribunal description of his attitude to decision-making: '. . . I operate a department on the basis of no long files, no long reports; put it on a single sheet and, if I need more information, I know where to get it. . . the one-sheet approach has got me through life very successfully in business and in politics.'

It was a perfectly tenable *modus operandi* — 'if I need more information, I know where to get it' was the important *caveat* — but it was skilfully used to portray him as virtually a semi-literate whose limitations dictated that he should not be taxed with more than could be kept to a single sheet of paper. In fact, the 'one sheet man' had a disquieting ability to absorb and retain reams of detail — we used to joke that it had something to do with a brain undamaged by alcohol — and I was present on occasion when economists and financial experts discovered that trying to faze him with jargon or technicalities almost always backfired.

Most who worked closely with him, including some of his sternest critics, remarked on how he could cut through obfuscatory 'officialese'. He said to me: 'Some of them will quite deliberately try to blind you with science, so you've got to show them straight off that you know the real score — I mean, the real score.'

29 June, 1992

> 'O'Malley goes into Tribunal. Danger, danger, danger! Says "if anything, I had understated the position" in the Dáil. But he stops short of calling Albert's honesty into question.' Pol corrs keep saying to me that the coalition is under fierce strain as O'Malley will be fired if he goes too far. No doubt, they are right. For the record, Albert merely says two sides to every story and he'll eventually tell his. . . .'

It was soon after our return from an EU summit in Lisbon that Des O'Malley began giving evidence before Mr Justice Liam Hamilton at Dublin Castle. Throughout the first day, he never once mentioned Albert Reynolds by name but he stood over his allegations in an earlier written submission to the Tribunal that the operation of the beef export credit insurance scheme represented a fraud on the taxpayer in some cases, and that it was abused to benefit two companies, Goodman International and Hibernia Meats.

Albert Reynolds was infuriated by O'Malley's accusations but, I felt, also somewhat relieved. If, over his remaining period in the witness box, O'Malley confined himself to similar generalities, then his evidence would be politically tolerable. Reynolds' certainly did not like the tone of "if anything, I had understated the position", but, that evening, I was able to go to the pol corrs with a reassuring line: 'Everybody is entitled to their view of past events; there are two sides to every story, and the Taoiseach will be only too delighted to give his side in due course.'

Off the record, I let them know that O'Malley's testimony could be lived with as far as Reynolds was concerned. I pointed out that the PD leader had told the Tribunal that 'the manner in which cover was given didn't constitute fraud, but was unusual'. That, I maintained, effectively exonerated the Department of Industry and Commerce. Reynolds' honesty and integrity had not been impugned — we could stomach allegations of incompetency although, of course, we totally rejected them — so, no provoke!

In reality, the Taoiseach was trying the same gambit later to be essayed by Labour during their campaign to prevent Harry becoming President of the High Court. He was ostentatiously drawing a line in the political sand beyond which O'Malley was not to go on pain of immediate and terrible retribution. I have always suspected that, over the course of six days giving evidence, O'Malley attempted to stay within that limit (Reynolds would not agree), that he sought to pressure Reynolds as much as possible without actually collapsing the government, but that he overestimated Reynolds' capacity to endure such a tongue-lashing from him of all people.

On his second day giving evidence, O'Malley drew a bead on Ray Burke who had succeeded Reynolds at Industry and Commerce. Burke, he said, had been 'seriously in error' in telling the Dáil in 1989 that there were no defaults in payments by the Iraqis to Irish exporters. Burke witheringly responded that O'Malley's attitude was 'dishonest, dishonourable and disgraceful'. That was probably the most scarifying criticism directed by one politician at another throughout the interminable course of the Tribunal. Only, significantly, it caused barely a ripple because Burke was by that time an ex-Minister, i.e. a backbencher who could use that kind of invective more or less with impunity.

Similarly, we scoured media coverage of O'Malley's week-long testimony for criticism of Charles Haughey, the original focus of his most swingeing attacks. Burke, Joe Walsh, Seamus Brennan and Michael O'Kennedy came in for critical attention, but the Haughey factor was curiously de-emphasised. McCreevy reminded me that CJH was no longer an inviting target: 'You don't waste ammunition on a dead duck.'

On his fifth day in the witness box, O'Malley threw his stiffest punch. Decisions taken by Albert Reynolds on export credit insurance had been 'wrong . . . grossly unwise, reckless and foolish.' I read and re-read the transcript, felt it stretched the outer limits of what was acceptable but, I also felt, it could be absorbed. Because, while offensive and insulting, it did stop short of the dreaded 'D' word, i.e. O'Malley was not directly accusing Reynolds of dishonesty.

Accordingly, Reynolds agreed that I should display the same forbearance as heretofore when briefing the pol corrs, i.e. the Taoiseach was not going to be provoked by anything which did not bear on his veracity or integrity; what was said was merely Mr O'Malley's opinion on the wisdom or otherwise of what the Taoiseach did five years ago, and the Taoiseach would deal fully with that allegation when he testified to the Beef Tribunal. That was the line and I carefully stuck to it. But I had seen the real Reynolds' reaction. He believed O'Malley had actually gone beyond what was admissible. He talked of a day of reckoning when he would set the record straight and sort O'Malley out in the process. I told Bart Cronin I had a sense of foreboding. 'He has that look in his eye,' agreed Bart. 'What look?' *'Tiocfaidh ár Lá!'*

5

'DON'T TELL ME LIES . . . DON'T TELL LIES ON ME'

ALBERT REYNOLDS was barely a month in power when I travelled to London to meet with my Downing Street opposite number, Gus O'Donnell, an extraordinarily relaxed press secretary despite having to deal with arguably the toughest media in the world, as well as a boss who then appeared fated to be a one-term Prime Minister.

Over a relaxed lunch with O'Donnell and his press section colleagues, Jonathan Haslam and Peter Bean, we mostly talked shop, and that led to comparison of the respective ways John Major and Albert Reynolds handled press relations. I casually mentioned that my man met every Thursday afternoon with the Leinster House political correspondents for a free-ranging on the record briefing which normally lasted an hour.

'You're joking, of course,' said Haslam. When I assured them that I was very much in earnest, all three were emphatic that Reynolds would come a cropper, sooner rather than later, if the arrangement were allowed to continue. No offence, but it was not possible for any Prime Minister to venture unprotected into the lions' den on a regular weekly basis.

They predicted that the pol corrs, constantly perfecting their skills for that precious hour, would become ever more effective in their interrogation techniques, while the opposition parties, knowing not just the day but the hour of the briefing, would save much of their best ammunition to prime the corrs before they went to confront the Taoiseach. 'It doesn't matter how you do it,' said O'Donnell. 'Find a way to break out of that system before it breaks the Taoiseach.'

It had seemed like a reasonably good idea at the time. At his first news conference, Reynolds breezily committed himself to open government adding that, if the question of media policy arose, he believed he had a good grasp of the industry. Then, almost as an afterthought, it was decided that he should meet each week with the pol corrs for an on the record briefing on current issues. It was not my idea, but neither did I object to the concept. I did check with press officers in a number of Irish embassies, mostly in the EU, and found that variations of the same system obtained in some Benelux and Nordic countries. Had I delved deeper, however, I would have discovered that there were crucial differences, not least regarding the extent to which journalists in these societies were more deferential, even compliant, in relation to authority figures than their Fleet Street and Dublin counterparts.

The Downing Street forebodings were soon borne out as the weekly briefing gradually took on the pattern of a hazardous obstacle course. News editors could generally rely on each session producing a front page and sometimes a main lead story, as well as abundant material for the inside pages. For his pains, Reynolds got more brickbats than kudos; appreciation turned to irritation; grillings felt more like roastings, and the net result was self-inflicted pain rather than gain. As if to add insult to injury, despite such unique media access, unparalleled before or since, Reynolds was soon being portrayed as unscrupulously plotting to subvert freedom of the press. Yet he kept this briefing system in place for the remaining nine months of the FF–PD coalition.

The notion dies hard among politicians that they can have 'friends' among the media. They know this can be done, they will tell you, because so many of their political opponents have manifestly pulled it off. Therefore, all they require is the right stroker with the right touch to massage the hacks into acknowledging their conspicuous worth. To this purpose, they cultivate a wide range of journalistic contacts, plying them with exclusive interviews, quotes and 'steers' and they almost invariably wind up in spluttering high dudgeon as the favoured ones bite the hand that feeds them.

Nevertheless, Albert Reynolds had some reason to think he possessed that elusive touch which seduces all but the most censorious scribes. He had been through alternately hard and heady times as a fiesty Longford newspaper owner. He had employed or been closely associated with some of the most celebrated and colourful journalists in the country. As a public representative, he had built up a rapport with the press which was the envy of almost every other politician. And, notwithstanding his meteoric rise, he took pride in being acquainted with, and accessible to, practically every reporter on the political beat at national and, indeed, local level.

To a large extent, he had led a charmed media existence since bursting onto the national scene in 1977. Even his political opponents saw him as at worst a genial go-getting operator, an astute self-made millionaire with an impressive ministerial track record. While Charles Haughey was being traduced as the epitome of all that was wrong with Fianna Fáil, Albert Reynolds was being touted as the acceptable face of the party. Garret FitzGerald, as Taoiseach, regularly singled him out in the Dáil as a notable exception to the shoddy Fianna Fáil rule.

Suddenly, in February 1992, Charles Haughey wasn't there to kick around any more. He had been supplanted by Uncle Albert who was proclaiming a new open system of government. Such uplifting tidings had hardened political reporters misty eyed, for all of twenty-four hours, which was about as long as it took to write the new testament. The Boss is dead. Long live the Boss!

The script was hastily rejigged. It now read that Reynolds, despite his protestations to the contrary, was indubitably the assassin who did for Haughey; his additional elimination of eight senior and nine junior ministers showed he was probably worse than CJH; he was already seeking to bully the press, actually threatening to take them on if they libelled him, which clearly smacked of intolerant and autocratic (possibly despotic) tendencies. 'They're going to come after me,' said Reynolds to me matter of factly. 'They need a substitute for Charlie, and I'll do.'

Few knew that, even as Reynolds addressed his first news conference as Taoiseach, he was already in dispute with *The Irish Times* over an article published two months previously. Written by outside contributor Raymond Crotty, it accused Reynolds of serious wrongdoing through abuse of ministerial privilege, while he was at Finance and Industry and Commerce, in order to obtain EC funds to assist his family firm, C. & D. Foods Limited.

Soon after becoming Taoiseach, he told me how he felt about such published allegations. Irrespective of the cost, he was not prepared to abide by Haughey's acceptance of the conventional wisdom that it would be counter productive for him (Haughey) to take legal proceedings against those who smeared and vilified him. I nervously tried to interrupt: 'But, Taoiseach . . . .' Reynolds was adamant: 'I don't care, Diggy. I'm not going to take that kind of thing lying down. Charlie felt there was nothing he could do about it, but if they tell lies about me, I will sue them, and to hell with the consequences.'

He claimed a prompt apology from *The Irish Times* would have satisfied him. He also maintained he never proceeded against those who promptly apologised for such transgressions. The problem with *The Irish Times*, he said, was that there had been foot dragging in D'Olier Street. The only way he could guard his reputation was by recourse to law. Neither would he be satisfied simply to go through the motions 'for the optics'. As part of any settlement, he would be seeking financial recompense and costs. 'Otherwise, they'll just laugh, and go on as before.'

Afterwards, he told the pol corrs that he had three such legal actions in train, including one against RTE over an assertion made on *Today Tonight* by Senator John A. Murphy that Reynolds told a 'monstrous lie' when he claimed that the Maastricht Treaty safeguarded Irish neutrality. I had already told him that most journalists and politicians took the view that John A. intended to make a political charge and was not impugning his personal integrity. He snapped back: 'Then let the "lie" word be withdrawn.'

After that, when there was no retraction, he rejected all *Today Tonight* and *Prime Time* interview requests. In fact, Albert Reynolds never appeared on *Prime Time* while he was Taoiseach. The day after he stepped down, he did go on the programme. When I asked him why, he replied: 'Because it's over.' 'I have a simple straightforward philosophy,' he said to the pol corrs. 'Don't tell me lies, and don't tell lies on me using twisted facts. Just tell the truth. This has nothing to do with me as Taoiseach, but it has everything to do with me as Albert Reynolds.'

Later, Conor Brady, editor of *The Irish Times*, told me that while they accepted the Taoiseach's submission on the Crotty article, and were prepared to publish an unqualified apology, they believed legal action was not the proper course for a Taoiseach to embark upon, and that they were particularly taken aback when he sought damages.

All of my former colleagues agreed with him. It was impossible for me to overcome the widespread impression that Reynolds suing a newspaper amounted to bullying of the most flagrant kind (not to mention conduct unbecoming of a Taoiseach or a gentleman) and that it was particularly reprehensible because it involved the most powerful personage in the land seeking to intimidate a gallant watchdog of democracy.

In vain, I tried to point out that, in the eyes of the law, Albert Reynolds was no better than any man on the street, so that a rich newspaper like *The Irish Times* need have no compunction about defending themselves in court if they had a legal leg to stand on (for the publicity and circulation boost alone), and that a Taoiseach would have infinitely more to lose (including possibly his job) should the verdict go against him. 'You're on a loser, Taoiseach,' I said 'the media stick together on this kind of thing, and they have long memories.' 'They would have come after me, at any rate,' he responded, 'but this might just make them that bit more careful.' It was then I told him that Conor Brady had emphasised to me that *The Irish Times* bore him no ill will, that they were prepared to pay substantial damages, etc. but they would like to know that the money went to charity. He reared up: 'They have a bloody cheek. That's their way of saying I should never have taken them on — that they're right and I'm wrong — tell them I'll spend every shagging penny of the money.'

I subsequently found out that he did give the money to charity. But that was never conveyed to *The Irish Times* or to any other section of the media. And I knew they were not likely to forgive or forget.

Being described as a 'spin doctor' never bothered me. So, when a Co. Donegal Fianna Fáil cumann presented the Taoiseach with a magnificent old spinning wheel, I commandeered it for my office. It served rather like worry beads as I absently pumped the foot pedal up and down through endless phone conversations — 'merrily, cheerily, noiselessly spinning.' Another of my opposite numbers, Sinn Féin's Rita O'Hare — '*An Bean Rua*' — was fascinated. She told me: 'I made two of them when I was inside.' It took a few moments to comprehend what she meant by 'inside'.

My main daily focus was on the Leinster House political correspondents, although writers and broadcasters of international, national or regional status, political or otherwise, were just as liable to demand attention. I held a weekly briefing for 'foreign' (including Northern Ireland!) correspondents based in Dublin and kept in regular contact with various other political writers and analysts, some of whom pontificated without ever penetrating the Houses of the Oireachtas.

However, the pol corrs who worked close to the parliamentary coalface were my main concern, especially for that tricky period each evening when I approached them with the 'spin' and then had to weather rigorous cross-examination. The slightest slip, and the Taoiseach could be walked into much trouble, with corresponding consequences for the unfortunate messenger.

Having been a pol corr myself for more than a decade, I knew more or less what to expect — hard but fair treatment — and that on balance is how it ultimately worked out, although Reynolds might not have always agreed. Typical of their approach to me was this from Tim Ryan of the *Irish Press* on one occasion: 'Diggy, what you're telling us won't wash. We'll be giving ye hell in the morning. Come on and I'll buy you a drink.'

The pol corrs room — actually two adjoining rooms — was where I once worked with Michael Mills of the *Irish Press* and the *The Irish Times'* Dick Walsh. Now, the denizens were Donal Kelly of RTE; Chris Glennon, Gene McKenna and Brian Dowling of the *Irish Independent*; Denis Coughlan and Joe Carroll of *The Irish Times*, Liam O'Neill and Mark Hennessy, *The Cork Examiner*; John Cooney and Tim Ryan of the *Irish Press* — and the 'Sisters'.

In 1976, when I began working as a pol corr, Geraldine Kennedy, then pol corr of *The Sunday Tribune*, was the self-styled 'token' woman in the room. Now, having weathered victory and defeat as a PD deputy, she was back wearing her new hat in *The Irish Times*, accompanied by D'Olier Street colleague Maol Muire Tynan, Úna Claffey of RTE, Emily O'Reilly of the *Irish Press* (later *The Sunday Business Post*) and Tara Buckley of the *Evening Press*. There was no question as to who dominated the room. The men readily acknowledged: 'The sisters are the stars.' I felt I got an easier time from the men corrs — due to male gender-bonding influence — while the women rarely succumbed to our insidious 'give the poor hoor a break' culture. That was part of why they were feted (and feared) as the best. Reynolds was hardly their feminist pin-up, and they gave him a hard enough time, but it was never personal. As Úna Claffey expressively shrugged after his 'There's women for you' remark in the Dáil: 'No big deal — that's Albert.'

Away from the pol corrs, some other political analysts made no attempt to hide the fact that they had a mission or agenda. Reynolds to them was a baddie and they unapologetically worked to bring about his downfall. But that too is par for the modern media course, i.e. the kind of heat one must be able to take in the political kitchen.

As for the running 'transparency' battle between Reynolds and his critics, genuinely open government and natural political secretiveness, in my admittedly cynical view, will never be reconciled. I was astonished when John Bruton declared as new Taoiseach: 'Government must be seen to be operating as if behind a pane of glass.' That'll be the day!

Hard on Des O'Malley's appearance at the Beef Tribunal came a development which sent relations between Taoiseach and PD leader spiralling further out of control.

Mr Justice Hamilton began to question witness Ray Burke about discussions at a government meeting on 8 June, 1988, when it was decided to raise the ceiling for Export Credit Insurance Scheme (ECIS) cover for Iraq. He particularly wanted to know whether it was decided that cover should be limited to two exporters, Goodmans (AIBP) and Hibernia Meats. But the Tribunal chairman's entitlement to raise the issue was immediately questioned by senior counsel for the State, Henry Hickey, citing Article 28.4.2. of the Constitution which states that the government must take collective responsibility for its decisions.

The issue, although not specifically mentioned in the Constitution, was cabinet confidentiality. Liam Hamilton insisted that it was necessary for him to inquire into decisions made at the meeting in question; Harry Whelehan was equally adamant that there could be no question of revealing details of the cabinet discussions involved, and the issue was referred to the High Court where Mr Justice Rory O'Hanlon rejected Harry's application to halt the Hamilton line of inquiry.

In the course of his judgment, the man sacked as President of the Law Commission, stated: 'It has not been unknown in the history of government in other countries for totally corrupt governments, and for members, to enrich themselves dishonestly at the cost of the public purse.'

8 July, 1992: Helskini (CSCE Conference)

> News of Rory O'Hanlon's judgment comes through to us in fancy Troikka restaurant. Earlier, Taoiseach had been predicting that it would go against the government. That still did not prevent him going ballistic when he heard it confirmed. No way can he run a government without cabinet confidentiality. I have drunk enough to say to him we have no judicial, political, media or public support on the issue. That makes me very popular indeed, and puts the final kibosh on the evening.'

Harry Whelehan promptly appealed the decision to the Supreme Court; Liam Hamilton thereupon adjourned the Tribunal for six weeks, and the skin and hair began flying. Albert Reynolds was cast as the chief culprit. He was accused by a succession of opposition leaders of having pushed the Attorney General into frustrating the work of the Tribunal in order to protect himself. His protestations that Harry had acted on his own initiative were derisively dismissed. Even in that unlikely event, argued most media commentators, he should never have supported such action. The PDs let it be known that they shared this view.

Then, to practically everybody's astonishment, the Supreme Court ruled by a majority that there was an absolute constitutional duty of secrecy in relation to cabinet discussions. 'An absurdity,' declared PD chairman, Michael McDowell. 'An absolute absurdity,' rowed in *The Irish Times*. Again, Reynolds took the brunt of the recrimination, and the pressure on him began noticeably increasing.

The Irish Times quoted five unnamed former FF ministers as disagreeing with his account of decisions taken at the notorious 8 June meeting four years previously. Ray McSharry furiously challenged these 'alleged ministers' to let their names be published — no more was heard of them — and then, reacting to an *Irish Independent* revelation, Reynolds maintained that he never knew that 70 percent of beef exports to Iraq came from intervention stock. The near universal reaction was: 'He must or should have known.'

Relations with the PDs were going from bad to worse. A long simmering row over the Culliton Report flared into open hostility between Reynolds and O'Malley. Culliton had suggested splitting the Industrial Development Authority into separate agencies — one to support indigenous industry, the other to attract inward investment — and O'Malley enthusiastically backed this formula while Reynolds was against a complete split. The upshot was what some regarded as compromise but most as a Reynolds victory. He had his way inasmuch as there was no complete separation — a 'variation' was agreed to provide for two divisions under the IDA roof — but O'Malley insisted, in the face of opposition and general media disbelief, that the PDs had prevailed. 'Never mind the reality,' said Bart, 'just feel the hostility.'

28 September, 1992

> 'Albert outlines to me the PDs "semi-detached" approach to government, e.g. Pat Cox announces that Albert's comments on Articles 2 and 3 are "not helpful"; Martin Cullen attacks the french letters bill as "a typical Fianna Fáil bill"; factories close in Tuam, Limerick, Ballinasloe — 290,000 unemployed — and McDowell attacks the government's employment record, as if the PDs weren't part of government. Albert also rails that unemployment seems to have nothing at all to do with O'Malley — the guy who is responsible for jobs — that O'Malley can never be found when that shit hits the fan. . . .'

About this time, relations came close to breaking point when the Taoiseach barred Minister of State Mary Harney from representing the

PDs at important North–South talks in Dublin Castle. She had been nominated by O'Malley but Reynolds ruled that out, and the talks went ahead without a PD presence. The Reynolds argument was that, on the government side, only members of the cabinet should attend. The PDs retorted that their two senior ministers, O'Malley and Bobby Molloy, were unable to do so because of prior engagements.

An unseemly row raged back and forth with Reynolds insisting that Molloy, at least, could have cancelled his engagement (the launch of a geological map in Co. Mayo) and the PDs arguing that Harney was eminently qualified to handle the assignment. I wrote:

> 'The Harney row is not really over her being just a junior minister. Albert does not like her line on the North. Says she has publicly attacked the government's northern policy, has shown she can't be trusted on the government team, and he is damned if she is going to screw things up — a 'wet'? — something's got to give, nothing surer.'

Meantime, in the 'real world' as Michael Smith called it, we were caught up in an international currency crisis as sterling collapsed; Britain and Italy pulled out of the EU Exchange Rate Mechanism; interest rates went up by three points; the punt rose to 107p against sterling, and Bertie Ahern began a long campaign to ward off devaluation. 'Where are the PDs now?' growled Reynolds.

They surfaced with a vengeance as the abortion spectre again reared its head. There was general political agreement on the wording of the government's travel and information proposals for the upcoming referendum. But the Fianna Fáil (Reynolds) formula on the so-called substantive issue of abortion seemed to be alienating most shades of opinion, including the PDs who were still publicly agitating for legislation rather than a referendum.

The proposed Article 40.3.3. amendment made abortion unlawful unless it was necessary to save the life ('as distinct from the health') of the mother. So it would only apply to a mother who had an illness or condition which gave rise to a real and substantive risk to her life — 'not being a risk of self destruction' — i.e. a threat of suicide would not be accepted as a reason for abortion.

The debate again raged. Who was to distinguish between what was life-threatening and 'merely' health-threatening to women? To what extent would women have to endure health-threatening illnesses because they were deemed not immediately life-threatening? Who would explain to the parents of a young pregnant rape victim who had committed suicide that there was nothing that could have been done for her in the circumstances? As against all that, on the Pro-Life side, the amendment was being opposed on the basis that it was the thin edge of the wedge for the eventual introduction of abortion on demand.

Reynolds warned (threatened!) the government would legislate to give effect to the Supreme Court 'X' case decision — provide for abortion in cases of threatened suicide — if the electorate rejected the wording. The Catholic bishops dithered for a fortnight, then let it be known that, although the wording was basically flawed, voters could in conscience vote either **Yes** or **No**. The opposition parties continued to press Reynolds to accept an amendment removing the distinction between the life and health of the mother, but Fine Gael seemed anxious for a deal. Then, to everyone's surprise, the PDs suddenly announced that they were not prepared to bring down the government on the issue.

'We were right . . . we told you so. . . they hadn't the balls!' There was a lot of Fianna Fáil crowing as O'Malley told the Dáil that to plunge the country into an abortion election would be unforgiveable. He had some difficulty in reconciling this forbearance with the fact that the PDs were on record that the amendment was dangerous for women. Still, the fact remained that the PDs had again pulled back, despite Mary Harney subsequently informing the House that the bill was a 'mistake' and PD sources briefing that they would campaign against the abortion clause even though this was in breach of collective cabinet responsibility.

I remembered what a PD deputy had said to me three weeks previously: 'We will not be forced into fighting a general election on an abortion platform. Neither will we bring down this government in advance of Albert Reynolds going into the Tribunal. Don't worry, we'll pick the right time.'

Ominously, too, Charles Haughey, Ray McSharry, Ray Burke, Seamus Brennan and Michael O'Kennedy had by now completed their Tribunal evidence and, with the notable exception of McSharry, had been conspicuously unsupportive of Albert Reynolds. They disclaimed responsibility for decisions taken by Reynolds at Industry and Commerce on export credit insurance cover.

O'Kennedy repeatedly stated that the responsibility for all aspects of the operation of such cover lay with Reynolds 'exclusively'. At no stage, said Haughey, was he aware of Reynolds' decision to limit export credit insurance to two companies, AIBP and Hibernia Meats. I told the pol corrs there was 'nothing new' in Haughey's evidence while slyly seeking to divert their attention to his withering Tribunal attack on the PD leader, as well as his retort, when reminded that he had appointed O'Malley a minister, that 'nobody's perfect'.

A fortnight later, Albert Reynolds began giving evidence at Dublin Castle. He almost immediately described Des O'Malley's evidence to the Tribunal as 'reckless, irresponsible and dishonest'. I went around dazedly repeating to FF ministers: 'I didn't know he was going to say that — "dishonest!" — did you know he was going to say that?'

Bart Cronin spoke just that one word to me when I returned to the office — "dishonest" — and then jerked his thumb floorwards.

6

'THE MESSAGE IS ALBERT IS THE BAD GUY'

WHY DID Albert Reynolds do it? Despite what many opposition and media observers maintained, it was not because he wanted to provoke an election (at least not arising from the wretched beef affair) and he never intended to be drawn into battle on the high moral ground, traditionally treacherous terrain for Fianna Fáil.

The problem was that he couldn't let it go with Des O'Malley, firstly for his declared determination to harass him on beef from within government, even after he became Taoiseach, and then for the relentless manner in which he gave effect to that threat when he went into the witness box in July. Like a footballer badly fouled in the first round of a cup-tie, Reynolds nursed his wrath until the second leg, and then put the boot in. Unfortunately, as often happens in such circumstances, it instantly earned him the red card.

He had more than three and a half months to brood about it, months when the relationship with O'Malley and the PDs continued to deteriorate. During that time, I don't believe he told either Tom Savage, Bart Cronin or myself that he was thinking of calling O'Malley dishonest, and I don't know if he consulted insiders like Flynn, Geoghegan Quinn, Cowen, Smith, McCreevy or Fallon, but I was subsequently told that a certain legal luminary advised him not just that he could get away with the 'D' word, but that O'Malley would be forced to grin and bear it. The closest I ever got to why Reynolds decided to call O'Malley 'dishonest' was the following from him long afterwards: 'Looking back on it from a political point of view, and I stress the word political, I was badly advised.'

The Taoiseach's counter attack changed public perception of the controversy. All interest in the substance of what he (or anyone else) had to say on the complex beef industry issues was swept aside by the hype over the political implications of his 'putting it up to' O'Malley. The public no longer had to grapple with the intricacies of intervention, export refunds or credit insurance. The affair had finally shaken down to a duel to the death between the most powerful politicians in the land.

In what sense was O'Malley deemed to be 'dishonest'? Reynolds related it to the PD leader's statement under oath that a claim by Goodman International against the State was for £170 million. The Taoiseach told the Tribunal: 'When he (O'Malley) said that to the Tribunal, he knew that the figures were wrong. He knew that the Iraqis had been paying right up to August, 1990. He gave no credit for that, but he knew the figures. He puffed up Goodman's claim for what I regard as cheap political gain. He was reckless, irresponsible and dishonest to do that here in the Tribunal.'

That particular issue eventually bogged down in confusion over the actual sum of money paid out by the State (£6.9m.) and the potential liability according to O'Malley (£170m. plus). We kept saying O'Malley had not told the Tribunal of £53m. paid by the Iraqis and notified to his own Department. O'Malley's defenders counter claimed that we were not comparing like with like, and that there were so many variables, that the real figures were probably incalculable. Few were interested — the issue was too complex — yet the case for and against Reynolds' dishonesty allegation was irretrievably bound up with this apparently impossible muddle. When I broached the subject with journalists, I was almost invariably told not to bother, that nobody understood it and, therefore, it did not matter.

The Taoiseach was also getting an increasingly bad press at the Tribunal. It related less to content than to presentation of his evidence. I subsequently accepted that, under intense cross-examination, he could be waspish, dismissive and disdainful. I was not prepared, however, for the level of denunciation of his demeanour in the witness box. His detractors dug deep for epithets — coarse, insolent, petulant, bullying, smirking, sneering — and it started to get to him and his family. I kept saying to Bart that attacking O'Malley was tantamount to going after President Robinson or Mother Teresa — 'nobody wants to hear' — and neither of us had any illusion about who would be saddled with the blame should the government collapse — Albert Reynolds.

Meantime, behind the scenes, the two sides were squaring up to each other with the usual huff and bluff: 'You kicked me/you kicked me first/ you kicked me harder' 'I did not/did so/so what?'. . . 'take it back/shag off/ok, you asked for it!'

They knew it was still possible to pull back from the brink. Either O'Malley could choose not to be provoked — an *Irish Times* editorial advised him to let Liam Hamilton be the one to eventually judge — or Reynolds could go the Alice in Wonderland escape route with the word 'dishonest' meaning whatever he wanted it to mean, e.g. incorrect, mistaken, wrong — anything other than 'dishonest'.

We started on the basis that there was no question of the Taoiseach backing down. I informed the pol corrs that he was totally unrepentant about having described O'Malley as dishonest because he had told it as it was without varnish or veneer. 'The Taoiseach feels duty bound to tell the truth as he knows it; facts are there on record and cannot be expunged from the record.'

Adrian Hardiman, senior counsel representing O'Malley at the Tribunal, spent two days pressing the Taoiseach to withdraw the charge of 'perjury' against O'Malley. Reynolds kept insisting that he had accused him not of perjury but of dishonesty. Hardiman maintained that describing O'Malley's sworn evidence as dishonest was the same as calling him a perjurer — Judge Hamilton observed that 'dishonest' meant 'telling an untruth' — but Reynolds kept repeating to Hardiman: 'Perjury is your word, dishonesty is my word.' Liam Hamilton commented that he found the whole wrangle 'unseemly and distasteful.'

It was slowly beginning to dawn on everyone that O'Malley would not blink on this occasion, and that we were on the brink of an election. I became more defensive — 'more desperate', Liam O'Neill of *The Cork Examiner* drily observed — and I told the corrs: 'An election is no more necessary now than when Des O'Malley accused the Taoiseach of recklessness, foolishness and telling untruths during the course of his evidence to the Tribunal.'

Stephen O'Byrnes promptly retorted that his leader had never used the word 'untruth or untruths' in relation to the Taoiseach, although he accepted that O'Malley had told the Tribunal that a statement made by Ray Burke in the Dáil was untrue. When I asked the Taoiseach about this — I could not recall him previously accusing O'Malley of it — he was adamant that the charge had been directed at him. I worried about it until Reynolds' chief media critic, Fintan O'Toole, asserted that O'Malley had, indeed, accused Reynolds of making untrue statements.

29 October, 1992

> 'Tribunal — I think he (Taoiseach) passed the point of no return today. He talked of O'Malley's £170 million figure as being 'incorrect'.
>
> 'Hardiman picked up on that, and asked him if he was now saying that O'Malley's evidence had merely been incorrect as distinct from dishonest. I kept willing him to say yes, to get back to defending his own decisions, to leave O'Malley out of the damn thing, get the show back on the road. Albert paused for what seemed ages (we all held our breath) and then he said that one word — "dishonest!". I think we're bollixed.'

At the weekend, Reynolds made a tentative move towards compromise. He agreed to speak exclusively to *The Sunday Tribune* political editor, Gerry Barry, at his Ballsbridge apartment. I accompanied Barry and recall the main thrust of the Taoiseach's remarks was that 'my door is open' to the PD ministers. As the interview wound up, Barry asked him for his reaction to allegations that he never spoke to Des O'Malley outside cabinet. Reynolds said something non-committal, then shook hands with Barry, left the room and I thought he had ignored or forgotten the question. As we were leaving, he reappeared: 'You want to know what I think of that — it's crap, pure crap.' Gerry chuckled at the word 'crap', appreciatively repeating it after Reynolds, and this elicited the following: 'I mean that — for the record — it's crap, total crap.'

I then made one of my worst mistakes. I knew that only *The Sunday Tribune* would have the quotation on the following day. I figured that, although it might raise eyebrows, it would pass off because most readers would assume the Taoiseach had not meant it for publication.

Indeed, throughout the following (Sun) day, there were no queries from the other newspapers even though *The Sunday Tribune* prominently ran the 'crap' reference. What had not occurred to me, however, was that the Taoiseach might actually relish the phrase, figure that it was within bounds and decide to recycle it.

As luck would have it, I was not with him when he travelled out of Dublin that Sunday morning. Later that evening, I watched the main RTE television news and could hardly believe it when the Taoiseach was doorstepped on arrival at a function and once again pronounced the O'Malley arguments 'crap, total crap'. This time, however, he was on camera, on 'mike' and on prime time national news. On screen, it looked and sounded wrong.

There is no doubt that I could have prevented that disaster. All it required was for me to say to him, after the Barry interview, that he should never again use such a word publicly. It cost Reynolds dearly during the upcoming election campaign, primarily because it perfectly fitted the grotesque Reynolds caricature being drawn by his opponents, that of a coarse and boorish man.

Hopes briefly flickered that the PDs might again step back from the brink as they continued to cling to office over the next few days, but we were disabused of this illusion when Bobby Molloy demanded an 'abject' withdrawal of Reynolds' dishonesty allegation, and the PDs told pol corrs that the only reason O'Malley was remaining on as Minister was to ensure that files were not tampered with, or a civil servant intimidated in relation to the beef tribunal.

After mechanically dismissing this as a 'disgraceful slur' I turned to Bart: 'tampering with files . . . intimidating a civil servant. . . the only surprise is that they held together for so long.' Bart replied: 'Believe me, they'd do so again, even with Albert as Taoiseach, because politicians will rationalise practically anything in the. . . er. . . national interest.' I didn't believe Bart at the time, but I should have known better than to doubt him.

3 November, 1992

> 'Albert's 60th birthday! Can it be his birthday present is that the PDs have blinked? They've certainly screwed up. They were to pull out today but, now, they say they must wait until Sean Dorgan, Sec. of O'Malley's Dept., gives evidence at Tribunal tomorrow re. credibility of Albert v. Des. Bedlam! O'Malley describes it as a "special investigation" and Hamilton erupts, accusing him of politicising the process, putting out inaccurate and misleading info, etc. Maybe they want out. Maybe they'll back off. Big party tonight in Hazeldene (Reynolds residence). The last supper? We'll know soon enough.'

4 November, 1992

> 'ALL OVER! PDs call a news conference in Montclare Hotel — "non-consultation and exploitation of loyalty (sic)" reason given by Dessie for break-up. Also says he considered asking Albert to replace him at cabinet by Mary Harney— "like hell he did," sez Albert — and that "dishonesty" was the straw that broke the camel's back. So that's it, finally. Go across to Dáil bar. Twilight of the gods. Stay too long. Home 2 a.m. Dusty reception from Marie!'

5 November, 1992

> 'End of 26th Dáil. It comes almost as a relief. Albert lashes PDs in final Dáil speech — stays clear of Labour. Bruton on about a "rainbow" coalition — how

is that going to work? PDs vote with opposition to defeat FF minority government. Meet O'Malley and later Ray Burke in the Dáil and shake their hands — Dessie just stares at me! We're to have Saatchi and Saatchi people in the campaign. Go with Albert to Áras an Uachtaráin. She was not there (New Zealand) but ceremony with Presidential Commission is strangely impressive. I think Albert has started badly off balance. Anyway, hooroo Pat and down the road!'

O'Malley told the Dáil: 'For some time, effective government has been choked by the pursuit of a political agenda directed towards its destruction.'

Reynolds maintained: 'I deeply regret the decision by our partners to create instability and effectively undermine my government under a poorly disguised pretext of self-righteous moral indignation.'

It would be a short campaign, voting in the general election to coincide with the abortion referendum on 25 November, with the opening state of the parties: FF 77; FG 55; Labour 16; PDs 6; DL 6; Others 4; WP 1; Greens 1.

On the following day, I went to Fianna Fáil headquarters in Mount Street to link up with the Taoiseach who was chairing an election strategy meeting prior to leaving for Athlone and Longford for the weekend. He invited me into the meeting just as it was about to get underway. Those present included Bertie Ahern, David Andrews, Seamus Brennan, Michael Woods, Pat Farrell, Sean Sherwin, Tom Savage and Terry Prone.

Brennan did most of the talking in the early stages. He outlined what he considered would be the main issues as well as the key constituencies requiring special targeting in the campaign. The Taoiseach was impatient and kept emphasising the urgency of getting the organisation and the troops motivated and activated. The ensuing discussion was ordered and business-like with nothing said that might give reason for undue concern. As I was leaving, however, I passed Ahern and Andrews and routinely asked them how they thought it was going. Andrews gave me an old-fashioned look, shook his head, then moved away. Ahern, as if taking that as his cue, rolled his eyes heavenwards. Nothing was said but when I arrived home I said to Marie: 'This has all the makings of a mega disaster.'

On Sunday, back from Athlone, I was phoned by *Irish Independent* pol corr Chris Glennon. He said the following day's *The Star* would carry an IMS poll showing that the Taoiseach's satisfaction rating had plunged a massive 20 points since the previous IMS survey three weeks earlier. He added: 'The message is Albert is the bad guy, that he tripped Dessie up, rather than vice versa. I'll be writing for the morning, not just that the overall majority is out, but that Fianna Fáil will actually lose seats.'

I rang the Taoiseach and gave him the bad news. He seemed to take it reasonably calmly but I knew he was shaken. I kept saying there was more than a fortnight left to turn the thing around. He would fight a whirlwind campaign, and the long haul back would begin within 48 hours at the first campaign walkabout in Killarney.

On the following morning, Tom Savage gave his assessment of the situation to the Taoiseach. There was no point in going into denial; the people had decided we were to blame for having provoked the election; the only way to deal with the situation was to accept that unpalatable fact. Above all, he said, there should be no excuses or attempts to change minds already made up on that issue. The only way forward was to put it behind us, and go on from there, and, if queried about the 'crap' word, he would have to say that it was 'totally inappropriate'.

The Taoiseach was not enamoured of any of this. I could see that he felt ill-done by, and that his every instinct was still to argue the toss as to who really was to blame. RTE's Charlie Bird was waiting to interview him, and it was important that the matter be resolved first. Eventually, he reluctantly agreed to take Savage's advice, even to the extent that it would be reflected in the Bird interview, but I could see that he was far from convinced.

I went to Killarney ahead of the Taoiseach and met Charlie Bird, Dick Hogan of *The Irish Times* and the *Irish Independent's* Miriam Lord just before the helicopter landed. Reynolds was immediately whisked to Killarney town centre where a suspiciously small group of FF activists were sheepishly waiting in the gathering gloom.

Five minutes after the walkabout began, Dick Hogan approached me: 'Do you hear that sound, Diggy?' 'What sound?' 'The only sound around — the sound of your own echoing footsteps on the streets of Killarney — ye're on ye're own, Diggy.'

True, the streets were practically empty. It was nearly 7 p.m. and there didn't even seem to be people in the shops and supermarkets. The Taoiseach was already muttering under his breath about lack of organisation on the ground. I was standing beside Denise Kavanagh of the Fianna Fáil press office who whispered to me that something must have gone badly wrong. She went to phone up ahead to Tralee and Listowel to warn them to 'get the finger out'.

10 November, 1992

'. . . Tralee was just as bad. Saw the mighty Eoin Liston coming out of a shop and the FF team clung to the poor devil like drowning men. There was a much better turn out in Listowel — John B., not exactly an FF man, passed by and good naturedly shook Albert's hand — but it didn't save him. Albert gave a briefing to reporters. The main thrust of their questions was the poor turn out. I asked Dick and Charlie what line they were going to take. They told me they would both be saying the same thing — "Albert's fucked!".'

7

'LABOUR WILL STRIKE A HARD BARGAIN'

'WELL, GENTLEMEN, we have nowhere to go but up.' Albert Reynolds was in defiant 'no surrender' mood, insisting that he had simply got off on the wrong foot, that he was already at his lowest campaign ebb, and that the tide would inevitably turn in the fortnight remaining before polling day.

I advised the pol corrs not to be too hasty in their judgments; the Taoiseach had taken and absorbed the best shots of his opponents, and the empire was now gathering itself to strike back. Reynolds said to me: 'Tell them Fianna Fáil traditionally start high and finish low, but this time we're starting low and we'll finish high.'

It was decided that I should accompany him wherever he went throughout the campaign. I looked forward to the opportunity of looking at an election from the inside for a change. I had been assigned by RTE to go on the stump with various Taoisigh — from dissolution to polling day — but I suspected this would be my only chance to savour actually being aboard the roller coaster. As it turned out, I got more than I bargained for, but I learned more about Albert Reynolds over the following fortnight than throughout my previous nine months as press secretary.

Fine Gael got their manifesto out first, a £267m. programme aimed at job creation and dealing with the monetary crisis. Labour proposed a £360m. borrowing programme, and the PDs plan featured proposals for income tax and PRSI reforms. The Fianna Fáil counter offensive was launched on Wednesday 11 October. The centrepiece was a six–point programme with the promise of a £750m. fund for job creation.

Padraig Flynn turned to me as the Taoiseach prepared to lead his frontbench team out onto the launch platform: 'If this doesn't fly, Diggy, we're all dead.'

It got a moderate welcome and drew surprisingly light fire. The pol corrs almost perfunctorily put Reynolds through his paces on the sums, and not even the financial corrs seemed particularly anxious to rubbish the package. FF ministers were still congratulating themselves when I got a call from Dick Walshe, Assistant Editor of *The Irish Times* to give me details of MRBI poll findings to be published the following morning. By the time he had finished, the full extent of the looming catastrophe had sunk in.

Support for Fianna Fáil had plunged a full nine points in less than six weeks. The Taoiseach's satisfaction rating had been halved — from 60 to 31 percent — over the same period. The main beneficiaries of the FF slump were Labour, up five points. In Dublin, the FF collapse was unprecedented, the party's approval rating down from 43 to 29 percent. Labour support in Dublin was up from 15 to 25 percent, five points ahead of Fine Gael.

11 November, 1992

> 'Albert looked blankly at me when I told him. I thought it hadn't sunk in, and began to read the figures again, until he interrupted me with a wave of his hand. 'OK'. he said, and no more. I reminded him that it had been taken before the FF manifesto launch, but he barely nodded. Pol corrs tell me the FF boys are already blaming Albert. Looks as if Chris (Glennon) was right and FF are going to lose seats. Bertie fought hard on *Market Place* tonight but he is clearly appalled. *Ca ndeacha muid amu?*'

I had become used to a lengthy line of courtiers seeking audience with the Prince. The long corridor and the waiting rooms now emptied practically overnight. I accepted most of them were back in their constituencies trying to salvage something from the shipwreck. 'But, Bart, they can't all be too busy to call him.'

We were on a roll, downhill. John Bruton was painting a multi-party 'rainbow' alternative to the FF–PD arrangement, and the idea was gaining momentum. Bruton clearly wanted to lead a Fine Gael–Labour–Progressive Democrat administration, but Dick Spring, with a fair wind filling Labour sails, began talking of becoming a 'rotating' Taoiseach in any new coalition, i.e. job-sharing with Bruton.

I could see, talking to FF ministers, that they already regarded themselves as primarily conducting a damage limitation exercise. If, in addition, the Reynolds era was about to end, personal survival would take precedence over all else. The air was thick with fear, frustration and fault-finding. Where did we go wrong? Who are we going to blame? And, jaysus, how are we going to get out of this?

Black Friday, 13 November, dawned with more bad news. Tom Savage, sounding utterly drained, rang me before 7 a.m. to tell me he was *hors de combat*. I knew he had not been well, but not that his blood count had been plunging dangerously. He would be in hospital and recuperating for at least the remainder of the campaign.

Savage was a big loss. He and Reynolds had seemed tense with each other leading up to and immediately following the dissolution. I got the impression that their old rapport had been strained by Reynolds' reaction to the sudden sequence of reverses. Savage remained one of the few Reynolds confidantes who was not only prepared to argue with him, but who regularly succeeded in changing his mind. Terry Prone was still there, but she frankly accepted that she did not have the same understanding with Reynolds as her husband had. Frank Dunlop was hurriedly drafted in, but he was being presented with a practically insurmountable task.

I went to FF headquarters to link up with Reynolds at the early morning strategy meeting and was sorry I did. Everybody was pointing the finger at everybody else, including me. An overburdened Pat Farrell was trying to cope with a stream of panic phone calls from the constituencies. I talked briefly to the Saatchi and Saatchi representative, Stephen Hilton, who understandably looked somewhat bewildered. I whispered to press officer Niamh O'Connor that this was how it must have been on the bridge of the Titanic.

I was struck by signs of indiscipline and even insubordination in the organisation at large. A steady stream of HQ instructions to FF notables, recommending particular responses to opposition criticisms, were being widely ignored. Certain Ministers and other personages who had been requested to represent Fianna Fáil on various TV and radio election programmes were begging off with all manner of specious excuses.

It seemed the prevailing party wisdom in the teeth of the storm was to remain well below decks. Heads dutifully poked through constituency portholes as we passed by, but were as quickly retracted. There was rarely any outright dissent, mostly regrets and evasions, but it struck me that the much vaunted iron discipline of Fianna Fáil was a myth. Many of the party warlords fought the election within their own territorial fastnesses— in their own way — with little or no reference to Mount Street.

That Black Friday weekend was instructive. The first sweep was across Co. Wexford on the Friday — Wexford, New Ross, Enniscorthy and Gorey. I talked to Minister of State John Browne who told me straight out that the 'smell' was not good. Seamus Cullimore, reckoned to have been among the few who voted for Michael Woods in the leadership contest, had a haunted look. He told me he was being squeezed out by his local FF rivals.

Later, at the Loc Gorman Hotel in Gorey, I listened to FF organisers including Hugh Byrne and Lorcan Allen telling the Taoiseach that the media and the pollsters had got it wrong. Reynolds expressed agreement but, at one stage, he left the room ostensibly to make a phone call and gestured to me to follow.

Away from the group, he quietly told me things were going badly, and he was worried about Kathleen who had undergone surgery for breast cancer ten months previously; the pressure was becoming too much for someone in her state of health, and he was afraid it could undermine all the remarkable progress she had made. He said: 'None of this is worth what it's doing to Kathleen.'

14 November, 1992

> 'Worse and worse. Near despair at FF Dublin Plan launch in Shelbourne. Albert and Bertie do their damnest but the vultures are circling. Chopper to Ennis/Limerick: good turn–outs, particularly in Limerick, but the inevitable bad news catches up with us at the Castletroy (hotel). *Sunday Indo* poll tomorrow will show Albert still on the skids. IMS estimate that FF support, over barely a week, has gone from 47 to 41 percent. Albert's own ratings keep tumbling. John (Bruton) is beginning to climb strongly, and support for the "rainbow" is up to 44 percent.' The manifesto, as 'Pee' feared, had failed to fly. Reynolds again took me aside. 'It's very bad, Diggy.' I said automatically: 'You've touched bottom: it's going to be all up from now on.' He looked at me intently, then said: 'They've made up their minds.' And, with even greater deliberation, he repeated: 'They've made up their minds.'

On Sunday morning, I felt tired for the first time but was still taken aback when I picked up the Taoiseach at his apartment. I had always marvelled at how fresh he could appear after just a few hours sleep, only now he was clearly exhausted. He had arrived back in Dublin soon after midnight but was on the phone until almost 5 a.m. It was a key Sunday because Reynolds was being interviewed on RTE's influential lunchtime radio programme *This Week*. A good performance by him was essential if he was to launch any kind of credible comeback. I could see he was tense, and I could also see he was bone tired.

I thought the interview, conducted by Joe Little, went well. I was aware of hesitancies, stumbles and glitches, but they seemed unimportant in the context of newsy answers to probing questions. Even before we left RTE, however, the corrs began coming through on my mobile phone querying verbal gaffes by Reynolds. One warned me that the newsline would be 'the stumblebum Taoiseach'.

In the course of the interview, Reynolds had called Bruton 'John Unionist' — he had been referring to him as a crypto-Unionist — and he described Belfast's *The Irish News* as *The Belfast News*. Then, unaccountably, speaking of Charlie McCreevy's objectives, he said he was trying to 'dehumanise' the social welfare system. Little intervened: 'To humanise it, surely?' Reynolds seemed not to hear: 'To dehumanise it, yes, to take it away from any harshness that's in it.' Afterwards, back in his apartment, he was mystified when I brought up the subject — he was not aware that he had made mistakes — and it took me several minutes to convince him that they had occurred. I never saw him so dispirited. He said to Kathleen: 'It's just that I'm so tired.'

The following day's election coverage was dominated by stories of a stumbling inarticulate man who appeared to be losing control. This fed the prevalent anti-Reynolds hype of someone staggering from one blunder to another. With just nine days to go, it contributed powerfully to the emerging image of a Taoiseach on the slide. As luck would have it, this coincided with an *Irish Press* lead story by Ann Cadwallader under the headline 'My Anguish'. The subject was an interview with a clearly distraught Kathleen Reynolds expressing shock at the personal attacks being directed at her husband. 'I just can't take it,' said a tearful Kathleen,' I can't believe what's happened over the past few days. I can't recognise the man I married in what's being said about him. In three weeks, he's gone from being the best man around to someone none of us recognise.'

There was sympathy on a personal level for Kathleen, but her contention that the mud-slinging went beyond acceptable bounds was shrugged off. Most journalists felt that picking up blisters in the political kitchen was an occupational hazard. In *The Irish Times*, Fintan O'Toole dismissed Kathleen's 'outburst' as part of that particular week's Fianna Fáil media campaign.

Nerves were becoming increasingly frayed. Shane Kenny interviewed the Taoiseach on *The News at One*. It was robust 'no quarter sought or given' stuff, and I thought it remained well within acceptable bounds. Terry Prone, however, rang me to say Albert was far too argumentative, abrasive and pushy. I disagreed — in retrospect, she may have been right

— I felt it was too late to try to re-invent the Longford Slasher (Albert the Cuddly Pet Food Pussy Cat) at that particular stage. Kathleen Reynolds told me: 'Asking him to change only saps his confidence. He won't change now. He is what he is.'

The next week passed in a blur of frenetic, if unrewarding, campaign forays. Wherever we went, Longford, Sligo, Donegal, Carlow, Kilkenny, Tipperary, Louth, Meath, Mayo, Galway, Cork, Leitrim, Cavan, I was continually being made aware of FF resentment at the deteriorating situation. And, while various factors were instanced as pertinent, there was little attempt to conceal the main focus of their frustration — 'Albert'.

The Fianna Fáil troops desperately needed a boost whether from some upward FF movement in the polls, a vigorous Reynolds counter-attack or even an opposition 'own goal'. A belated promise by Bertie Ahern to increase the rate of mortgage interest relief was having no discernible effect. FF support in Dublin was at an historic low, and some polls had Labour ahead of all other parties in the capital. I felt Bertie Ahern and Minister of State, Mary O'Rourke, were among the few FF notables who were punching their weight throughout the campaign.

The only good news had been on the referendum front. Less than two weeks from polling day, an MRBI poll reported clear majorities in favour of the right to travel and access to abortion information, as well as a comfortable majority for the government wording on the substantive issue, distinguishing between the life and health of the mother, although the number of undecided was very high — **Yes** 48 percent, **No** 30 percent, **Don't Know** 22 percent. Suddenly, John Bruton abandoned his neutral stance on the amendment. He advised the electorate to vote **No** promising legislation if the amendment were defeated. This happened after some of the hitherto irresolute Catholic hierarchy — most notably the Archbishop of Dublin, Dr Connell — had come off the Maynooth fence to also declare against the government's wording. Practically overnight, with opposition building from both ends of the spectrum — the anti-abortion and womens' rights lobbies — there was a dramatic switch in voting intentions. Now, MRBI said 56 percent were against and 44 for the amendment. Significantly, Fianna Fáil supporters were most noticeably associated with the trend towards a **No** vote.

19 November, 1992

'Carlow–Kilkenny–Clonmel–Waterford — Reynolds girls are good troopers. They take it in turns to accompany their dad. They know the score but keep up a good front. Andrea is something else — a born up–and–at–'em politician — he's lucky with the *famiglia* . . . . Still nothing but gloom and doom. Have a chat with Noel Davern in Clonmel. He says FF will lose a lot of seats. The boys on the bus say: 'He would say that, wouldn't he!' But I don't think it's that with Davern. He really believes the thing is bloody awful . . . .

'Albert was talking on the phone to Pat Farrell. Didn't say a word until we were flying home from Waterford. Then told me that Pat gave him the latest MRBI figures — Fianna Fáil still stuck on 40 percent. Fine Gael 25 percent (up one). PDs, DL, WP, Greens all down a point or two. But Labour are up 5 points to 22 percent. In Dublin, Labour at 32 percent, more than double Fine Gael (15 percent). Dick's satisfaction rating 71 percent (!) with Albert down to 28. We're running out of polls! Albert very quiet. Then he says, almost to himself: "Labour will strike a hard bargain." Labour will strike a hard bargain! Is that the way he thinks we'll escape? — *L'appertura a sinistra?* — Politicians are something else.'

On the following day, Padraig Flynn was waiting to greet the Taoiseach when we arrived in Westport. Driving into the town, after a brief council of war, 'Pee' suddenly came to the point. There were, he said, 'elements' within Fianna Fáil trying to push the party into a post-election alliance with Labour. That, he declared, would have to be firmly resisted.

Well, now . . . . I glanced at the Taoiseach to see how he was taking the advice of his close confidante. Reynolds kept listening and nodding as if Flynn were pointing out some interesting sights along the route. The hortatory monologue continued but Reynolds never ventured yea or nay. Flynn didn't seem to notice.

The post-election penny had finally dropped for me. Reynolds was waiting until it was all over before going big game hunting. Like Charles Haughey before him, he was prepared to break historic moulds if that was what was required to continue as Taoiseach.

22 November, 1992

'I have a not so fine sense of the ridiculous. Can't help seeing a "funny" side. Its probably hysteria born of sheer terror. Stephen from Saatchi and Saatchi materialises in Macroom as a cattle fair ends. Albert's up on the back of a lorry, belting away. A deputation of local farmers approach me and say they want to talk about "headage". Insanely, I point them in the direction of Stephen who had just told me he had never been in Ireland (never mind Macroom) before. Charlie Bird and I can see them surrounding the poor hoor and still haranguing him five minutes later. The two of us rolling around like bold children. Doesn't even occur to me that it'll probably cost Albert votes, apart from screwing

Stephen around. Albert heard about it afterwards and was furious. Stupid, stupid, stupid!'

The traditional eve of poll TV 'head to head' debate between the Taoiseach and John Bruton ended with both camps claiming victory. The pol corrs were divided as to who won out. The talk was of it being 'shaded' by one or the other, i.e. it was so close as to make no difference to the election outcome. On the same day, Ray McSharry came into the Taoiseach's office for a photo call relating to GATT. He spent some considerable time talking privately to Reynolds before emerging and beckoning me aside: 'It is absolutely essential that he publicly announces he will not go into coalition under any circumstances.' I was taken aback but found myself nodding in the same way as Albert had done with Flynn. 'He must do it now,' persisted McSharry, 'If he says "no" to any form of coalition, it could add another 2 to 3 percent to our vote.'

I was intrigued by the Flynn–McSharry pincer movement. McSharry had stood shoulder to shoulder with Reynolds on the beef crisis; he had been offered another term as EU Commissioner, then decided not to seek re-appointment and to retire from public life. 'Pee' was determined to be his successor which would mean both of them removing themselves from active politics. In these circumstances, I couldn't understand why they took it upon themselves to be the most outspoken and persistent of all FF insiders against coalition.

An hour later, Donie Cassidy was also telling me he believed, along with most party activists, that Fianna Fáil should go into principled opposition. Donal Kelly of RTE rang and mentioned a strong anti-coalition lobby emerging in Fianna Fáil. Interestingly, the Taoiseach never referred either to McSharry or to anything remotely pertaining to coalition when I got back to him. Someone did draw my attention to Brian Lenihan writing in *In Dublin* that, if another coalition were necessary after the election, Fianna Fáil should do a deal with Labour. Brian had expressed views along those lines on a number of occasions in the past. There were no indications that he had any real support now.

I met with Fine Gael Director of Elections Sean O'Leary whose radio election count analyses I had admired for years. 'OK, Sean, call it,' I said. He immediately complied: 'Fianna Fáil down to 70; Fine Gael will also lose seats. The ones to watch are Labour. I figure they'll get maybe 30 or more.' I said: 'You must be joking.' O'Leary grinned: 'Remember I said it to you.'

On the night before polling, Reynolds attended an emotional FF gathering in Rakish Paddy's pub deep in his Longford heartland. The speeches were alternately denunciatory, defensive and defiant. The media — 'the anti–Albert press' — was the main target, with 'Dublin 4' and 'PD types' close runners-up. There was a mood almost of rural betrayal and abandonment at the hands of the eastern establishment. It reflected a gut instinct which, apart from any moral or sociological validity, augured ill for the morrow.

Polling day dawned with another full blown currency crisis. The Spanish and the Portuguese had been forced to devalue. The Punt was under severe threat with international investors and analysts predicting it too would be devalued. In their last throw of the campaign, Fianna Fáil argued that stable government rather than the insubstantial 'rainbow' was what such a crisis situation demanded.

26 November, 1992: Longford

> The Count— DISASTER — based on early tallies Garret FitzGerald and Gerry Barry are calculating (on RTE radio) Fianna Fáil will be down close to 70. Gerry actually predicting 69! The FF people here, however, are confident they'll hold 73/74. Fine Gael also getting a hammering. Labour are sweeping the land. Albert does interview with Charlie (Bird) at his home. Goes to count centre where he gets a big reception. He seems in reasonable form, as if he expected this, but I only have to look at the faces of Kathleen, Philip and the girls to see the real picture. Brennan (Seamus) says FF should have no truck with Labour. . . . Albert goes home and big session develops in Longford Arms (shades of the Berlin bunker) with Michael Hand, Sean O'Rourke, Stephen Collins, Miriam Lord and *mé fhéin*, of course, in full flight. Just like at a good funeral. . . .'

I awoke with a serious hangover to be confronted by more incoming missiles. The seats were still tumbling against FF and kept doing so throughout the day. I wrote:

> 'Albert acts as if he were a slightly detached observer . . . FF keep missing (seats) out by a whisker at the finish — O'Kennedy in Tipp, Fahey in Waterford, Abbott in Westmeath, Tunney in Dublin North, Daly in Clare, Briscoe in Dublin S.C. Substantive abortion amendment banjaxed by 2 to 1 margin (Albert points finger at bishops) although right to travel and information comfortably carried. Flynn says it means legislation required to bring in some form of limited abortion. Now, that's one for the *méar fada!* Spring talking again about a "rotating" Taoiseach, i.e. John and he take it in turns! Mickey Doherty announces cabinet meeting on currency crisis tomorrow (doing his best to explain away Albert's late arrival at the count)

causing all kinds of panic on the international exchanges — "Jaysus, Mickey," sez someone, "you've taken two effing phennigs off the mark!" which is true! — Albert insists on pouring me a chain of brandies and starts talking . . . . Labour, Labour, Labour! . . . . he's fooling himself.'

With some results still to come in, the new Dáil make-up seemed likely to be: Fianna Fáil 67 seats (down 10), Fine Gael 45 (down 10), Labour 32 (up 17), Progressive Democrats 10 (up 4), Democratic Left 5, Others 6. Fianna Fáil, to retain power, would require a deal with Labour. I believed that would not happen — Fine Gael had already ruled themselves out of any association with Fianna Fáil — and, more significantly, the figures showed that the 'rainbow' was very much 'on' On that count night in Longford, the Taoiseach also insisted to me that the substantive abortion issue could have been won. The problem, he said, was that he was forced to simultaneously fight on two fronts. 'In the circumstances, we were bound to take our eye off the referendum ball.' It was around midnight when we got back to Dublin, but McCreevy and Cowen were waiting to talk to the Taoiseach. Martin Mansergh told me early signals were coming from Ruairi Quinn that Labour might be 'interested'. The problem was that the ball was now firmly in the opposition court; there could be no overt FF advances unless, or until, the others exhausted all the possible 'rainbow' permutations.

28 November, 1992

'Albert forced to sit an wait, to watch from the shadows for the gleam of hope. He's up to something though. I can tell. *An t-é nach bfhuil láidir, ni foláir do bheith glic.*'

On my way home, I bought the early morning editions of the newspapers. All of the pol corrs and analysts agreed that Fianna Fáil's only hope of continuing in power was via an arrangement with Labour. But they also agreed this would not happen, particularly in the light of Spring's virulent anti–FF attacks right up to polling day. The headline on Drapier's column in *The Irish Times* reflected the general view: 'The Rainbow Will Materialise Before the Next Dáil Meets.' Next day, senior *Independent Newspapers* executive Joe Hayes , with Vinnie Doyle, editor of the *Irish Independent,* mused with Albert Reynolds on what might have been had he not 'lost' the election. 'Any particular regrets, Albert?' 'Just one. I had something going which I think could have brought an end to the Troubles in the North. Other than that, no, no regrets.'

8

'BINGO — EIGHT BILLION SMACKEROOS!'

ON 5 NOVEMBER, 1992, in his contribution to the confidence debate at the end of the 26th Dáil, Dick Spring delivered one of the most devastating anti–Fianna Fáil speeches in modern Oireachtas history.

He first targeted Albert Reynolds whom he described as a Taoiseach without any mandate from the people, one who was viciously cruel to those who lived on the margins of society, who had broken all his promises of open government and who preached respect for the institutions of State but lacked the ability to conduct himself with dignity in any crisis. As for Fianna Fáil in government, low standards and the cheapening and debasement of political life was their hallmark.

> *Given these (standards), it must surely be considered amazing that any party would consider coalescing with them. . . we will not get involved in any government that are willing to bring politics into disrepute, as this government has done. . . . I believe one political party in this House has gone so far down the road of blindness to standards, and of blindness to the people they are supposed to represent, that it is impossible to see how anyone could support them in the future without seeing them first undergo the most radical transformation. We will not support any government with the track record of this one.*

Des O'Malley, who had more experience of supping with the devil, was noticeably more circumspect, despite having effectively brought down the Government. Asked if he might be prepared to go back into government with Reynolds after the election, he did not rule out the possibility. 'I don't rule out working with anyone,' he said, 'if the people and the party concerned work reasonably in a spirit of cabinet government. . . . If we were to go back in the same circumstances, then that would not be an effective government, and we would not go into it. It would hardly be a propitious circumstance if the allegation of 'dishonest' evidence stood.'

A few days later, asked once again if he would consider working with Fianna Fáil under Albert Reynolds, O'Malley edged further: 'That is very much up to him,' adding that he could not do so in 'present' circumstances. He was keeping his post-election options open. Said Bart Cronin: 'The PDs, if they get the chance, will be back knocking on the Fianna Fáil door — in the national interest.'

When Election '92 was over, however, John Bruton, for whatever reason, laid down various pre-conditions, including no rotating Taoiseach and, vitally, no question of accepting the Democratic Left, as part of any 'rainbow' arrangement; this although DL maintained that Fine Gael, three years previously, had offered to do a deal with them in return for support for Alan Dukes as Taoiseach. Bruton was now fixated on the formation a FG–Lab–PD administration.

His problem was that he was not in any position to dictate. Fine Gael had lost ten seats, proportionately more than Fianna Fáil, despite being in opposition. It behoved them to be extremely attentive to the Labour point of view. To make matters worse, Bruton himself had a struggle to reach the quota in his native Meath, being elected third, and losing his running mate John Farrelly in the process. A post-election opinion poll in the *Sunday Independent* showed Fine Gael down to 19 percent support with Labour up to 30 percent, making Labour for the first time the second most popular party in the State.

More urgently, Fine Gael frontbencher, Austin Currie, the party's standard bearer in the 1990 presidential election, had announced from the Dublin West count that his leader should accept the job of Tánaiste and serve under Dick Spring as Taoiseach in the new government. Currie was to eventually withdraw that suggestion, but the damage in those horse-trading days was incalculable.

1 December, 1992

> 'All, except Albert, say it's the "rainbow". McCreevy says it on *Questions and Answers*. Flynn again tells us any attempt to deal with Labour will "destroy" Fianna Fáil. Bart also says it has to be the "rainbow". Lunch with Maurice Manning who says "rainbow" is already being put together. *Evening Press* has Michael McDowell suddenly discovering that the PDs and Labour have a great deal in common. Have a long chat with Albert who says Currie's intervention may be sign that signals are coming to Fine Gael that Labour won't do business with Bruton. He seems to think it's not over yet. Meet Donal Kelly who tells me the word is that Dick is making John (Bruton) "eat dirt". What the hell is going on?'

Meantime, Dick Spring, protecting his left flank, kept insisting that Democratic Left were essential to any 'rainbow' in which Labour participated. Fine Gael pointed out that Labour had previously refused to allow Proinsias de Rossa and his colleague, MEP Des Geraghty, into the Socialist Group in the European Parliament, but nobody was listening. Spring could do no wrong as he went on to also firmly rule out any dealings with the Progressive Democrats. As for Fianna Fáil, he said, they would be better occupied seeking an accommodation with Fine Gael to form a government which would facilitate the emergence of left–right politics in the country.

Spring now entered into lengthy negotiations with Democratic Left despite (or perhaps because of) the fact that they had been emphatically rejected by the PDs as well as by Fine Gael. At the same time, he gradually increased his attacks on Fine Gael and the PDs while taking a noticeably softer line with Fianna Fáil. All this time, Albert Reynolds was bashfully acknowledging that Fianna Fáil were out of the frame as things stood. He told reporters: 'We haven't had an approach from anybody. Labour are talking to the other parties. The sooner a government is formed the better.' He was asked: 'But what if Labour can't reach agreement with them, Taoiseach?' 'Well, I suppose when they've talked to the rest, if they don't agree, they'll come and talk to us then.' I was aware that key figures in Fianna Fáil and Labour were already talking.

A few days after the election, Bart and I were in my office when the Taoiseach came in accompanied by Padraig Flynn and Seamus Brennan. They had clearly been discussing post-election options and, almost immediately, Flynn resumed his pre-election line of argument. There should be no question of an FF/Labour coalition; any such deal would be calamitous for Fianna Fáil; the proper course was for Fianna Fáil to go into principled opposition. Seamus Brennan agreed.

Again, I carefully watched Reynolds' reaction. He listened intently but, as before, he did not venture an opinion. What struck both Bart and me was the openness with which the anti-coalition view was being propagated. I knew Flynn was Labour's *bête noire* and that a number of FF ministerial places would have to be forfeited if Labour were to be accommodated at cabinet. It was still fascinating to watch Flynn finger-wagging — don't even think about it, Albert!

Already, Gerry Collins, Ray Burke, Jim McDaid, Seamus Kirk, Michael J. Noonan, John O'Donoghue, Mary Wallace and Ned O'Keeffe were being spoken of as against any deal for government. Even Reynolds loyalists such as Charlie McCreevy and Noel Dempsey were believed to favour going into opposition. We wondered too about a possible heave against Reynolds. Former FF Chief Whip Vincent Brady was preaching mutiny and rumours swept Leinster House that the 'dispossessed'. along with the newly disenchanted, were busily plotting.

A move to float the name of David Andrews as a potential successor was torpedoed by Andrews himself when he described the idea as unprincipled and even obscene. All eyes turned to Bertie Ahern but he too made it clear he would have nothing to do with a heave.

Labour were presenting their flirtation with Democratic Left as based on shared leftist beliefs as well as on the likely final allocation of Dáil seats, one of which remained to be decided. A marathon series of recounts was still going on for the last Dublin South Central place which was being contested by Ben Briscoe of Fianna Fáil and Democratic Left's Eric Byrne. The first recount left Byrne ahead by nine votes, and it was widely believed that the final figures would confirm that outcome, as a recount result had never before been overturned. That would then allow for an 83-seat FG–Lab–DL administration, complete with Dáil majority, albeit of just one seat.

As to why Labour should favour such a precarious arrangement, they told the corrs they wanted their volatile left-wing DL cousins where they could keep an eye on them, safely inside the government tent; this could then lead to an eventual Lab–DL merger; it would also rule out having to negotiate with the detested PDs. Most importantly, a combination of Lab–DL numbers would greatly increase their negotiating strength when dealing with Fine Gael. At least, that was the story for the record.

Off the record, key Labour insiders were steadily and unremittingly bad-mouthing John Bruton. Their insistence that he was either stupid or crazy, or both, was almost eerie in its intensity. It seemed to be based on their experiences of Bruton in the Fine Gael–Labour administrations of the early Eighties. I asked Reynolds: 'What on earth did John do to Labour back then?' He replied: 'It's nothing to do with Labour. The question is, what did John do to Dick?'

3 December, 1992

'. . . Albert finally talks to me of the Flynn objection to Labour. He and "Pee" simply disagree on the subject, he says. It doesn't seem to bother him (Reynolds) much either. In fact, Joe Walsh is sent out to run it (coalition) up the flag pole to see who'll salute it —" There is no reason to presume changed government cannot involve Fianna Fáil" — so diffident and unassuming! Albert doesn't tell me in so many words, but there's no doubt there's already been behind-the-scenes contacts with Labour — some of these guys are very pally with Bertie — and Albert clearly believes they're "coming"! Still, Seamus Brennan keeps telling me most senior ministers want to go into opposition. . . MM (Martin Mansergh) tells me maybe Collins will be sent to Europe — surely not on as Flynn would go bananas —and the bould McCreevy says Albert will do anything to get into bed with Labour, but that he won't get away with it. . . oooohhh. . . *Seachain tú fhéin, Diggy!*'

The media were still giving long odds on a Fianna Fáil–Labour deal, not least because of Dick Spring's imminent appearance at the beef tribunal — it had now emerged that he would be going into the witness box in advance of the formation of a government — and there seemed to be no doubt about the nature of the evidence he would give.

Spring's charges against Reynolds, both in his Dáil and his written Tribunal statements, were regarded as practically on a par with O'Malley's allegations. There was general agreement that he would not back off when he appeared before Mr Justice Hamilton and, therefore, the consensus was that he could not contemplate government with Reynolds. *The Irish Times* put it succinctly: 'Could Mr Spring credibly enter a historic partnership government with Fianna Fáil, only to begin his period in office in the witness box at the Beef Tribunal?'

Then, to everyone's surprise, Spring, along with Barry Desmond, Pat Rabbitte and Tomas MacGiolla, invoked parliamentary privilege in relation to their sources of information. Within days, Liam Hamilton duly ruled that all of them were entitled to claim privilege. He rejected the Attorney General's contention that they had effectively waived Dáil privilege when they submitted written statements to the Tribunal.

About this time, after ten days of the Dublin South Central recount — the longest recount on record — four votes finally lay between the two candidates. The original plurality in favour of Byrne had been reversed and Briscoe was adjudged to have taken the last seat. This left any FG–Lab–DL coalition a vote short of a Dáil majority, so it would require Greens and/or Independents to make up the numbers.

I remarked to the Taoiseach that this was a lucky break, and could swing the balance in favour of a Fianna Fáil–Labour arrangement. He replied to the effect that it probably wouldn't have made any difference if Eric Byrne had won. The majority in Labour wanted to do business with

Fianna Fáil in any event. Byrne's defeat would merely help get them off the DL hook.

'How can you be so sure?' I asked. 'Are you telling me you've already got a deal with Labour?' 'No,' he replied. 'It's just adding two and two. Dick has made an offer to John (Bruton) that he can — that he must — refuse. John can't go for the rotating Taoiseach bit, and Dick knows that.' On Sunday, 6 December, armed with an IMS poll showing Labour with a 30 percent rating (up eleven points) and Fine Gael at 19 (down six) since the election — Fianna Fáil were still languishing on 39 percent — Dick Spring went to talk about the formation of a government with John Bruton in the Constitution Room of the Shelbourne Hotel. Soon after that meeting concluded, a Labour TD took me aside in a Baggot Street bar: 'Dick put Bruton in his box today — now John knows he won't be Taoiseach.'

7 December, 1992

> 'For the first time, I'm beginning to believe Albert might survive all of this. There's an extraordinary pic in *The Irish Times* today which backs up everything I'm being told. It shows John and Dick standing all by themselves in the Constitution Room with their backs to each other. They say Dick wouldn't even do him the courtesy of sitting down for the meeting, that he marched up and down lecturing him on what was wrong with him, why he was unsuitable to head a government, etc. . . . Normally, I would take that kind of story with a grain of salt — an FF flier — but it's all coming from the Labour lads themselves — and even from FG!'

On 10 December, just before our departure for a crucial EU Summit in Edinburgh, Labour finally made their first formal approach to Fianna Fáil. They sent the Taoiseach a copy of the joint Labour/Democratic Left policy document accompanied by a request for a meeting. They probably calculated that Reynolds would not be in a position to respond until, at the earliest, his return from Edinburgh four days later. However, within an hour, even before the Taoiseach's plane took off, a considered 20-page response from Fianna Fáil was lobbed back over the Labour fence. And, to their amazement, it was not just a pre-prepared variation on the FF manifesto but a negotiating formula bristling with positive reactions to specific proposals contained in the Labour document.

Martin Mansergh had drawn up the FF response in anticipation of the Labour approach — he had been made aware of practically all the Labour and DL proposals before they sent Fianna Fáil their document — and Mansergh's rapid fire rejoinder was distinguished by its readiness to accept, word for word in some cases, the Labour proposals. We were acutely aware that this was in stark contrast to the many *caveats* and preconditions laid down by Fine Gael. So, as the Taoiseach headed for Scotland, the mood aboard the government jet was: 'Now, let Labour put that in their pipe and smoke it.'

I later heard that Labour were especially taken by the FF document's commitment to the concept that 'a partnership Government between two substantial parties would inevitably be different in character to a traditional coalition involving one large and one small party.'

Albert Reynolds also had other things on his mind as he headed for the EU Summit in Edinburgh. Since coming to office, he had maintained that he could secure an unprecedented doubling of Ireland's EU funding entitlement, bringing the total to £6 billion over a five year period, and now his promise was about to be put to the test.

He would have been determined to fulfil his pledge whatever the circumstances. With Labour 'watching for a sign', as Bertie Ahern put it to him, it was now literally a matter of political life and death. He was committed to meeting Dick Spring as soon as we arrived back from Edinburgh. The betting amongst almost all the experts was that he had already got the funding issue badly wrong.

The practically unanimous view of the Brussels-based Irish media was that Reynolds had originally exaggerated the EU structural and cohesion funds potential and was now either too stubborn or scared to admit it. For months, they had been citing various developments in support of this contention, including the currency crisis, the EU budgetary problem, the Danish rejection of Maastricht, the cost of German unification, allegedly superior claims of poorer countries such as Greece and Portugal, and opposition to the Irish case by the richer member states. On the eve of his departure for Edinburgh, *The Irish Times* editorialised that the Taoiseach had 'unwisely' hung himself up on the £6 billion objective.

The political consensus supported this analysis. EU Commission President Jacques Delors admitted that his original targets on funding for the poorer countries were 'over ambitious'. Most EU finance ministers were opposed to Delors' plan for an expanded Community budget. Reynolds himself admitted to me that, ever since the EU Summit in Lisbon, he was fighting practically a lone battle — 'even the Spanish have deserted us'— so Irish opposition MEPs such as the PDs Pat Cox and John Cushnahan of Fine Gael took to rubbishing the Reynolds claim, with Cox maintaining he would be lucky to secure £4.5 billion.

11 December, 1992: Edinburgh

'All day talks at creepy Holyrood Palace. Hope Albert isn't in some cloud cuckoo land. He keeps telling me we're going to do better than £6 billion. But he warns me not to hype it to the corrs —that'll be a change! — just to say that we're still aiming for the £6 billion, that it'll be tough going, etc. . . . Also here are Bertie, David Andrews, Tom Kitt. The official heavies P. O hUiginn, Dermot Nally, Sean Cromien, Maurice O'Connell, Michael Tutty, Paddy McKernan, Ted Barrington go back and forth clutching lists of figures and calculators (they're sure earning their pay here).

'It's hard to tell anything from their professional poker faces. Albert and Bertie keep going into huddles together "on the margin". It's not all about EU funding. They're discussing developments on the FF–Lab front much of the time. I think Bertie is in constant touch with Labour (Ruairi Quinn?). They'd bloody well better get this funding thing right. . . .'

I hosted a dinner for journalists covering the Summit as the Taoiseach, Bertie Ahern, David Andrews and top Irish officials attended a banquet aboard the royal yacht Britannia with Queen Elizabeth, Prince Charles and Princess Diana, although Charles and Di had just announced they were breaking up. At that stage, the pol corrs were still unanimously of the view that Reynolds was about to lose power, so I made easily the booziest speech of my brief period as press secretary, much to the amusement of Annette Andrews, wife of David Andrews, who delighted us by agreeing to be guest of honour but who still must have wondered at my maudlin message — 'You won't have Diggy to kick around any more although, mind you, we're always willing to deal — is there anyone out there?'

Padraig O hUiginn played an important role liaising with key figures of the EU Secretariat and the British Presidency. He was centrally involved in the incorporation of what was regarded as a key paragraph in the final Summit declaration, stating that the Commission would have to take account of issues such as unemployment and rural development in allocating structural funds. This was designed to prevent any future attempt to reduce Ireland's 13.5 percent share of the funds. At least, that was the calculation.

At one stage, the Taoiseach almost casually told me he had decided Padraig Flynn should succeed Ray McSharry as EU Commissioner. I recalled what he had said to me after McSharry announced his departure in August. At that time, he didn't want Flynn in the job.

Musing then on the competing claims of Flynn and Máire Geoghegan Quinn, he said Geoghegan Quinn going to Europe could confront him with an unwinnable Galway West by-election, so that wasn't on. Neither could Flynn go, he added, because he needed him beside him as an adviser. 'What about O'Malley for Europe?' he said suddenly. 'It would split the PDs, lop off their head, get Dessie out of everyone's hair, and maybe we'd win the East Limerick by-election to boot.'

In jest? You could never be sure with Albert Reynolds. Immediately after the election count, he talked straight-faced to Bart and I about going to Europe himself — 'how would you both like to be in my cabinet?' — and it took a moment to realise he was winding us up. In any event, Flynn could now book his ticket for Brussels. But, warned Reynolds, it was essential that I say nothing about it to the media pending certain further developments.

12 December, 1992: Edinburgh

> 'Bingo! — EIGHT billion smackeroos — 10.30 p.m. after marathon session. Albert walks out of the conference room and heads straight at me, his eyes blazing: "Eight billion, Diggy, eight billion. . . tell that to the begrudgers. . . now watch me put a government together!" At news conference, the Irish corrs (Brussels based) look stunned — the foreign press must have thought we'd suffered a national disaster — Albert says afterwards: "If I came out with nothing, that shower would have stood up and cheered.". . . However, John Downing, the *Indo's* (the *Irish Independent*) man in Brussels gets stuck in — says the money is over a longer period and queries the basis (13.5 percent?) for Albert's figures — and Albert is annoyed. He more or less tells John to shag off. . . . But is it too late? Will it all be handed over to the rainbow? Home at 2 a.m. Woods, Dempsey and Brennan waiting at airport. More huddling. We go tiger hunting tomorrow.'

In the afternoon (13 Dec.), I arrived ahead of the Taoiseach at Dublin's Berkeley Court Hotel for the crucial meeting with Dick Spring. Chatting with reporters in the lobby, I became aware of considerable background to-ing and fro-ing involving many familiar Labour faces. When Reynolds arrived, I was able to inform him: 'Practically the entire Labour frontbench is here, presumably to assess whatever you and Dick may come up with.' He nodded: 'They seem to be taking a page out of Martin's (Mansergh) book. They're certainly not wasting any time. Looks like they may want to do business.'

Dick Spring was accompanied by his chief adviser, Fergus Finlay, whom I had known for more than a decade. We had lost touch to a large extent due probably to my move away from Leinster House to front *Six-One*.

The four of us went by lift to the sumptuous penthouse suite where the two leaders immediately proceeded to an inner room, leaving Finlay and me on our own.

I nervously tried small talk. 'Do you think this is going to take . . . ?' Finlay interrupted: 'Can Albert deliver? 'How do you mean "deliver"?' 'Can he deliver, if they agree in there?' 'Oh, you mean can he get it through the Fianna Fáil parliamentary party?. . . get them to buy it?. . . absolutely. They'll not hit him, not with the eight billion pound baby in his arms, not if he's dealing to get back into government.' 'We can't take Flynn.' said Finlay. 'You mean "Pee"?' 'We can't take him. We don't care what job he gets, Europe, whatever, but we can't take him.'

I paused: 'All I can tell you, Fergus, is that I don't think Padraig Flynn is going to be a problem.'

That was all. We sat making small talk for what seemed almost a half hour but I cannot remember what else was said. It seemed to me that Finlay had two items to enquire about and that, once I responded, there was little else to say.

When the two leaders emerged, we all simply shook hands and walked away. When I asked the Taoiseach how it had gone, he said absent-mindedly: 'Fine, fine.'

Days later, the newspapers, radio and TV were still full of speculation as to 'will they, won't they?' But I was already convinced of the outcome on foot of not much more than 30 seconds of a conversation with Fergus Finlay. On that Sunday 13 December, 1992, several weeks before the formation of the new government, I left the Berkeley Court, dropped into the Baggot Inn, rang Marie and said: 'It's all over. Albert and Dick are getting hitched. Come on out and we'll celebrate.' She, a long-time Labour voter, said: 'Are you sure it calls for a celebration?'

9

'ALL BLUSTER, BLUFF AND BOOZE'

DICK SPRING must have known that any Labour move towards Fianna Fáil under Albert Reynolds was going to be difficult to justify. He could hardly have anticipated, however, the outrage it provoked among most of his hitherto uncritical admirers, particularly in the media.

From being the hero of the hour, Spring spiralled downwards through initial taunts of being 'flea-infested' (having laid down with dogs) via a later charge in *The Irish Times* that he was guilty of 'Caribbean-style nepotism' to the *Sunday Independent* columnist Eamon Dunphy's considered view that he was 'a bollocks of the highest order'.

A few days after Spring's meeting with Reynolds, *The Irish Times* devoted a half-page spread to reprinting his lacerating anti-Fianna Fáil contribution to the 'no confidence' debate at the close of the 26th Dáil. An accompanying editorial asked whether what he said then about Fianna Fáil was contrived merely to secure political advantage and if he was willing to share power with people who were morally outside the pale which he inhabited.

On RTE's *Prime Time* programme, presenter Olivia O'Leary reminded Spring of what she described as pledges in his Dáil speech that Labour would not enter government with Fianna Fáil. She asked: 'Did you mean any of that?' Then, as he hesitated, she twisted the knife: 'Do you mean anything you say?' They were not long, the days of wine and red Labour roses.

15 December, 1992

> 'Albert meets with Dick for an hour. Fergus waits in my office. Pleasant chat. He makes it clear they (Labour) won't do business with John (Bruton) whom he doesn't think much of, to put it mildly. Mind you, he is clearly not enamoured of Albert either — the lesser of two evils? Dick comes in and, over tea and biscuits, tells me that press speculation that Padraig Flynn will be one of the three FF negotiators tomorrow is not true . . . what's with these guys and

'Pee' then talks about the "future" in a roundabout way. It's real North Kerry speak — if, if, if . . . maybe, maybe, maybe — but I understand North Kerry, even if I'm not a native speaker. He's coming, all right.'

A few hours later, Padraig Flynn was passing the impressive Sycamore Room next to my office when it was mentioned to him that it was being suggested as a venue for the Fianna Fáil and Labour talks on the formation of a government. Without breaking stride, pointing his finger dramatically at the room door, Flynn exclaimed: 'If Labour go in there, they will not be let out.'

On 16 December, the two sides began their deliberations in Leinster House. Fianna Fáil were represented by Bertie Ahern, Brian Cowen and Noel Dempsey; Labour by Ruairi Quinn, Brendan Howlin and Mervyn Taylor. Afterwards, they said that they had decided *inter alia* it would be 'more convenient' to hold the remainder of their meetings in the Sycamore Room. The whisper down the long corridor was: 'Ruairi is coming like an express train.'

Hell hath no fury like a politician played for a patsy. John Bruton, despite all the straws in the wind, seemed genuinely dumbfounded by what he called Dick Spring's perfidious somersault: 'It diminishes not only his credibility, but also the credibility of all politicians.' Des O'Malley accused Spring of having operated to a dishonourable gameplan from the outset: 'Labour has sought to marginalise and to rubbish our (PD) role in government formation.' Mary Harney agreed: 'I suspect Labour have already done a secret deal with Fianna Fáil.' Interestingly, Stephen Collins subsequently wrote that Spring's closest advisers were evenly divided, leaving him with the decision.

Now, as Reynolds no longer offered an option, the PD assaults on him resumed with renewed fervour. Predictably, it was back to the Beef Tribunal as well as to the luckless Harry Whelehan. O'Malley accused Harry of being politically influenced in instructing counsel at the Tribunal to seek the dropping of certain allegations which could be a threat to the FF/Lab talks on the formation of a new government. This, he said, was particularly relevant in light of the pending appearance of Spring before the Tribunal. Harry responded that he was offended and disturbed by the allegation — he said his role had always been exercised wholly independently of government — and he pointed out that O'Malley's counsel had made no objection to the State team's line at the Tribunal.

John Bruton concentrated on Spring and his stated intention to refuse to name his sources of information at the tribunal. It would be an unprecedented abuse of the privilege of the Dáil, and a culpable waste of public monies, if the tribunal was consequently prevented from finishing its work. The Labour leader was forced to issue vehement assurances that he would not support any curbing of the tribunal 'by anybody'. But it was observed that he confined himself to dismissing the Bruton source of information claims and made no direct reference to what O'Malley was alleging.

The movement towards a FF–Lab 'Partnership' — their mutually preferred word for coalition — also continued to be opposed within Fianna Fáil. Gerry Collins, backed by a number of ex-Ministers, spoke forcibly in favour of going into opposition. Then Ray McSharry, who had stood by Reynolds through thick and thin until the talks began with Labour, fired a Parthian shot from Brussels. On the evening of 16 December, shortly after the first meeting of the Fianna Fáil and Labour negotiators, the Taoiseach told me that he had a disturbing report from Brussels.

Irish correspondents there had been briefed by a top Commission source that the Irish claim of having secured an £8 billion package of EU funds at Edinburgh was not valid. He added: 'I understand that the source is Mac.'

17 December, 1992

> 'All papers carry the "£8 Billion In Doubt" story. They quote unidentified EC officials as their source. They say Albert based his £8 billion figure on the assumption that Ireland would retain its existing 13.5 percent share-out of the structural funds, but that this share-out level is now highly unlikely. Albert tells me of how Maurice O'Connell held up piece of paper, so Albert could see it, at end of Edinburgh bargaining. Maurice, he says, had written on paper the figure £8.7 bn. (Eight point seven!) I'm told it's been confirmed about Mac; that he said the £8 billion was not on, no way; that it'll only amount to over £6 billion over seven years; that even if there's some private deal with Delors — which he (Mac) doubts — it ain't going to happen. . . .

> 'Padraig O hUiginn onto Williamson (Secretary General of Commission) and I'm told he gets assurance that reports are without foundation — I gather Albert has been onto Delors — and we're getting all kinds of Brussels promises that it will be all right on the night. So what's Mac on about? We announce that Padraig Flynn is the new EC Commissioner — at least that should suit both Albert and Dick — and ain't "Pee" lucky to be outa here.'

If Albert Reynolds was unfortunate when assuming office on the day the 'X' case broke, Labour were now having to enter government at the precise moment of the State's most intractable economic crisis since the 1970s. Unemployment was close to an all-time high. The value of the pound was under unprecedented pressure. And interest rates were again threatening to soar.

Other bullets were also waiting to be bitten. The long simmering Aer Lingus unprofitability crisis, with its attendant TEAM aircraft maintenance problem, and the question of the compulsory Shannon Airport stopover for transatlantic carriers, could no longer be kept on the back burner. The giant Digital factory in Galway was about to close down most of its operation with the loss of close on a thousand jobs. An election campaign row over the siting of three interpretative centres in environmentally sensitive locations was shaping to divide Labour progressives and Fianna Fáil 'philistines'. And Labour's protective device to ensure maximum protection in bed with Fianna Fáil — the so-called 'Ethics Pill' — was already being rubbished by the Soldiers of Destiny.

Labour insistence on this new code of government ethics upset Fianna Fáil sensitivities from the outset, despite Albert Reynolds' determination to honour that part of the deal. There was talk of compulsory registration of parliamentarians' interests (to include inspection of bank and other financial statements), limits on spending on election campaigns, a register of gifts to office holders, and disclosure of the source of substantial party donations.

More worryingly, there was Labour's liberal agenda on such issues as divorce, abortion and homosexuality. Fianna Fáil accepted that a new divorce referendum was a nettle which had to be grasped — Reynolds kept telling me it would be a close-run thing despite what the polls might indicate — but they were chary of anything to do with abortion. Until the day he left office, Albert Reynolds regularly reminded me: 'I am anti–abortion.'

As for homosexuality, Reynolds had never made a secret of the fact that the issue was 'at the bottom of my list of priorities' despite the fact that four years had elapsed since Irish laws on homosexuality were found to be in violation of the European Convention on Human Rights. Tom Savage, an instinctive liberal who had regularly urged the Taoiseach to decriminalise homosexuality, now saw his opportunity. Reynolds grumbled and warned that such as former Minister Noel Davern had clearly indicated that he would not support decriminalisation. Apart from

Reynolds putting down that perfunctory marker, Savage found that he was now practically pushing an open door on the issue. The bottom line was that Labour would not tolerate any further procrastination.

21 December, 1992

> 'Dick (Spring) goes into witness box. I couldn't get down to the Castle, so listened to RTE coverage. I have a piece of his original written statement to the Tribunal in front of me (it repeatedly sticks it to Albert, allegation after allegation) but Dick's evidence today was conspicuous for the absence of two words. He went on and on and on, but never mentioned "Albert Reynolds", and then everything was adjourned until after Christmas!'

Now, barring accidents, e.g. an undetected time-bomb, the 'Partnership' would come together in the new year. I noted:

> 'Labour terrified that there may be skeletons in the FF closet which will fall out when it's too late for them to back off. Niamh Breathnach said to me that they were worried about this — "after all, we know Fianna Fáil!" — and I was stung to reply that I wouldn't be surprised if the first skeleton to fall out of the new administration closet came from the Labour side. She kind of blinked at me. She actually believes all that stuff.'

Then, right on cue, with the dawn of the new year, the complacent mood of seasonal goodwill came to an abrupt end. Just as the 'Partnership' was about to be launched, Des O'Malley fired a political Exocet which almost scuppered the new ship of state as it was being launched. Subsequently, O'Malley vehemently denied that he timed his move in a last ditch attempt to sink the partnership. He told the Dáil that he had no control over the timing of his revelations. It had nothing to do, he said, with the fact that Fianna Fáil and Labour were coincidentally negotiating a government deal. Albert Reynolds said to me: 'He could have fooled me.'

On 5 January, O'Malley sought a meeting with Dick Spring and told him that one of the State's legal team at the Beef Tribunal, Gerry Danaher, had tried to intimidate his (O'Malley's) legal representative at the tribunal, Adrian Hardiman, and also that confidential O'Malley documents had been furnished to Fianna Fáil and subsequently used by the State's team.

The so-called 'Horseshoe Bar' affair centred on a number of conversations, some of them on various dates in 1992, when Danaher allegedly threatened that the Revenue Commissioners might take a keen interest in the financial affairs of Adrian Hardiman if his cross-examination of the Taoiseach at the Tribunal caused unnecessary offence;

and certain other conversations, over the 1992 Christmas period, in the bar of the Shelbourne Hotel, when Danaher allegedly told another member of O'Malley's legal team, Diarmuid McGuinness, that confidential documents belonging to O'Malley had been furnished to Fianna Fáil head office 'in a brown envelope' and subsequently used by the State team at the Tribunal.

This latest development had a galvanic effect on Dick Spring. He immediately went to see Albert Reynolds who, when he had finished listening, called in the Attorney General and Garda Commissioner PJ Culligan. Later that afternoon, Harry and Paddy Culligan had a meeting lasting about an hour with O'Malley. Afterwards, Harry consulted with members of the State's legal team and then announced he was satisfied that no documents belonging to O'Malley had got into their hands. He subsequently came in for severe criticism, mainly from the Progressive Democrats, for having delivered this verdict before talking to those who made the allegations. Dick Spring announced that he wanted a full inquiry, irrespective of the consequences: 'We cannot go into government if there are clouds hanging around.'

6 January, 1993

> 'Labour are in a bad state. Their reaction to Danaher shows that they're terrified of stepping on old FF landmines. Some of them clearly have qualms about the deal too, and there's still considerable anti–FF feeling in the party. Quinn and Howlin are definitely aboard, so too most of the frontbench, but Dick's kitchen cabinet led by Fergus is another matter entirely. I think Fergus goes along with the logic of dealing with Fianna Fáil, but it's not what his gut tells him. I don't think he likes or trusts Fianna Fáil. . . Inevitably, Harry is wham bang in the middle of the Danaher mess. O'Malley and McDowell say he jumped the gun and got it all wrong. Harry's game always ends in trouble — although I'm assured that he acted properly — or is it that he just naturally attracts hassle?'

Labour hesitated — 'their knees buckled for a moment' Reynolds said to me — then they recovered their nerve as the Fianna Fáil ministers emphasised to them that the tawdry affair was basically 'a falling out of auld acquaintances while alcoholic drink was being consumed'.

Eventually, the Barristers' Professional Conduct Tribunal announced that Gerry Danaher was guilty of conduct unbecoming a barrister (this judgement was subsequently reversed on appeal) but they rejected the two main charges against him, the alleged intimidation of Adrian

Hardiman, and the allegation that O'Malley documents had been furnished by Fianna Fáil to the State team at Dublin Castle.

To many observers, the Tribunal's most significant finding was that Danaher had misused information that he had in order to 'concoct a story which was fundamentally untrue'. Afterwards, I wrote:

> '... All bluster, bluff and booze. At the end of the day, Danaher was just winding them up. Only he should have known better than to fool around with these particular "friends" of his. There's a lesson here. Brilliant PD use of a messy episode others would have walked away from. Brilliant moral indignation at satanic Danaher machinations... Fianna Fáil haven't a clue how to deal with this stuff. They look guilty even when they're totally innocent — "did we do it?"— if they're told often enough that they are guilty, they'll believe it. A piece of stupid boozy tomfoolery expertly manipulated into nearly frightening Labour off. These geezers in the Shelbourne were old school-tie Law Library chums, but business is business.'

On 12 January, the FF–Lab knot was finally tied, providing a government with the biggest majority — 42 seats — in the history of the State. Labour obtained six cabinet places — Dick Spring (Tánaiste and Foreign Affairs), Ruairi Quinn (Finance), Brendan Howlin (Health), Niamh Breathnach (Education), Michael D. Higgins (Arts, Culture, Gaeltacht) and Mervyn Taylor (Equality and Law Reform). Reynolds' words came back to me: 'Labour will drive a hard bargain.'

Fianna Fáil survivors were Albert Reynolds (Taoiseach), Bertie Ahern (Finance), Michael Woods (Social Welfare), Maire Geoghegan Quinn (Justice), Michael Smith (Environment), Joe Walsh (Agriculture), David Andrews (Defence and Marine), Charlie McCreevy (Tourism and Trade), Brian Cowen (Transport, Energy, Communications).

McCreevy seemed as surprised as everyone else at being still in cabinet. Typically, he teased Reynolds about it: 'You couldn't bring yourself to drop me — the (Reynolds) girls wouldn't let you.' Reynolds flashed back: 'At least, I've got you out of Social Welfare.' FF cabinet representation had been reduced from 13 to 9 to accommodate Labour. Fortuitously, Padraig Flynn was on his way to Brussels; former Tánaiste John Wilson had retired from the Dáil, and Health Minister, Dr John O'Connell, ruled himself out of cabinet, so the only FF Minister actually dropped from cabinet was Seamus Brennan (Education) who was made Minister of State.

The Taoiseach was surprised by O'Connell's decision to step down. The personable doctor's original appointment to Health represented the achievement of a life ambition, and he had worked effectively in the office. Afterwards, Reynolds told me he felt O'Connell's decision to retire had to do with his having personal health worries combined with 'frustration' at not being able, despite being in office, to more rapidly implement his ambitious (and costly) plans for Health.

Nevertheless, the Taoiseach was euphoric about the new partnership — he kept telling me — 'this will be a great government' — and it looked for a time that his relationship with the new Tanaiste would be relaxed and even good humoured. They teased each other while divvying up the portfolios. 'We would be very interested in having the Culture ministry, Albert.' 'Well, Dick, I don't know about that. It belongs to the Department of An Taoiseach, you know.' 'Come on, Albert. That was Charlie Haughey's trick. He loved all that stuff. You don't give a fuck about Culture.' 'Well, since you put like that, Dick. . . ooh, all right. . . but tell Michael D. I refuse to give up the ballet classes.' Guffaws and knee-slapping all round.

I complacently figured Labour were securely locked in and that, given the favourable long range economic outlook (plus £8 billion due over six years), they would gear themselves for the long haul and to staying aboard for at least four and a half years.

14 January, 1993

> 'Albert tells me Labour will now have to come to terms with budgetary reality — we're also into this currency crisis — and that they must accept the rough side of being in government. Still, I suppose, if you're going to be unpopular, it may as well be at the start of a five-year term. Down 'scope. Secure hatch. Crash-dive!'

Neither I — nor the media — paid much attention to what Spring had told Labour delegates during the special conference at which they decided to enter government with Fianna Fáil. He said: 'This government will stand or fall on the issue of trust, and no one should be mistaken about that. It will be a policy-driven government, and not a scandal-driven government. If it does not conform to the highest standards of accountability and openness, it will cease to exist — it is as simple as that.'

10

'TONIGHT MEANS THE BEGINNING OF THE END OF THIS GOVERNMENT'

FROM THE start, I was impressed by the Labour operation. Despite having doubled the party's Dáil seats at a stroke, the team of advisers surrounding the party leader stayed small, cohesive and constantly focused. They were also, from beginning to end, fiercely protective of Dick Spring and inveterately suspicious of Albert Reynolds.

An early Fianna Fáil miscalculation was to place too much emphasis on good relations with Labour at cabinet level. Undoubtedly, such as Quinn, Howlin and Taylor 'frolicked' with FF ministers, but insufficient attention was paid to Spring's insiders, and their majority distrust of both Fianna Fáil and Reynolds.

This inner cabinet was headed by Fergus Finlay, Spring's friend, confidant and chief counsellor; John Rogers, former Attorney General, also a friend since their days at Trinity College together; Willie Scally, chief economic adviser; Greg Sparks, chief partnership programme manager; Senator Pat Magner, expert on the parliamentary Labour party and organisation, and John Foley, former *Irish Independent* political correspondent, now Head of the Government Information Service, and my press secretary opposite number.

Finlay and Foley were the two I knew best. Finlay was highly intelligent, astute and volatile. He had extraordinary influence over Spring; he decided quite early on, in my view, that the Reynolds–Spring union wasn't working, that Reynolds could not be let have his way to the extent that he desired and, if that were not achievable, that Spring would have to be prepared to pull out of government. Foley was a friend of mine, and we remained friends to the end.

We had worked on and off together in journalism for more than 25 years. From the outset, we liaised closely on media briefings, etc.

although our agendas generally diverged. He was also given direct access to the Taoiseach, in contrast to the non-communication with his predecessor, Stephen O'Byrnes, in the FF/PD administration. Within a few weeks, I wrote in my diary:

'John (Foley) plays a vital role for Labour. I rarely go in to see the Taoiseach without John being invited along. I gather part of the deal (with Spring) was that this access to Albert be afforded to John. It must be invaluable to Labour — talk of being a fly on the wall — and Albert encourages John to "speak out", which he does. I cannot imagine Dick reciprocating.'

Initially, I agreed with the Taoiseach that he was heading a potentially great government. Indeed, it was many months before it dawned on me that he had probably landed himself in at least as bad a tangle as with the Progressive Democrats. In relation to the previous government, it had been widely acknowledged that Reynolds had no choice but to cohabit with the PDs, having been presented with a *fait accompli* by Haughey.

Now, however, he was seen as primarily responsible for Fianna Fáil having to share close to half the seats in cabinet with Labour. The Soldiers of Destiny were still smarting from that humiliation, and Noel Dempsey was echoing a representative FF grassroots view when he said to me: 'It's important that Labour realise that we're still the majority party, and that we're not going to be pushed around.'

Unfortunately, Labour were also in defensive mood. They had been badly shaken by widespread media antipathy to the deal with Fianna Fáil. They were to become progressively more dispirited by opinion poll verification that the public were similarly unimpressed. Therefore, it became of the utmost importance to Labour that they be seen, not just to hold their own with Fianna Fáil, but to actually dominate the partnership in key areas.

These conflicting FF–Lab priorities were compounded by the different character and personality of Taoiseach and Tanaiste. Reynolds was manipulative and impatient of opposition to his wishes. Spring was moody and quick to take offence. Given these characteristics, it was always going to be a bumpy ride, but I was still convinced that they were both sufficiently astute to arrive at a *modus vivendi*.

27 February, 1993

'I kind of like Spring, but he's touchy, and, when he's not being touchy, Fergus is touchy for him. Anyone who has studied Dick knows he demands "respect"

— don't they all! — that he stands on his dignity at all times. It seems he never really wanted to get into bed with Albert either, but that's OK. It'll work out.'

Some Labour ministers had still not entered their new departments when headlines blazoned the first great test of the Partnership. International investors and market players were speculating that the exchange rate of the Irish pound within the EU Exchange Rate Mechanism (ERM) could no longer be sustained.

Bertie Ahern kept insisting that the disadvantages of devaluation far outweighed any short-term benefits, but for how long could the new government support a pound trading at as much as 110p sterling? Government strategy was to try to secure EU support in general and German support, in particular, for Irish resistance to the speculators. Ahern, meantime, was hanging on for either a reduction in German interest rates or recovery in the value of sterling.

There was initial all-party and media backing for the government stance, but then John Bruton came out in favour of devaluation, to the dismay of his own Fine Gael colleagues. Reynolds, the businessman, had few illusions. He told me: 'We can only hold out for so long. We're really only midgets in this league. We're gone if the Germans don't throw us a lifeline.' The Germans never did. The Bundesbank had already helped the French franc, and would eventually move to protect the Danish krone, but not the Irish punt.

So, faced with unavoidable increases in already punitive mortgage and other borrowing rates, the government finally capitulated on 30 January and devalued by 10 percent. I noted:

> 'We get the message. We're no core currency. Like it or not, we're in the junior EU league. But Labour stood shoulder to shoulder with FF in the *bearna baoil.* A good sign.'

Bertie Ahern, who had worked tirelessly to get the Community to underpin the ERM, was uncharacteristically bitter: 'At the end of the day, Diggy, it didn't suit them to help us. We didn't have sufficient clout. They threw us to the sharks. It's a hard monetary lesson.'

Little did we know that we were soon to learn an even harder monetary lesson from Europe.

The first internal partnership power battle was also developing. Michael D. Higgins, new Minister for Arts, Culture and the Gaeltacht, was at odds with Noel Dempsey in his capacity as Minister of State for the Office of Public Works, over the building of an interpretative centre in the heart of the nation's most ecologically unique tableland, Mullaghmore, on the Burren, in Co. Clare. It was being presented as a confrontation between enlightened Labour environmentalists and Fianna Fáil vulgarians, between protectors of the national heritage and hucksters whose only concern was cash, campers and carparks.

The Taoiseach and Dempsey told me there was no question of ceding authority to Michael D. either over Mullaghmore or two other interpretative centres being built at Luggala, Co. Wicklow, and in the Boyne Valley. Dempsey said to me: 'Tell Fergus and John these projects are too far advanced to be dropped. Tell them that, if Labour only accept that, Michael D. can have authority over all future projects of this kind.'

I duly conveyed that message to Foley who soon rang back with Labour's answer — 'no deal'. Personally, I had an open mind on the issue. I was merely anxious that fellow Clare/Galway man Michael D., one of my heroes, emerge undamaged from the fray. The singer, not the song.

Now, with 302,000 registered unemployed, the worst figures in the history of the State, the new government had to produce its first Budget. Even allowing for devaluation, it turned out a political dud. Taxes were increased, notably with the introduction of a detested new 1 percent income levy, and Foley told me it seemed to Labour ministers that they, rather than Fianna Fáil, were having to bear the public opprobrium for this.

By far the most devastating early verdict on the new government, or rather on its Labour element, came as a result of Labour appointments to jobs ranging from powerful Programme Managers to special advisers and, not least, a bevy of secretaries, organisers and drivers. Those appointed were widely represented as Labour activists, protegés, friends and even relatives. Jobs for the boys, nepotism, graft!

These charges were not just being levelled by the opposition against Labour but by some of the most influential sections of the media. Labour ministers were profoundly shaken by this unexpected assault, much of it from erstwhile admirers. And Fianna Fáil could hardly believe that the moral barrage had been lifted from their positions and was now being directed at the Labour trenches. Cowen shook his head mournfully at his Labour colleagues: 'Jaze, lads, ye're giving us an awful bad name.' Labour were not amused.

The Irish Times editorialised: 'Mr Spring and his party were perceived as being different from those who had gone before, Fianna Fáil and others. There was a vote for change, for a fresh start, for new standards. Less than two months into government, a lot of illusions have been shattered.' Albert Reynolds chuckled: 'There are no better lads than Labour for ethics in politics, and there are no better lads than Labour for grabbing every job they possibly can when they get half a chance. With no apologies to anyone either.'

An MRBI poll mirrored media disillusionment with Labour in the wake of what Denis Coughlan of *The Irish Times* described as the shortest-lived political honeymoon in decades. As support for Fianna Fáil and Albert Reynolds began edging upwards again, Labour dropped 6 percentage points on their pre-election showing, and Dick Spring's satisfaction rating plummeted, cut by half from 71 to 36 percent.

Labour counter attacked on the two levels at which they were superior to Fianna Fáil, first, using their tightly integrated approach to every aspect of government, with Labour members of the cabinet, junior ministers, Programme Managers and special advisers uniting in highly effective common cause and action, and also through use of their imaginative and betimes audacious handling of the media.

Labour, for example, consistently outmanoeuvred Fianna Fáil at Programme Manager level, particularly when it came to the allocation of Euro structural and cohesion funds, and I told the Taoiseach that Labour could also 'buy and sell' us in the field of media briefs, tweaks and leaks. His answering look meant: 'So, what the hell are you doing to counter it?' I subsequently wrote:

> 'The key to leaking is to just do it, then blithely deny it, irrespective of speculation, accusation or even verification. In politics, it is not a 'lie' to deny a currency devaluation intention, even as you prepare to do it, nor, it would seem, to disclaim responsibility for leaking even when the whole world knows you're guilty. It's just business — *realpolitik* in polite terms — and my only regret is that I'm just not as good at leaking as Labour. Mind you, as "Pee" Flynn said yesterday, that doesn't stop them and the PDs caterwauling on and on, like demented monks, with that awful "can't chant" — trust, openness, transparency and accountability. The more I hear this pious claptrap from certain of these tulips, the more, like Goering, I feel like reaching for my "Pee" shooter.'

True, Reynolds was ultimately accused of the most notorious partnership 'leak' of all, i.e. the somewhat 'previous' release of our interpretation of the Beef Tribunal judgement but, of course, that was not a leak, but rather a full frontal attempt at a pre-emptive strike which badly boomeranged.

1 March, 1993

> 'FF getting pissed off. Ruairi (Quinn) boasts "Labour are now in control of foreign affairs". All the corrs tell me Labour are claiming to control the Programme Managers plus Dempsey says Dame Eithne (Fitzgerald) is driving FF nuts with her endless ethics lectures — "I don't want a Ferdinand Marcos (for Marcos read Reynolds) situation developing here", on top of her self-appointed role as "Minister for the £8 Billion". Hardly a wet week in office, and this stuff already. Is it going to be worse than with the PDs?'

In early March, media attacks on Labour had reached a dismaying level of intensity when Spring made his first move to publicly assert himself within government. He accused Reynolds of trying to ram a £60–£70 million deal through cabinet in order to sell the government's 30 percent shareholding in the giant agribusiness group, Greencore, to a big US multinational food company, rather than to an Irish consortium. Labour proclaimed that they would not tolerate such a deal.

3 March, 1993

> 'Why did Labour go public? Why not sort it out behind cabinet closed doors? Albert tells me Dick admitted straight up why — Labour ministers felt they had to "publicly" pre-empt today's parliamentary Labour party meeting by "revealing" how they had stood up to FF and stopped the deal. Albert shrugs, later tells me Finance and Greencore themselves are mainly to blame. He doesn't really seem upset, more intrigued than anything else, but he tells me Dick is in bits over the way he's being attacked in the media.'

Now, with the Aer Lingus problem going from bad to worse, came near simultaneous crises on two other fronts, one involving reports that the giant Cable and Wireless multinational was negotiating to buy 25 percent of Telecom Eireann, the state telecommunications service, for £1 billion; and the other, a government decision to introduce a once-off tax defaulters' 'hot money' amnesty intended to channel hundreds of millions of black economy punts back into the State coffers. I wrote:

> 'Taoiseach doesn't seem to be on top of the Telecom thing. Labour again laying down the law, just as with Greencore. Albert is being coy (says it's no big deal) but Cowen can't hide his fury. Have they been downfaced by Dick again? He seems to be calling the shots. . . . Not only does he (Spring) say Labour will leave government if there's any attempt to go down the Cable and Wireless road, but he maintains there will be no further sale of State assets for the lifetime of this government. Albert shrugs again. No provoke?'

Next day, the tables were reversed on the tax amnesty. Despite opposition from Bertie Ahern, from the Department of Finance and the Revenue Commissioners, as well as majority Labour ministerial resistance to the idea, the amnesty was approved by the cabinet.

25 March, 1993

> 'Hot money amnesty — John Foley tells me it will be 13–2 against at cabinet. I tell this to Albert who says: "I can carry the cabinet if I want!" I'm told maybe Quinn and Taylor will back it, that the other Labour ministers are against, that Bertie is not in favour either. . . . Cabinet adjourned because Bertie is caught up in Seanad committee stage debate of Finance Bill (resumes at 6. 45 p.m.) and then, two hours later, Albert walks into my room and says amnesty is agreed. Apparently, he persuaded Labour that if they wanted to get rid of the 1 percent levy, this was the only way to raise the money. . . .
>
> Afterwards, John (Foley) tells me Dick said it was a choice between Labour giving in to Albert or undermining him as Taoiseach. When I see Albert, he insists it's a victory over Finance, not over Labour (tell that to Labour!), that the government governs, etc. . . . . . So, is this to be the caper? — Labour "wins" on Greencore and Telecom to be balanced by FF "victories" on such as the amnesty? This is where I came in with the PDs.'

The most worrying aspect was that Spring felt he had to threaten the ultimate sanction on Telecom in order that his view should prevail. I had always known that Labour's strategy in all coalitions was based on figuring not whether but when to pull the plug. But, surely, I said to John Foley, it was too soon for that to happen. He replied: 'We've seen enough of Albert to recognise that he is the most pleasant and reasonable of men — provided he gets his own way.'

Having agreed to the amnesty, which provided for a mere 15 percent penalty on disclosed untaxed funds, Labour were appalled by the public and media reaction. 'Cheats' charter' fiddlers' freebie' and 'tax dodgers' whitewash' were typical of the denunciations heaped on the measure. I met Greg Sparks who made it clear to me that Labour felt deeply aggrieved at being seen as 'forced' to cave into Fianna Fáil on the issue. Reynolds subsequently made a number of attempts to mollify Labour. A plum post at the Court of Auditors in Luxembourg went to Labour MEP Barry Desmond despite widespread media and Fianna Fáil expectation that it would go to former Fianna Fáil minister, Gerry Collins, whom Reynolds had dismissed the previous year. I wrote:

> 'It seems Spring, for whatever reason, didn't want it to go to Barry (Desmond). In fact, Barry had to put pressure on his own leader to move his ass. Albert tells me he himself had to actually put it up to Spring and Co. to say they wanted the

job for Barry. Really weird stuff. . . . In fact, Albert could have mended some FF fences if he gave it to Gerry (Collins). . . .'

Subsequently, when Labour pushed for a Residential Property Tax (RPT) clause in the '94 Budget, to effectively lower the tax threshold on the family home from £91,000 to £75,000, Reynolds told me he and Bertie Ahern could make no sense of the concept, but Labour were set on having it, so it would have to be. He also ruefully admitted to me that, despite his own resistance to the RPT, neither he nor any member of the cabinet (nor, indeed, any of their top officials or advisers) had anticipated the extent of middle-class resistance to the measure. In fact, before going into the House to present the Budget, they all conferred on which measure would attract the most criticism, and still not one of them got it right. Said Reynolds: 'It goes to show you, Diggy. We figured there could be a public backlash on everything from mortgage interest or VHI relief to taxing of widows' pensions. We figured everything and anything but that Mickey Mouse house tax which will raise five million lousy quid. You never can tell in this business.'

Not long afterwards, following media exposés of a sex scandal involving Labour Minister of State, Emmet Stagg, Reynolds sent out instructions to the FF parliamentary party and organisation to 'lay off' and not to get involved in the controversy, this despite the fact that several of the pol corrs — predominantly female — were maintaining that Stagg should either step down or be dismissed. Spring insiders clearly dreaded the implications — strained relations between Spring and Stagg were a complicating factor — and the Spring advisers I spoke with said they wanted Stagg to resign which, to their unconcealable chagrin, he adamantly refused to do. Meantime, Fianna Fáil kept out of it, and media interest eventually waned.

Behind the scenes, another Reynolds–Spring row erupted on proposed new 'residency' loopholes in the Finance Bill. Reynolds was on holiday in Cyprus when Spring faxed him with warnings that the measures would merely ease taxes on the super rich such as Tony O'Reilly, Michael Smurfit and Dermot Desmond. Labour would not countenance such a move under any circumstances. I noted:

> 'Taoiseach phones from Limassol, tells me he will not be dictated to — "I will not be a half Taoiseach. . . this could be the breakpoint." Jaysus! I ring John Foley who says, yes, it's a "principle" thing for Labour and could lead to a general election!'

On the following day, I wrote:

> 'Row defused. Agreement to drop "residency" either on Finance Bill committee stage, or leave it over until the autumn. Albert flies back in apparently good form. Before leaving Limassol, he and I have long chat. I relay message to Labour — I feel like a character in a B movie — we don't want to see no Albert Backed Down story nowhere, and that means no leaks, no spins, no steers, no nothing, capisch? — some partnership!'

Relations went on in this kind of give-and-take vein, with sudden squalls followed by periods of calm, until the Masri Affair in June '94. It had emerged that two Arabs, Khalid and Najwa Masri, a mother and son, had been granted Irish citizenship for a substantial financial consideration under the Business Migration Scheme which had been set up as an inducement to foreign investment. The scheme was similar to ones in many other countries, including Canada and Australia, and had been utilised by successive Irish governments. For an investment of upwards of £500,000 in an approved job creation enterprise, a foreign national could get Irish naturalisation while the Irish company concerned could get money at attractively low interest rates.

It was revealed that the Masris had invested £1 million in C & D Foods, the Reynolds family petfood company, in which the Taoiseach was still the major shareholder. Charlie Bird rang me: 'They're giving odds that he won't be able to talk his way out of this one, Diggy.'

Now, with Labour preparing to publish their Ethics Bill, a bitter 'Passports for Sale' row erupted. Reynolds was accused of using his influence to attract the Masri investment to his family firm. He denied any involvement in the transaction, insisting that he no longer had anything to do with the day-to-day running of the company, and asked why C & D Foods should be 'victimised' just because the Managing Director, Philip, was his son i.e. why should they be prevented from seeking to benefit from a scheme open to every other business firm.

Labour agonised, wrestling with the ethical implications, and Reynolds told me he eventually suggested to Spring, that he was welcome to inspect the Department of Justice files on the Masri deal. Spring, he said, then coolly informed him that he had already done so. Reynolds told me he could hardly believe Spring had gone ahead without first informing him. 'I have to admit that, for once, I was speechless.'

Nevertheless, Spring, having perused the file, pronounced the deal conducted in an 'ethical, above board and arms length way.' This brought an avalanche of criticism down upon his head. The PDs' Michael

McDowell told the Dáil that Spring was now 'morally brain dead'. Spring, under attack from practically all sides, promised new, tougher legislation as part of placing the passport scheme 'on a statutory basis'. In the Dáil, however, when pressed by McDowell on this 'promise', the Taoiseach insisted no legislation had been promised 'as yet. . . in due course, when the Government has decided on it, if legislation is to be introduced, it will be brought before the House.'

With less than a week to go before the European elections and two key by-elections, this routinely reported exchange enraged Spring. He was to become progressively more embittered as, on the run in to the elections, Reynolds continued to stonewall in response to more Dáil questions on 'promised' legislation to change the system. After the elections, in which the overall Labour vote slumped significantly, and Fianna Fáil lost the two by-elections.

12 June, 1993

> John Foley still saying Spring and his entire team deeply bitter. They insist Dick went to the wall for Albert on passports — I think they now see it as a major blunder that Dick went anywhere near the Justice files — and that Albert showed his appreciation by kicking Dick in the balls.
>
> 'I keep telling John I've put this to Albert — twice — and that he insists he was just tactically kicking to touch, on the basis that the Opposition can take procedural Dáil advantage of any acknowledgement of "promised" legislation to keep harrying the government on the matter in the House. John says he has told them (Labour) what Albert's saying, and they still insist Albert hung Dick out to dry.'

On the following day, Spring said on RTE's *This Week* programme that Labour would henceforth be much more assertive. A fortnight later, Labour broke government ranks on the crisis at TEAM, the Aer Lingus aircraft maintenance company, then losing money at a rate of £1 million a month. The government had repeatedly announced it would not intervene — Cowen told the Dáil: 'We have run out of time, out of cash and out of work.' — and the TEAM unions were being urged by the cabinet to accept cost-cutting Labour Relations Commission (LRC) recommendations.

In the Dáil, however, Labour Minister for Enterprise and Employment, Ruairi Quinn, suddenly launched an 'initiative' which sparked a violent FF–Lab flare-up that went largely undetected by the media. Quinn proposed new talks between the TEAM parties to consider the LRC recommendations as well as the unions' counter proposals 'without prejudice or preconditions'.

As it transpired, four Labour TDs, under pressure from their Aer Lingus/TEAM constituents, saw this as too little too late, and refused to vote for government motions on the TEAM issue. Two of them voted against, the other two formally abstained.

But, as far as Fianna Fáil were concerned, Quinn was still guilty of desertion in face of the enemy. Immediately after the vote, Cowen and Dempsey stormed into my room. Quinn, they said, had changed his circulated script which had included specific confirmation of the government's intention to 'implement' the LRC terms. Now, they maintained, certain Labour ministers were trying to save their skins by betraying their FF colleagues.

29 June, 1993

> '. . . Cowen absolutely livid. Says he'll resign if Quinn is allowed to get away with it. Keeps saying Fianna Fáil held the line on Shannon Airport when Tony Killeen and Síle de Valera jumped ship. Albert comes in and tries to calm the pair of them. Eventually, he gets them to cool down a bit, and they both go away. I relax — just another hiccup — but then Albert says to me, as calmly as if he were making a comment on the weather: "Mark my words, tonight means the beginning of the end of this government!"'

11

'THE HUME–ADAMS REPORT DOES NOT EXIST'

ON 26 FEBRUARY, 1992, a fortnight after coming into office, Albert Reynolds paid his first call as Taoiseach on British Prime Minister, John Major, in London. Afterwards, as the two leaders spoke about Northern Ireland to reporters outside 10, Downing Street, Reynolds referred to developments 'here on the mainland'.

I spent the next few days trying to fend off criticism of Reynolds for this 'proof' of his basic lack of experience or understanding of the Northern problem. Most pol corrs and analysts — Irish and British — told me it was the gaffe of a man with little or no feel for Northern Ireland.

More than a year later — the PDs had gone and been replaced by Labour. Reynolds was still being portrayed as a second rater on the North. On 6 May, 1993, *The Irish Times* editorialised: 'He acts like a politician, rather than a statesman. . . it would not happen in a state that genuinely believed in its ability to articulate "the common name of Irishman".'

Two months earlier, Reynolds had shown me a draft of a proposed joint Anglo–Irish declaration which he had been working on since taking office.

4 March, 1993

> 'Albert gives Bart and me sneak preview of draft document on N.I., plus rundown on what he's up to, which scares the bejasus out of both of us. He is convinced he can sell it to Major, and he insists Sinn Féin and the Army Council of the IRA will also buy it. He says: "This is about the IRA being persuaded to lay down their arms. . . ." He says it will involve the Republican movement accepting Irish unity coming about only by consent (that doesn't sound like the IRA to me!) but what's really scary is that he seems to be fixing

to contact these guys. Bart and I so worried we go back in to warn him he could be destroyed if he goes down that road. He says maybe so, but he's going to go all the way . . . .'

I subsequently asked him if Spring knew about pulling in the Provos. I made a diary note of how Reynolds responded: 'Yes, I told him.' 'And what did he say, Taoiseach?' 'You're on your own, Albert.' I also jotted down something else Reynolds said when Bart and I were telling him of our fears: 'I'm a dealer — not a wheeler-dealer or a double-dealer — just a dealer. That's what I do, hard straight dealing. And that's what I think I can pull off on the North, something they'll all accept as an even deal.' I remember he also said he had a rule of thumb when dealing: 'Always leave something for the other fellow.'

Northern Ireland happened to be my particular interest in the business of government. I had walked through burning Bombay Street after the first shots were exchanged in August 1969. I was at Sunningdale, in 1973, when Liam Cosgrave and Edward Heath were among the signatories to the Northern power-sharing agreement. Twelve years later, I was in Hillsborough Castle when Garret FitzGerald and Margaret Thatcher signed the Anglo–Irish Agreement. Now, after 25 years of the Troubles, I saw an opportunity to get an even better close-up view of the next major development in the long drawn-out agony. It did not occur to me that I might be about to witness an actual end to the conflict.

Despite my unease at what the Taoiseach had told me, I was fascinated by the nature of the initiative he contemplated, not least because I had always questioned the orthodoxy that there could be no contacts of any kind between governments and paramilitaries.

Soon after that first Reynolds–Major meeting at No. 10, I was struck by the words of two former Presbyterian Church Moderators, Dr Jack Weir and Dr Godfrey Brown, who had just held much criticised talks with Sinn Féin: 'Somebody has to start talking to them'. I particularly admired SDLP leader John Hume's decision to enter into dialogue with Sinn Féin leader, Gerry Adams, which he did on a number of occasions from 1987 onwards. However, I was acutely aware of the difference between Hume and/or Presbyterian churchmen talking to Sinn Féin/IRA, and the government making contact with them.

In April 1993, Hume and Adams held further meetings and then issued a joint statement ruling out an internal Northern settlement, but they also committed themselves to a peaceful accommodation of the differences between Ireland and Britain, on the basis of the right of the

Irish people as a whole to national self-determination. Hume said: 'If I fail to achieve the objective of bringing violence to an end, the only damage will be that I have failed, but not a single person extra will be supporting violence as a result. However, if the talks succeed, then the entire atmosphere will be transformed.'

Reynolds, at Arbour Hill, warned: 'If we in this part of the island appear to walk away from constitutional nationalism, by unilaterally abandoning our long-standing position with regard to Northern Ireland, the only form of nationalism left in entire possession of the field is a violent form of nationalism, which we all repudiate.'

4 May, 1993

> 'Albert the only one who has welcomed Hume–Adams talks. Bruton has come out against them, particularly "self-determination". That means Fine Gael, the PDs and Democratic Left have now all condemned Hume. Garret (FitzGerald) supports him, but he doesn't believe talks with Adams will succeed. . . .
>
> 'He (Hume) looked dreadful when he came into see Albert. Tells me he's got hypertension. He's a hypochondriac. He'll bury us all. Albert says John blew it by letting it out that he talked to Adams, but he may not have been responsible for leak.'

Now, listening more intently to the Taoiseach and Martin Mansergh whenever the North was discussed, I began piecing together what had transpired since 1987 when Charles Haughey first met with Redemptorist priest, Fr Alex Reid, of Clonard Monastery, Belfast, and his colleague Fr Gerry Reynolds, to explore the possibility of a new joint Anglo–Irish declaration as well as intermediary contacts between government and Sinn Féin, and by extension the IRA. Critical to the overall process was Hume's subsequent acceptance of the then Northern Secretary Peter Brooke's insistence that Britain no longer had any selfish, strategic or economic interest in Northern Ireland. Indeed, there is evidence that Hume may have encouraged Brooke to make the announcement.

Although Sinn Féin publicly dismissed Brooke's contention, Haughey and Hume, with some assistance from Fr Reid, produced a preliminary draft of the proposed joint declaration which was still being worked upon when Haughey was replaced as Taoiseach by Reynolds.

Afterwards, Mansergh said to me that Haughey, had he continued in office, would undoubtedly have pressed the peace initiative, but that he would have been constrained by his 'green' reputation and controversial background on the North. Reynolds, he said, carried no such baggage;

he simply embraced the process and was prepared to hazard all to press it to fruition. Said Mansergh: 'The process called for a risk-taker, and Albert Reynolds was certainly that.'

I asked Reynolds about his reputedly close relationship with John Major. He described to me how they had been introduced at a European finance ministers meeting in Brussels in the 1980s soon after Major's appointment as Chancellor of the Exchequer. 'What do I need to know about this place?' said Major conversationally. 'That you're the bad guys,' replied Reynolds, 'bad Europeans, bad partners, bad everything. The game here is for the rest of us to gang up against the anti-EC Brits. But I think you and I are going to do business.'

Initially, I wondered if Reynolds was hyping the relationship, but as the peace process advanced, I realised that there was a peculiar empathy between the two leaders. Certainly, it required more than mere mutual esteem to surmount the succession of mostly behind the scenes crises which were to bedevil the relationship.

Reynolds told me: 'I'm breaking a few rules. First, instead of continuing to marginalise these people (IRA/Sinn Féin), I'm going to try to pull them in. To do that, they must be shown the benefits of ending the "armed struggle" and going the constitutional road. And that means they'll have to be talked to, by whatever means, but they'll have to be talked to. . . .

'As for the other talks process, everyone says the talks must first produce a political settlement before we can have peace. Well, I'm going to put the cart before the horse. We could be talking for another 25 years, reach no agreement, and still be no nearer an end to the violence. . . . So, my instinct is peace first — then we can all sit around discussing the new Ireland — but with nobody being killed while we're at it.'

This fascinated me because of my interest in W.T. Cosgrave, President of the Executive Council of the original Irish Free State, who successfully inveigled 'slightly constitutional' Fianna Fáil elements of the defeated Civil War republicans — including my own father — into the democratic snare in the late 1920s, even though it was at Cosgrave's own political expense. Over the next eighteen months, as Reynolds' critics accused him of pan–nationalist and even militant republican tendencies, he repeatedly told me nothing would be achieved if he continued to maintain the traditional attitude of successive Irish governments to the paramilitaries, i.e. treating them as criminal 'untouchable'. Neither was he prepared to cede the republican high ground to Sinn Féin or the IRA.

After the fall of the Fianna Fáil–Progressive Democrats government in late 1992, the former PD Minister for Energy, Bobby Molloy, had accused Reynolds of having hindered the talks process and of displaying a lack of generosity towards the Northern Unionists, particularly in relation to Articles 2 and 3 of the Irish Constitution which proclaimed Dublin's right to exercise jurisdiction over the whole of Ireland, though confining the exercise in practise to the twenty-six counties, 'pending the re-integration of the national territory'.

Earlier that year, following persistent unionist demands for the dropping of the Dublin claim, Reynolds had controversially declared that Articles 2 and 3 were 'not for sale', although he also spoke of any changes to the Articles requiring reciprocal changes to the Government of Ireland Act 1920, which partitioned Ireland but also provided for re-unification if the parliaments in Dublin and Belfast agreed.

Subsequently, during the FF–Lab partnership, Dick Spring, in his capacity as Minister for Foreign Affairs, took what was described as a more 'flexible' line on Articles 2 and 3. Indeed, Reynolds was widely criticised for dragging his feet before confirming the obvious — that if an overall Northern settlement were agreed, there 'would' as distinct from 'could' be a referendum on amendments to the Articles.

19 May, 1993

> 'I don't believe Albert gives a tuppenny damn about Articles 2 and 3. As he says himself, he's a "dealer". The point is, of course, the Unionists do give a damn, and the more they shout about them, the more Albert is going to say they're pearls beyond price, so there can be no question of giving them up unilaterally — what are they worth to you, boys? The Unionists are stupid to make a song and dance about them. They're no big deal to FF, no matter what they say. They'd flog them — and a lot more besides — for the right price.'

A week later, aboard a flight to Malaysia, I had a long conversation with Reynolds about the Northern 'state of play'. He told me contact had been made with 'Republicans' with a view to an IRA ceasefire partially based on British acceptance of Irish national self-determination and the holding of plebiscites, north and south of the border.

26 May, 1993

> 'On way to Kuala Lumpur. . . I notice he (Reynolds) refers to the IRA Army Council without the slightest emotion — they're just there — he might as well be talking about the PLO. He sees killing as the ultimate stupidity — so everything is the deal, the deal, the deal. Says only he and Major are involved.

"Mayhew doesn't know." Doesn't know what? — about the document or contacts with the Provos?'

I was becoming increasingly aware of comings and goings around the Taoiseach's department. Mansergh would disappear at intervals for a day or two at a time — it was considered indelicate to refer to his absences — and Nally would suddenly materialise from what were called 'roving missions' for private meetings with the Taoiseach. Reynolds repeatedly told me that their contacts were always through intermediaries and, although he chaffed at the inevitable communications delays, he would not take 'short cuts'.

Then there was the man Reynolds referred to only as 'the priest'. Slightly built, almost wraith-like, he would 'appear' and invariably make a bee-line for Mansergh's room. When we first met there, he did not introduce himself, merely shook hands. I recognised Fr Alex Reid from the famous photograph of him kneeling over the bodies of two British soldiers shot dead by the IRA in Belfast. I knew from the way Reynolds referred to him that he was a vital link to Sinn Féin and the IRA.

Much later, Church of Ireland Archbishop Robin Eames paid regular calls on the Taoiseach, who admitted to me that he originally underestimated the Archbishop. Reynolds, in fact, soon became an Eames admirer and told me he played an important role in the peace process, particularly in terms of mainstream Unionist and British opinion. The name of Presbyterian minister, Rev. Dr Roy Magee, also began cropping up in the autumn of 1993, but I saw him only once, and I was left under the impression that contacts with him took place mainly in the North or around the border. In September, 1992, Dr Magee had hailed a speech by Sinn Féin Ard Comhairle member, Jim Gibney, at a Wolfe Tone commemoration in Bodenstown, as 'exceedingly significant'. Magee, who had earlier been involved in talks with the UDA, placed particular emphasis on Gibney's assertion that a sustained period of peace would have to 'precede' any British withdrawal from the North. In that event, said Magee, he believed the loyalist paramilitaries would reciprocate — 'and we would be into a new scenario'.

Six months later, however, there was still no sign of any IRA let-up as bombs exploded in the British town of Warrington, killing two young boys. The universally admired Senator Gordon Wilson, survivor of a 1987 IRA bombing in which his daughter died with 10 others at Enniskillen, then held talks with IRA representatives. He emerged in near despair pronouncing the exercise 'useless. . . a complete waste of time'.

Soon afterwards, as if to reinforce that view, the IRA struck at the City of London, heart of the British capital's financial district, killing a press photographer and causing damage estimated at more than £1 billion.

This incident produced the only division of opinion on the process that I observed between the Taoiseach and his chief adviser. Mansergh did not believe, then or subsequently, that the British government was materially swayed by the City of London bomb. Reynolds, however, suspected the British were deeply shaken — the IRA had hit the same district a year previously — and that the vulnerability of London to such attacks was a factor in terms of subsequent developments.

The incident coincided with publication of the joint Hume–Adams 'national self-determination' statement which signalled a renewed anti-Hume campaign (Adams was already demonised) in British and Irish political and media circles. It was to bring Hume as near to physical and mental collapse as anything in his 25 year involvement with the 'nationalist nightmare'.

Meantime, the SDLP leader's many faceted approach to the problem had dovetailed with Irish government efforts and yielded results in Washington DC. Reynolds and Spring, capitalising on continuously increasing Irish–American influence on Capitol Hill, were making considerable play of President Bill Clinton's long-standing commitment to the appointment of a US peace envoy to Northern Ireland.

In the past, in crunch situations, sympathetic pro-Irish US tendencies were insufficient to counter the 'special' Anglo–American relationship forged in two World Wars and decades of the Cold War. Now, despite unconcealed British anger at the prospect of a peace envoy, Clinton was preparing to honour his pre-election promise. But, Reynolds, notwithstanding deep Irish–American lobby suspicion of what was going on, quietly moved to have the appointment put on hold. He gradually manoeuvred White House acceptance of an Irish–American fact-finding mission to the North rather than the sending of the peace envoy. This was done as a Reynolds favour to Major at considerable risk of an Irish–American backlash. 'In life, business and politics,' Reynolds told me, 'there is a time to give, and a time to take. If I give on this issue, it is only so that I gain on a more important one. John (Major) owes me on the peace envoy.'

The British now let it be known that there were powerful lobbies other than on Capitol Hill. John Major's narrow parliamentary majority meant he required the support of the unionist parties in the House of

Commons. So when James Molyneaux, respected leader of the Ulster Unionist Party, maintained London and Dublin were on collision course because of Irish demands for joint sovereignty over the North, most analysts took the view that there was a Major–Molyneaux deal which would negate any pan–nationalist Dublin agenda. Interestingly, Reynolds' persistent denials of any joint sovereignty intent were consistently dismissed by Irish as well as by British political and media opinion. Reynolds had to enlist the help of Rev. Roy Magee to reassure Loyalist paramilitaries, who were now responsible for more fatalities than the IRA, that Dublin wanted peace for its own sake, not to impose joint authority or any other system on the North.

6 June, 1993

'Taoiseach rings me from Mayo. Tells me the "peace" document has been completed, that he talked twice on the phone to Major today, and even suggested going secretly to Britain to give it to the PM himself. But Major against the idea, says no way it could be kept secret, that Albert would inevitably be spotted. . . I don't think Major really wants to know. He doesn't trust it, probably thinks the Provos had a hand in it.'

9 June, 1993

'Taoiseach meets Danish PM Rasmussen, then tells me Major now has the completed document, that Sir Robin Butler (British Cabinet Secretary) flew secretly into Ireland to get it from him personally. . . .'

Later, Reynolds told me the venue for his rendezvous with Sir Robin was the military air base at Baldonnel. He handed the document to Sir Robin in a sealed envelope. He then briefed him for almost an hour before Sir Robin flew back to London. Throughout this period, I was acutely aware that Dick Spring, as both Tánaiste and Minister for Foreign Affairs, had a crucial role to play; also, that this could generate fresh tensions between Taoiseach and Tánaiste.

Fortunately, a two-pronged approach to the Northern situation was already in place. There was the long-running political dialogue, initiated by Peter Brooke, with its complex three-stranded Northern, North–South and Anglo–Irish dimensions; and alongside that was the new separate process which Reynolds had dubbed the 'formula for peace'. It suited both Reynolds and Spring — initially at least — that Spring should retain day-to-day charge of the complex 'talks' element while Reynolds concentrated on the high-risk 'peace' initiative. However, the problem for Spring was that Reynolds regularly became involved in key aspects of the talks process.

15 June, 1993

> 'Spring understandably sensitive on North. A lot of his achievements unsexy and unsung. The punters can't figure all this on again–off again "three strand, talks about talks, nothing agreed until all is agreed" stuff. Everyone, on the other hand, understands Albert's message — let's end the war! On top of that, there's a Catch 22 which means that whenever Spring gets anything even half interesting going with Mayhew, it's moved onto "Prime Ministerial" level, i.e. Albert and John take over and grab the headlines. . . .'

On 3 September 1993, as an Irish–American fact-finding group approached Northern Ireland, the IRA made a significant gesture. Just before the group's arrival, a massive bomb ravaged the centre of Armagh, but over the next week, while the US visitors were actually in Ireland, there was no IRA offensive action of any kind. The fact that the fact-finding group, headed by former US Congressman, Bruce Morrison, had agreed to talks with Sinn Féin while in the North, was seen as one reason for the temporary ceasefire, also that Sinn Féin wanted to show they could influence the IRA to suspend military operations to allow political options to be explored.

Meantime, the Reynolds 'peace' document, the draft of a proposed joint Anglo–Irish declaration, was being examined in London practically as if it were booby-trapped. Despite Dublin protestations to the contrary, the British shied away from what they regarded as a large Hume–Adams input to the document. They maintained that they were reluctantly prepared to discuss but not to negotiate it. Mansergh confirmed later that many of them would have preferred to sideline it altogether.

On 24 September, Hume and Adams moved to end the stalemate by disconcertingly upping the ante. They announced they had ended their discussions and would put their conclusions to the Irish government. Hume then departed on a trade mission to the United States, saying he would make contact with the government upon his return in a fortnight.

27 September, 1993

> 'What's Hume up to? I have rarely seen Taoiseach or Mansergh so upset. And not a peep from John. Haven't a clue where he is. I keep issuing "we look forward to hearing what progress may have been made" rubbish. Either he's lost the head or he is crafty as a fox — or both? — because we're getting conflicting reports from US quoting him as having already given Dublin the report, then that he'll give Albert the report when he gets back. Mansergh says we've got nothing from Hume or Adams. Still, nobody here wants a public row with John. So I go on as if everything is perfect. What a way to make a living!'

Hume finally returned from the US and had a highly publicised meeting with Reynolds and Spring at the end of which I said he had presented them with both a written and verbal report.

7 October, 1993

'I tell corrs the report has "significant potential", that it will be "part of the process", etc. But I gather the "written" report is in the form of notes, i.e. practically back of envelope stuff. . . Albert at one stage says to me: "The Hume–Adams report does not exist." He seems to be saying it's somehow part of the document he handed Sir Robin to give to Major. I haven't the faintest idea. Is it "subsumed" into the draft joint declaration? Is there something Hume and Adams committed themselves to which they don't want revealed? The words "consent" and "persuasion" (by the Brits?) keep cropping up. . .'

19 October, 1993

'Sir Robin Butler flies in secretly again to meet Taoiseach and Tánaiste. Albert tells me Sir Robin totally dismissive of Hume–Adams — "Downing Street is not interested" and Albert tells him British will regret this — He says he warned Sir Robin that the Provos would now concentrate their attacks on the British mainland, also that the British will get a US peace envoy who will "harass" them with all kinds of peace propositions and demands. Charming.'

At one stage during this period, Reynolds received a letter from Major, in the PM's own handwriting, dismissing Hume–Adams and effectively ruling out a joint Anglo–Irish declaration for the forseeable future. I did not find out whether the letter was conveyed to the Taoiseach by Sir Robin or through some other channel, but I was aware that the contents were regarded as so profoundly negative as to offer practically no prospect of a Dublin–London agreement.

On 23 October, a bomb exploded in a shop on the ground floor of a premises which had also been formerly used as an Ulster Defence Association office on the Shankill Road in Belfast. Ten Protestant men, women and children, along with the IRA bomber, died in the blast. Within little more than a week, the death toll rose to 23 as loyalist paramilitaries exacted bloody revenge. On Halloween, seven died as loyalist, gunmen burst into a licensed premises in Greysteel, Co. Derry, and raked the crowded bar with gunfire.

The 'formula for peace' was widely dismissed as collapsed. Dáil Éireann and the House of Commons echoed to derisive condemnation of Hume–Adams. Hume burst into tears at the funeral of the Greysteel victims. He told friends he was being 'hung out to dry'. Reynolds worried over reports that the SDLP Leader was close to a breakdown.

Then, on the eve of a crucial meeting between Reynolds and Major in Brussels, Gerry Adams, despite having described the Shankill Road bombing as 'wrong' helped to carry the coffin of the IRA bomber who died in the explosion.

29 October, 1993: Brussels

> 'Hume and Adams told to get off the pitch! Albert and Major met (no officials present) for more than an hour. Joint statement afterwards sent a clear message to John (Hume) to butt out and leave it to the two governments. . . . When Brendan McMahon (Dept of Foreign Affairs) and I read it together, we just looked at one another. Brendan said: "Doesn't look great to me." That's for sure. It says only the two governments can take an initiative; no question of adopting the report (Hume–Adams) given to Albert which, it is emphasised, he (Reynolds) did not pass on to the British government. Brits happy at having dumped on Hume. Albert says to me it had to be done, that only the two governments can do the job, but I can see he's not happy. . . .'

Hume and Adams had no doubts about the significance of what had transpired in Brussels. Adams said it meant that Major had jettisoned their peace initiative.

Hume dramatically addressed the House of Commons: 'I say it is the best opportunity in 20 years that I have seen. . . why has he (Major) rejected my proposals. . . ?' Major responded: '. . . I reached the conclusion, after having been informed of them by the Taoiseach. . . that it was not the right way to proceed.' It was many weeks later before Reynolds told me something of what transpired in Brussels. I wrote:

> 'Albert tells me Brits at Brussels demanded that joint (Reynolds–Major) statement contain "lecture" directly addressed to IRA to renounce violence, and that his own (Irish) negotiators all advised him that it had to be, that it was their duty to protect their political masters, and they would be failing in their duty if they didn't inform him of the serious consequences of not doing so. Albert says he told them: "Now you see the difference between me and other politicians — I believe in life after politics — so, I'm not going to do it.
>
> 'He tells me Hume–Adams was still alive and kicking after Brussels, that Major actually accepted this, insisting that he just couldn't publicly wear it. Albert says Major and he reasoned it out together: "Hume–Adams was being declared dead, in order to keep it alive, in the same way as Adams carried the bomber's coffin, because otherwise he couldn't deliver the IRA." He says Major agreed with this reasoning. Albert added: "So it had to be done — but I hated that Brussels joint statement."'

12

'TELL THE POL CORRS I'M VINDICATED'

RELATIONS BETWEEN Reynolds and Spring waxed and waned through 1993 with Reynolds largely setting the agenda while Spring at times appeared marginalised and off balance, particularly in relation to Reynolds' front running on the North.

In mid-June, I travelled with the Taoiseach and Tánaiste on a flight to London for a meeting with the Prime Minister. Practically the only topic of conversation aboard the aircraft was the upcoming visit of President Mary Robinson to Belfast amid reports that she intended to meet and shake hands with Gerry Adams. The meeting with John Major lasted 90 minutes longer than scheduled. Afterwards, I learned that British anger at the President's plans accounted for the overrun.

17 June, 1993

> 'Brits said (16 June) they wanted the whole Belfast thing stopped. Dick is livid with her. Albert shakes his head too, but I know him. . . . Dick goes up to Áras (again!). But the lady is not for turning. She insists she is going to go. Albert goes up around 5 p.m. She is still adamant. Dick furious. "Some woman" sez Albert. "She is determined to make history" sez Dick. . . . '

18 June, 1993

> 'President goes North. Meets Adams and shakes the hand. Peter Robinson goes ape. So too the SDLP. The NIO say they raised their concerns "at the highest level" with Irish government. . . . I tell pol corrs that Mayhew and Blatherwick (British Ambassador to Ireland) pressed Albert and Dick at Downing Street to persuade her not to do it plus I tell them Albert resisted Brit pressure to stop her, i.e. no question of Albert not giving her permission to go to Northern Ireland. Understandably, Dick's boys not amused — they let us know: "She shouldn't be given permission to go to Disneyland." Ouch!'

We had known for a considerable time that something had gone significantly wrong in the ostensibly rapturous relationship between the President and the Labour Party — Labour, behind the scenes, made no secret of the breach — and the general assumption was that it had something to do with the President, despite their election campaign togetherness, refusing to maintain a 'special' relationship with Labour once she had been elected.

Reynolds viewed the President with a mixture of mild awe and wariness. He might privately share some of Spring's reservations about her peripatetic tendencies, but, he was also pleased that he got on well with her at a personal level, and he assiduously avoided unnecessary friction between Merrion Street and Áras an Uachtaráin. He would regularly draw my attention to the latest opinion poll showing overwhelming public support, on whatever issue, for the President. This comment after one such poll was typical: 'No arguing with that. We walk around that. Let her off.'

In February, 1994, there was another bitter behind-the-scenes row between Labour and Áras an Uachtaráin. It arose following publication of an Emily O'Reilly report in the *Irish Press* which revealed that the President had sought independent legal advice following a government decision, two months earlier, not to allow her to accept an invitation to co-chair a high level committee on the future of the United Nations.

17 February, 1994

> 'President writes to Taoiseach hinting strongly that leak to Emily was via Dick Spring. . . . I have been told that the President has also written directly to Dick more or less accusing him of being the leaker, and that Dick has furiously written back to her demanding a retraction . . . .'

On the following day, I wrote:

> 'Dick pulls what seems like neat headline-grabbing stroke — "Tánaiste Favours Expanded Role for Presidency" — only Áras are onto us like a flash. They say that's the last thing they want, and well the Tánaiste knows it! Albert gives me a look that says we stay well clear of this one. Between them it is!'

It was at times like this that I sympathised with the new Secretary to the Government, Frank Murray, who also had responsibility for Departmental communications with the Presidency. Monitoring cabinet ankle-tapping between Taoiseach and Tánaiste was one thing, but being caught between the two of them and the 'Lady in the Park' must have been nerve shattering. I couldn't resist winding him up occasionally, just to see his eyes bulge: 'Frank, the Taoiseach says she's told him she wants to go to East Timor next.'

I was also getting to know Padraig O hUiginn's successor, the new Secretary of the Taoiseach's Department, Paddy Teahon. Another of that distinguished line of St Brendan's of Killarney luminaries, I took an instant liking to him. He was the quintessential man in the 'Hill 16' crowd — less of a mandarin it was hard to imagine — only he was also one of the seriously brilliant (he told me he had given up being mad) North Kerry variety. Teahon, I quickly realised, possessed that most underrated of qualifications for a top public servant — basic common sense — and I often thought afterwards that we might have found ourselves in far less trouble if we had paid more heed to his advice.

There was also a key new arrival in my office, Grace Fagan, former secretary with Bart Cronin. Suffice to say that, long before the final collapse, Grace had taken over where Bart left off as a friend and counsellor.

Another major FF–Lab embarrassment was developing and, this time, it was difficult not to sympathise with Labour. The '£8 Billion in Doubt' spectre was rearing its head again. Word from Irish officials in Brussels was that the Commission would soon publicly renege on the Edinburgh 'deal'. Spring, who had nothing to do with the original negotiations, was being forced, as Minister for Foreign Affairs, to spearhead the Irish 'We Want Our £8 Billion' Euro offensive.

At an EU Summit meeting in Copenhagen, Jacques Delors and the Taoiseach discussed the prospects. Afterwards, Reynolds told me Delors said £8 billion was going to be a problem. Reynolds told Danish Prime Minister Rasmussen that he would still be insisting on the full amount. He then went to Paris and pledged *quid pro quo* Irish support for the French position on GATT to Prime Minister Balladur. Afterwards, I wrote:

11 June, 1993: Paris

> 'All emerge from the meeting reeking of grandeur. Then I'm casually told that — in return for Irish support — Balladur referred to us throughout as having left the ERM. With knowledgeable friends like that, how can we miss? The danger in this business is to believe in Great Helmsmen with grand cosmic designs. *Le tout ensemble* chancing their arm.'

Subsequent developments gave me further insight into the Reynolds style of high-wire deal making. 'You aim high to score high' was one of his favourite axioms. Now, he added: 'You have no friends when you're divvying up money. All the niceties go out the window. Also, when you're dealing, the slightest sign of uncertainty, and you're gone.'

As the doubters multiplied, Reynolds forbade any 'defeatist' talk about the £8 billion, even berating Teahon when he pointed out that his Euro soundings confirmed the fragility of the Irish position, and sending repeated messages through me to First Secretary Dan Mulhall of our EU embassy in Brussels — Mulhall dealt primarily with the media there — that he impress on all journalists that Ireland would not accept a penny less than £8 billion.

The Irish *bête noire* in the EU was Regional Commissioner Bruce Millan whose officials had taken to predicting that the Irish could still wind up with as low as £6.5 billion. Reynolds responded by telling the Dáil that the government would veto the regulations governing the release of the EC structural funds — effectively preventing distribution of the funds — unless Ireland maintained its 13.5 percent share. I kept briefing that Jacques Delors had given both written and verbal assurances to that effect at Edinburgh.

After weeks of hard and often bitter haggling, Dick Spring finally emerged with a new deal, again based on a verbal assurance, but this time, we emphasised, with two important witnesses to a handshake on the deal between Spring and Delors — Paddy Teahon and the Irish Ambassador to the EC, Paddy McKernan. Bertie Ahern became involved at one stage, but Spring signalled that Ahern was to get off the pitch — this was a Spring operation — and Ahern duly withdrew. The dominant Irish mood was one of relief at what we presented, and was widely accepted, as an honourable £7.8 billion compromise.

20 July, 1993

> 'Claremorris. Good news! Early morning agreement in Brussels that Ireland gets £7.8 billion. Met Albert at Ballinrobe Races yesterday before the news came through. In great form, even though he told me it was going to go down to the wire, and that the going in Brussels was tough. Albert is a born gambler — at the track, in business and politics. He had that same look in his eye yesterday as during the election. When the chips are finally down, and there's nothing more that can be done, he just stands back and watches — fascinated, fatalistic, almost stoic. *Les jeux sont fait. Rien va plus!*'

Three months later, almost to the day, the £7.8 billion construction disintegrated. Delors announced in Brussels that the Irish had got it wrong; that he had never given them a £7.8 billion commitment, and that the most Ireland could now get was £7.2 billion. Reynolds, in a rage, demanded an all-out offensive to force Delors to honour his 'word?'.

21 October, 1993

> 'McSharry was right. I'm sorry for Spring. He had to go to Brussels last night to try to salvage something from the wreck. In fact, he tells us he thought he had patched something together when Delors walks out to be door-stepped by Tommie Gorman (RTE's European correspondent) and blows the gaffe. Never, never, he says, did he promise £7.84 billion. Indeed, he says, the Irish knew very well it was not on. And then he claims Bertie (Ahern) had pleaded with him to postpone announcement of that decision until after the launch of the National Plan last week. Suffering shit . . . .'

I wrote:

> 'Again, I notice, as the dice come to rest (snake eyes!) that when it's over, and as we all rant and rage at Delors' perfidy, Albert is suddenly calm, even as ministers start wailing about how they're going to be screwed in the Dáil. "You just tough it out" he tells them. "We made a straight deal. We got Delors' word on it. We overlooked one thing. We never figured on Delors not being able to deliver. He's no longer the man he was. So, he couldn't deliver. So, end of story. Now, we put the best face we can on it." He says to me. "Mark my words. We'll get every penny of the eight billion at the end of the day."'

23 October, 1993

> 'Galway. Connemara Coast Hotel. Kathleen is Albert's best adviser and toughest critic. Albert, in dressing gown, watching TV about all the flak we're taking re the dwindling £8 billion. Kathleen walks in just as he's arguing with the TV set — "that's all bullshit", etc. — and, suddenly, eyes flashing, she wires into him: "Why do you do it?. . . why do you stress the maximum rather the minimum or a reasonable compromise?" Albert tries to fight back; accuses her of talking like the opposition, but he hasn't a chance. The only time I've seen him bested. "I know you, Albert," says Kathleen. He'd take it from nobody else. She's the Boss. Makes my day.'

Emily O'Reilly began a series on the government in the *Irish Press* maintaining that Labour effectively ran the administration through their superior Programme Managers and Spring's outstanding team of personal advisers. It included something along the lines that Albert woke up each morning, checked that he was still Taoiseach, and this kept him happy for the rest of the day.

Not for the first time, I marvelled at the impact of a newspaper 'think' piece (well based or otherwise) on the powers that be. I thought I could discern the fingerprints of one or other of the Spring entourage on the series, but, to me, it was still merely an irritation. Albert Reynolds, however, was deeply offended. He told John Foley: 'This is how the split with the PDs began.'

Over the next few days, arising from the O'Reilly articles, I first had a telephone conversation with the Taoiseach lasting more than an hour; he subsequently conferred with Spring for three hours, and then there was a lengthy 'private' cabinet discussion (Frank Murray remained outside the room for the first three-quarters of an hour) on the same subject.

5 October, 1994

> 'Albert tells me the message to Dick and Labour at cabinet was: "It's not on, lads". He blamed Sparks, Scally, FitzGerald (Eithne), Burton (Joan) and I can't remember who else. Says he told Dick we can take the opposition on and prevail, but the real danger will come from within. Labour later tell me Eithne walks into their rooms, clenches her fist, points to the knuckles, and says: "I've been rapped on these."'

Subsequently, FF–Lab relations sharply deteriorated and there followed, in quick succession, the Finance Bill 'residency loophole' election threat by Spring, the 'Passports for Sale' trauma and the row between Ruairi Quinn and Brian Cowen over the TEAM/Aer Lingus crisis which culminated in Reynolds telling me that it marked the beginning of the end for the government.

On 1 July 1994, two days after that Reynolds forecast, during the summer adjournment debate in the Dáil, Dick Spring warned that, under no circumstances, would Labour 'hide or walk away' from the implications of the Beef Tribunal verdict.

3 July, 1994

> 'Emily O'Reilly has SBP *(The Sunday Business Post)* story headlined "Spring Ready to Leave Coalition If Tribunal Report Censures Reynolds". It's straight from the horse's mouth stuff. Albert swears it's from an "unidentified, bearded, Labour source". Significantly, Labour are not denying the story. More significantly, Albert says: "No government can survive this kind of thing." Why do Labour do these things publicly? Why hang themselves on that hook unless or until it's necessary? What message does it send to Hammo (Mr Justice Hamilton)? I'm hearing "reports" that the tribunal verdict will be "non judgmental" and not require recalling the Dáil. Is that it? Do Labour think it will be OK for Albert and, therefore, feel free to talk macho? It's hard to read.'

26 July, 1994

> 'Government meeting before Albert goes to Galway Races. I'm told that the Labour ministers warned that they would not allow themselves to be frog-marched into "rush to judgement" ramroding of the Report through the Dáil one week after publication this Friday? Dick (Spring) rings me and warns me

to be "careful" about briefing the pol corrs. Greg Sparks and Willie Scally drop in and also tell me to be careful re briefings . . . .'

27 July, 1994

'Something's up! Niamh Breathnach goes on solo run re free university education. Albert rings me from Galway. Says there was no government decision on it yesterday. "X" (a senior civil servant) says he's convinced she did it because she's scared Labour won't be around after Tribunal report. I'm told Fergus calmly told the Programme Managers meeting that, yes, it was he who briefed Emily about bringing down government. Alarm bells ringing!'

Late in the evening of Friday 29 July, I was summoned to the Taoiseach's office where members of his Beef Tribunal legal team, senior counsel Henry Hickey and Conor Maguire, along with Paddy Teahon, Frank Murray, Tom Savage and Donal Cronin, were examining a copy of the Tribunal report which had been obtained through the Department of Agriculture.

Hickey, Maguire and Savage had divided the report into a number of sections which were being simultaneously scrutinised between them while the Taoiseach sat awaiting their verdict. After about a half hour, a quick check around the table produced a consensus that the findings, apart from criticising certain of the Taoiseach's decisions, did not question his motives or impugn his integrity.

Someone said: 'You're in the clear.' 'Are you sure?' asked Reynolds. 'Yes,' came the reply. 'OK,' said Reynolds,' I've taken this shit long enough. I'm not taking another minute of it. Tell the pol corrs I'm vindicated, Diggy.' I hesitated: 'Taoiseach, Labour are going to go spare. They've warned me against this.' Teahon rowed in: 'You don't need to do this, Taoiseach. You don't need to have a row with Labour. You've won.' Reynolds said: 'They told the dogs in the street they would bring me down on this if they didn't like the judgement. Now, I've been cleared, and I don't need their permission to tell it as it is.'

Then, as I made no move, he glanced at his watch and said: 'You're already losing the country editions of the papers, Diggy. Now, if you don't do it, I'll bloody well do it myself.' 'OK. But I still believe we should tell Labour what we're doing. Let me at least ring John Foley.' 'I don't care who you ring. Just do it. Tell Foley if you want, but do it.' I rang Foley who already suspected what was afoot. After I confirmed his fears, he said: 'Don't do it, Diggy. They made a deal at cabinet that this would not be done.' Reynolds has always denied there was any such deal.

With time now of the essence, I rapidly jotted down a number of quotations from the report which bolstered the Reynolds 'vindication' argument. In order to confirm that they were selective and drawn from different parts of the report I separated them with punctuation marks. This was later represented as an attempt to mislead the media. As if even a cursory perusal of this public document was not going to reveal that they were 'cherry picked'. I should, of course, have put the report page numbers in parentheses after each quotation. I should have done (and not done) a lot of things that night.

30 July, 1994

> 'The worst part is Fergus (Finlay). I'm phoning the papers when the door opens and I'm confronted by this Old Testament whirlwind of wrath, biblical beard quivering, like Moses about to smite the idolators of the Golden Calf, and he's thundering that Albert is refusing to talk to Dick, that his staff are saying he is gone home when he (Fergus) knows damn well he is skulking down there in his office. Repent, repent! All I can clearly remember is him fiercely proclaiming: 'This could mean the end of the government — you have been WARNED!'. He picks up the phone (can't remember if he got through) then slams it back on the receiver with such force that it goes flying off the table. PJ (Mara) was right: "Diggy, you'll be sorrreee. . . !" I ring around. Jackie Gallagher in *The Irish Times* insists that I'm purporting to speak on Spring's behalf as well as Albert's. He subsequently tells this to Labour which drives Dick around the twist. He (Spring) rings Frank Murray and warns of "implications for government". I get back to Albert, fill him in, and he starts saying he won't be threatened by Spring or Finlay. Dick finally contacts Albert around 1 a.m. Albert tells me afterwards that he said to Dick: "Would you deny me my hour in the sun?" and that Dick replied: "There may be no sun, Albert. This is bad."'

Perhaps the most enduring image of that chaotic night was the so-called 'locked door' episode. Fergus Finlay told reporters that he could not get into the Taoiseach's private offices because a corridor door leading to them had been locked, presumably in a deliberate attempt to prevent Labour gaining access to Reynolds. Finlay certainly believed the door was locked — he described seeing a person knocking and failing to gain entrance and others using 'coded' knocks to get through — and I could not contradict that. But I don't remember it being locked, although I do recall it was closed which was unusual. However, I went back and forth through the door to the Taoiseach's office on a number of occasions that night and have no memory of encountering any hindrance or delay. I later queried senior and other officials who were in the Taoiseach's office on that occasion, and they maintained they knew nothing of locked doors.

In any event, Reynolds' 'hour in the sun' cost him dearly. The object of the exercise was submerged in the furore over the so-called 'leaking' controversy. The Hamilton judgement, viewed in isolation, was politically tolerable — its contents did not pose a significant threat to either Reynolds or his government — but, after the row of 29 July, the public perception was of a Taoiseach who was seeking to misrepresent the findings. True, his claim of 'total vindication' overstated the position, although I felt this was understandable in terms of normal political hyperbole. The key point, however, was that Mr Justice Hamilton's findings did not throw doubt on Reynolds' integrity.

As *The Irish Times* concluded: 'There is no evidence to suggest that Mr Reynolds' decisions were in any way based on improper motives, either political or personal, the report states. And there is no evidence, it says, that either the Taoiseach at any time, or the Minister for Industry and Commerce at the time, was personally close to Mr Goodman, or that Mr Goodman had any political association with either of them or with Fianna Fáil. Mr Reynolds is thus fully entitled to claim that his personal integrity has been vindicated. And Judge Hamilton does not reject his plea that he acted in the national interest, as he saw it, in taking the decisions he did regarding export credit insurance for Iraq. What the judge says is that Mr Reynolds ought to have taken a more thoroughly informed view of what constituted the national interest.

'A more detailed investigation or analysis of the benefits to the economy was called for. Such an investigation would in all probability have disclosed that a large proportion of the beef to be exported was to be sourced outside the jurisdiction, the report says. The benefits to the Irish economy were "illusory rather than real".

29 July, 1994 (evening)

> 'It was a total balls-up, and it happened because neither FF or Labour trusted each other at that stage. Albert comes from the hard "get your retaliation in first" school. He really believed, given the way Labour were shaping, that they were fixing to put an anti-Reynolds spin on the findings. So he was obsessed with getting his "spoke" in first. Pity, because it obscured a reasonably acceptable outcome for him — most people, unfortunately, now think Liam Hamilton must have come out totally against him — and probably resulted in Labour finally deciding the next move was to get out. Game, set and match (due to unforced error) to the opposition.'

As a result, John Bruton reminded Spring that he could collapse the administration and become part of a new government, without having to face a general election. Geraldine Kennedy wrote: 'Mr Spring and his Labour ministers have not even contemplated Mr John Bruton's wistful aspiration of the week that they would cross the floor to form the rainbow coalition which he mooted after the last general election. The presence of Democratic Left would no longer be an obstacle for the Fine Gael leader.'

Spring, in fact, although deciding against the Bruton scenario, almost certainly did contemplate the possibilities arising from the Fine Gael leader's belated preparedness to work with Democratic Left, marking it down for future reference. It is doubtful if Reynolds and his ministers gave similar weight to this fresh option.

14 September, 1994

'Harry's back in the frame! I'm like Inspector Clouseau's boss in "The Pink Panther" whenever he hears Clouseau's name. The mere mention of Harry and I get this twitch of my right eyelid. Albert wants to appoint him President of the High Court (Dick away in Tokyo) but Labour say "no way". And they're making a big deal out of it. What the hell are they at now? Who cares who becomes whatever it is of the High Court?'

14 September, 1994 (cont.)

'Suddenly departure for Australia put back three hours as cabinet crisis develops. . . . Appointments of Chief Justice and sequential jobs, President of High Court and AG (Attorney General), on cabinet agenda. Ruairi Quinn tells Taoiseach they (Labour) will walk out if he tries to push it through. Accuse Albert of trying to slip appointments through while Dick out of country. Albert insists they were on last week's cabinet agenda, but not dealt with, therefore go automatically onto this week's agenda. Quinn/Howlin in touch with Spring at Tokyo Airport. They say no deal on Liam Hamilton's appointment as Chief Justice unless it's agreed that Harry doesn't get President of H.C.

'Albert tells me they say "Hamilton not our man!", that they wanted Donal Barrington (Mr Justice Donal Barrington) which can't be constitutionally done. Taoiseach says: "I'm going down there and I'm going to appoint Liam Hamilton without conditions — they walk out, they walk out — they want to bring the thing down, so be it." Cabinet delayed for hours. Quinn comes back up looking like death. I do my Diggy shrugging bit as he passes out from Taoiseach's office. He looks right through me. I go into room. Albert is carefully explaining to Kathleen on phone: "Look, you weren't all that anxious to go (to Australia) at any rate. We have to be prepared for the possibility that these guys mean what they say."'

Soon afterwards, Quinn tells him they'll come in for Hamilton appointment without conditions, and that the other jobs will be sorted out between Albert and Dick when they're both back in the country. . . We ask Labour to keep quiet about the row — not to leak — it can be dealt with when we get back . . . . We head for Australia. Just like that!'

Before we left, Fergus Finlay came into my office. Later, aboard the flight, I jotted down my recollection of what he said: 'Make no mistake, this is a resigning matter . . . . Incidentally, Sean, I know what you're thinking, that it's me, but it's not me behind this one . . . I'm just telling you, if he tries to force Harry on us, we will make the Beef Tribunal row look like a storm in a teacup.'

23 September, 1994

'Sydney — I think we're all insane. Albert Reynolds is being treated like God down here. He's headline news right across Australia for what he's done on the North. And we're talking about bringing down the government over Harry and some job people hardly know exists. Madness!!!'

13

'You're Supposed to be My Pal, John Major'

IT HAD not been all distrust and discord between Reynolds and Spring. There were times, particularly on Northern Ireland and in relation to the peace process, when they cooperated to significant effect. And, in these circumstances, Martin Mansergh, Sean O Huiginn, Dermot Nally and Fergus Finlay were reportedly at least a match for their British opposite numbers.

Soon after the October '93 EU Summit in Brussels, when John Major told the Commons he and Albert Reynolds agreed that Hume–Adams was a non-runner, Spring moved during the ensuing hiatus to help keep the process alive by coming up with what became known as the Six Democratic Principles. They incorporated, I was told, elements of Hume–Adams, as well as guarantees to the unionists.

Gerry Adams, however, was not impressed, and there was a tense Dublin meeting between Reynolds and Hume — I had briefed journalists that it was time for the SDLP leader to 'stand back' — and Hume could not conceal his anger at being sidelined. He never publicly criticised Reynolds, but he told the Commons that if the Prime Minister had not totally disagreed with him,' I think we would have peace within the next week in Northern Ireland.'

Reynolds now told me that he had gone as far as he was prepared to go down that road with Major. He resented the Prime Minister's repeated harping on the theme that he (Reynolds) was totally in support of his rejection of Hume–Adams. 'I've done my bit. It's up to him now. It will have to be done within a month — certainly before the end of the year — and, if he doesn't come by then, I'll walk away.'

I did not know whether this was a wise attitude to take or not, but I had no doubt that Reynolds meant what he said. He was always convinced that he knew better than Major on the North. Supremely confident that his way was the right one, Reynolds regarded it as his duty to act as a 'persuader' of the sceptical Prime Minister, particularly as he worried that Major was susceptible to inept and betimes mischievous advice on Ireland.

I was constantly intrigued by his certitude: 'If I have him (Major) on a one-to-one basis, I can talk sense to him. It's when these anti-Irish Tory headbangers and spymasters get to him that he weakens. I've told him the IRA have better intelligence than British Intelligence. . . . I've told him that I won't see him wrong; that if I think they (the IRA) are not coming, I'll warn him even at the eleventh hour, but that he's got to trust me.'

At the beginning of November, Reynolds began turning up the heat on Major. After what I thought was an excellent FF Ard Fheis speech — "history will not forgive us if we waste this opportunity" — he went on to give a series of British TV, radio and newspaper interviews, journeying twice to London for the purpose, with a core message summed up by what he told the BBC's John Humphreys on *On the Record*: 'It is now up to the two Prime Ministers to run with the ball.'

'Peace first,' was his message to the Ard Fheis, publicly confirming his long held belief that peace must come in advance of progress on the talks process. He also maintained that the beginning of the peace process had to become a 'reality' before the end of the year.

8 November, 1993

> 'Carrick-on-Shannon — Get phone message that Mayhew has challenged Albert's "peace first" proposal — he (Mayhew) says talks and peace process must run in "parallel" — and he says setting a time frame (end of year) for agreement is not helpful to the peace process. I tell Albert. He instantly barks out sound bite reaction: "Peace can't wait. The killing must be stopped. Time is not on our side."'

Two days later, British Ambassador David Blatherwick told Mansergh that Reynolds should stop pressing for a pre-Christmas breakthrough. That evening, at Dublin's Point Theatre, Reynolds delivered himself of what was to become known as the 'Houston Declaration' although it was intended to be off the record. Two journalists he encountered later accepted that Reynolds meant it to be so, but they then decided: 'It is too important not to publish.' At a Whitney Houston concert, Reynolds told the *Cork Examiner's* T. P. O'Mahony and Tim Ryan of the *Irish Press*: 'If it comes to it, I will walk away from John Major, and put forward a set of proposals myself. . . . I am not prepared to let this opportunity pass.'

12 November, 1993

> 'Anglo–Irish relations badly strained. Envoy from UK (not sure if it is Sir Robin) in with David Blatherwick. Taoiseach says he told them the British don't have a veto on the peace process. Warns them not to pull out or else! They reply that we're reneging on the Brussels joint communique and reactivating Hume–Adams. Albert later tells me that, if Brits don't come, it may still be possible to appeal to the Provos. His hunch is that the Provos want out of the "armed struggle". . . '

Despite the brouhaha, Dick Spring was impressively supportive of Reynolds. He said, in Limerick, that he was fully behind the Taoiseach's search for a cessation of violence. He then went to Washington and made an excellent speech at John Hopkins University insisting that now was the time to go for the 'window of opportunity?' He also had a critical meeting with President Clinton who subsequently phoned Major to pointedly 'encourage' him to press forward on the peace initiative.

It was around this time that Fergus Finlay told me he admired Reynolds' guts, judgement and tenacity on the peace process. I was somewhat taken aback given that such encomiums were not lightly dispensed by Finlay, particularly not in the direction of Reynolds. In fact, Finlay remained highly supportive — despite yet another major FF–Lab row — right through to the 15 December denouement at Downing Street.

On 15 November, at the Lord Mayor's banquet in London's Guild Hall, Major indicated that he did not wish to be deflected by the rift in Anglo–Irish relations. He declared: 'There may now be a better opportunity for peace in Northern Ireland than for many years.'

The Major speech was headlined on the same day as a statement by Gerry Adams was relegated to the inside pages. Adams had said that Sinn Féin representatives had engaged in 'protracted contact and dialogue' with the British government, a claim that was emphatically denied by No. 10 Downing Street. Reynolds observed: 'If that is the IRA saying they were involved in talks with the Brits, I believe them. They kill people. They don't tell lies.

18 November, 1993

> 'Taoiseach totally focused on peace. He is striking a fine balance between denying any attempt to impose peace deadline, and keeping up the pressure on the Brits. He is still working behind the scenes on a pre-Christmas agenda. Says he can't let it go into 1994 and the Euro elections.'

On the following day, Emily O'Reilly had an *Irish Press* exclusive revealing the contents of an Irish position paper, drafted by the Department of Foreign Affairs, calling on the British government to acknowledge 'the full legitimacy and value of the goal of Irish unity by agreement' in return for reciprocal change to Articles 2 and 3 of the Constitution. Reynolds and Mansergh were appalled — they regarded the leak as almost criminally irresponsible — while Spring described it as a 'vile deed' saying he would number the perpetrator of the leak as among the real 'betrayers' of both communities in the North. James Molyneaux, Ian Paisley and John Taylor maintained the document provided proof of a planned sell-out of Unionism.

There was widespread speculation that the leak came either from Foreign Affairs or from Spring's personal entourage. Reynolds blamed it on Finlay who vehemently denied the allegation. It became such a contentious issue that Emily O'Reilly sent a message through me to Reynolds that Finlay was not the source. Her defence of Finlay was couched in such trenchant terms that Reynolds told me he would accept it, but the incident still left him deeply upset and resentful.

Intriguingly, O'Reilly later told me that her source had given her a copy of the document to quickly peruse, then when he (she allowed that the subject was male) felt she was too slow in taking notes of its contents, almost casually told her to hold onto it. The matter was viewed with such seriousness that there was a Garda inquiry. O'Reilly, among others, was subjected to intensive questioning by detectives. Needless to say, the identity of her source was never revealed.

Ian Paisley, after a meeting with John Major at No. 10, emerged quoting the PM as saying he would have kicked the leaked Irish government document over the rooftops. Paisley, who had previously had frequent clashes with Major, expressed himself pleased with such language, adding that he now believed Major would not do a deal with Reynolds.

The Taoiseach was worried. He was awaiting news of the outcome of a special British cabinet meeting at which ministers were due to make a final decision on the proposed joint declaration. But three days had elapsed since the declared date of the meeting without any communication from the British side.

Finally, Reynolds told me to telephone Major's press secretary, Gus O'Donnell, to suss out what was going on. O'Donnell told me a 'person' was due in Dublin in forty-eight hours (Friday, 26 Oct.) with the final

British decision. Within 24 hours, I was back onto O'Donnell querying a Downing Street press briefing that the British could not advance work on the joint communique for the upcoming (3 Dec.) Anglo–Irish Summit in Dublin because they were still awaiting the Irish position paper.

I told O'Donnell: 'The Taoiseach says that is deliberately misleading. We have given you over our paper on the peace process. Your people are referring to a paper on the separate talks process which you know is not relevant to December the 3rd. O'Donnell said: 'Be careful. Things are at a delicate stage. Watch tomorrow for questions here on contacts with the IRA.'

On the following morning, the BBC's Jim Dougal, in the course of a *Panorama* interview with Reynolds, asked if it was true that Mansergh had been having direct talks with IRA representatives. Reynolds emphatically denied this and, afterwards, instructed me to again ring O'Donnell. The message was blunt: 'Gus, the Taoiseach says he resents British Intelligence seeking to undermine the peace process by misrepresenting a top Irish official as having had direct contact with Sinn Fein or the IRA.'

On that evening of 26 November, I wrote:

> 'Sir Robin Butler in from London. Produces alternative paper to Irish position paper, including proposals for unilateral changes to Articles 2 and 3. Albert gives him hell. Tells him he hasn't a clue. He also tells him that his (Major) alternative to the Summit peace proposal, which involves the two leaders finding some kind of "middle way", won't wash. He (Reynolds) will not buy some kind of "sticking plaster" anodyne cover-up. Why bother to have the Summit at all? Who is trying to bluff who?'

27 November, 1993

> 'Taoiseach rings: "Tell Gus (O'Donnell) I always said I would play straight and warn him (PM) even at the eleventh hour. I now want him to know that whoever has advised him to go the route he seems to have chosen has no understanding of the peace process. His (yesterday) communication has no peace focus. Consequently, it is not worth proceeding with. Not even an Irish government could stay with it." He tells me to remind Gus that three weeks of non paramilitary violence — since Greysteel — is important, and as a result of "quiet" approaches to the two sets of paramilitaries. Suddenly, around 8.55 p.m., story breaks — NIO admit British talking to Provos for many months.'

29 November, 1993

> '. . . Taoiseach has 40-minute chat with Major — No dice, John; you double-dealed on links with Provos; you never told us, plus your communication

> through Sir Robin Butler on Friday was a disaster. We will not deal on it; not much point in having summit; no prospect of success; we will not collude in anodyne joint statement afterwards. Major pleads for 3 Dec. summit. "I'll sit for eight hours and more, if necessary." Taoiseach does not trust him . . . . It hangs on a knife-edge.'

On the following day, I wrote:

> 'Gus O'Donnell rings. Been to see PM. Wants to brief lobby that last night's PM/T phone call very friendly, positive, etc. I go to Taoiseach who is with Dick and they say no way; we'll contradict him; Brits have used duplicity. "We're sore and angry" says Spring. Mansergh rings Rod Lyne (Roderic Lyne, chief private secretary to the PM) at night. He (Lyne) is desperate for Friday (3 Dec.) summit but insists on Friday's (26 Nov.) Brit document, cementing the union and pushing for Constitutional stuff (Articles 2 and 3), being on table. John Foley, Mansergh and I, with Taoiseach, discuss. Mansergh goes back to say "no way"— we want to see significantly more progress on peace initiative before agreeing to 3 Dec.'

> 'Lyne suddenly agrees. Brits to withdraw their document and everyone to concentrate on Irish peace proposals. He is so anxious to come to Dublin (Friday) that he suggests second summit pre-Christmas to finalise the thing.'

Rod Lyne rang me on the following morning to confirm that what he called the 'hop, step and jump' was on. This I took to mean the Friday summit in Dublin followed by a scheduled meeting between the two leaders 'on the margin' at an upcoming EU summit in Brussels, and then a final pre-Christmas meeting in London in order to conclude an agreement. However, Lyne stressed to me that the post-Brussels meeting at Downing Street would only take place 'subject to progress'.

After I told this to the Taoiseach, I wrote:

> 'Taoiseach rants that Mansergh must go back and tell them it's all off — don't come! Martin comes back in minutes to say: "OK, the three meetings are definitely on." We started all this by pushing for 3 Dec. Brits told us to back off. Now, we're saying to them forget 3 Dec. And they're pleading for it! Gus rings me to say all is still well, but mentions negative vibes from Dublin as relayed to British papers. I tell him: "Gus, that was me. We briefed about duplicity, hurt and anger. We particularly resented you guys telling us we had to keep a million miles away from Hume–Adams when you were inviting the IRA to have three of their boys meet three of yours — 'tea on the veranda, etc."' Gus says effectively: "Keep the faith."'

On the eve of the Dublin summit, Mansergh told me that Martin McGuinness was saying the British had kept Sinn Féin–IRA briefed on what was happening throughout the period of the inter-party talks at

Stormont during the previous year. Reynolds reminded me that Major had said it would 'turn my stomach' to talk to the IRA. I told the pol corrs we accepted that the morrow's fixture could now be described as just a 'working meeting' effectively confirming the parlous state of Anglo–Irish relations going into the long heralded Summit. I wrote:

> 'T. tells me he'll bring tomorrow's talks to an end with a major rift in Anglo-Irish relations, if necessary. Not a pretty sight on the eve of the Summit.'

As expected, the 3 December Anglo–Irish meeting at Dublin Castle was a contentious and bad tempered affair. Reynolds and Major clashed on a number of issues, including the *Irish Press* procural of the draft Irish position paper and the secret British talks with the IRA. Again, Gus O'Donnell and I, with John Foley, became involved. For several hours, we consistently contradicted each other at impromptu media briefings held in the same press area of Dublin Castle. I was taken aback as I had assumed there was agreement based on Rod Lyne's acceptance of the Irish position paper three days earlier. I later learned from Reynolds that a bitter row had erupted in the nearby conference room. Essentially, they differed on the key issue of whether the two sides were working off the one agenda, i.e. the Irish peace position paper or, as the British maintained, on two documents, one Irish and one British. They also disagreed on whether Articles 2 and 3 were on the agenda.

Suddenly, Gus O'Donnell conceded that the negotiations were, indeed, confined to the Irish position paper which incorporated amendments proposed by the British over the previous five months. This was an important admission by the British, but there was not any agreement on Articles 2 and 3. O'Donnell maintained they were very much 'on the table'. Foley and I insisted they were not on the agenda; all such constitutional considerations would be dealt with 'downstream' when the violence was over.

3 December, 1993

> '. . . Major, Hurd, Mayhew look tense afterwards. Conversation strained. Taoiseach winks at me while Marie (McLoughlin) removes make-up. "Tough stuff, but we shall see" he says. He tells me he was stuck into Major all day: "You're supposed to be my pal, and you're dealing with the Provos. I don't mind you talking to them, but you're not telling us the truth about it, and, worst of all, not telling me. My cabinet people say 'some pal!' Major, during document negotiations, snaps a pencil in frustration, but no Reynolds give. . . Earlier, Nally says: "They think they're dealing with the King of Lesotho." Gerry Barry spots how the two "pals" take leave of each other as Major leaves Castle. They shake hands before PM gets into car, but Albert then turns away

and is gone before Major is even seated in the car. Still, end of day, Mansergh says: "We did a bit better than we're admitting." Taoiseach allows: "It's not gone yet."'

Two days later, I wrote:

'... Brits say Articles 2 and 3 have to be written in .... He (Reynolds) says he'll put Articles 2 and 3 "in writing" only if there's British acceptance that this will require reciprocal movement on Government of Ireland Act. Taoiseach also sends message that while we're talking to republicans, etc. in order to get them to move, Major should decide that, if Unionists won't talk to us, he or his people will do the business with them ....'

On 10 December, a meeting between Reynolds and Major at an EU Summit in Brussels ended in apparent deadlock. Reynolds told me he wouldn't give an inch, and that he told Major he would not come to London if the document remained as it was. Also, at Brussels, Reynolds told me the British were signalling that they found Mansergh acceptable, but they couldn't 'stand' Sean O Huiginn. Reynolds said: 'That's because O Huiginn is so bloody good'. Then he chuckled: 'He's (O Huiginn) tough — a real Republican, you know.'

12 December, 1993

'S. O'Rourke's *This Week* interview, pushing it a little further. Done at Taoiseach's apartment. Kathleen tells me he is tired. Suddenly, he stands reading me the document. I listen to key Par. 4 and decide it is sufficient for Provos. He tells me he is still fighting for reciprocal "by right" obverse of majority right to at present defy a united Ireland. He is telling Major that if the majority changes, then the new majority has similar rights to go for united Ireland.'

Afterwards, Reynolds, the 'one page man', told me: 'I can close my eyes and quote you practically any sentence you like from any page, complete with every comma, colon, semicolon and full stop.'

14 December, 1993

'It's on! I talk to Gus. He says PM anxious to go ahead tomorrow (leak "something" could happen). Taoiseach shows Bart (Cronin) document. Mansergh says we're more or less agreed. Decide to take out reference to IRA being brought into process within three months (too condescending to IRA, says Albert). Apparently, Provos feel same way. Gus and I agree details of tomorrow's meeting. Taoiseach tells me he cannot do it (document) any better.'

'I have a distinct feeling that Albert has got his way on practically everything except, perhaps, the Brits agreeing to be persuaders for Irish unity ....'

The Downing Street Declaration was signed at a ceremony in No. 10 on 15 December, 1993. At 11. 40 a.m, after putting the finishing touches to the document, Albert Reynolds and John Major announced the accord — 'an agreed framework for peace' — and called on the men of violence on both sides to lay down their arms. The Declaration contained a commitment, for the first time, that the British government 'will uphold the democratic wish of a greater number of the people of Northern Ireland on the issue of whether they prefer to support the Union or a sovereign united Ireland'.

It declared that the British had no selfish, strategic or economic interest in the North, adding that their role would be to encourage, facilitate and enable the achievement of agreement 'among all the people who inhabit the island'. 'They (the British) accept that such agreement may, as of right, take the form of agreed structures for the island as a whole, including a united Ireland achieved by peaceful means . . .'

The Declaration stated that it was for the people of Ireland alone, by agreement between the two parts respectively, to exercise their right of self-determination on the basis of consent, freely and concurrently given, North and South, to bring about a united Ireland, 'if that is their wish'. Self-determination would have to be achieved and exercised with and subject to the agreement and consent of a majority of the people of Northern Ireland.

Reynolds was proud of the Irish government commitment in the document to six 'rights' conveyed to him via Rev. Roy Magee. They included rights of free political thought, freedom and expression of religion; the right to pursue democratically national and political aspirations; to seek constitutional change by peaceful and legitimate means; to live wherever one chose without hindrance, and to equal opportunity in all social and economic activity, regardless of class, creed, sex or colour.

At No. 10, John Major warmly welcomed Albert Reynolds, Dick Spring, Máire Geoghegan Quinn and the Irish officials. Major seemed somewhat tense and nervous to me. We were told more than once that the two leaders' joint news conference should not be 'lengthy'. I remarked to Martin Mansergh that the occasion had all the strained bonhomie of a shotgun wedding reception, but Mansergh said it was just their natural (British) reserve.

Douglas Hurd did give an impression of vaguely tolerant approval. Sir Patrick Mayhew, however, made no attempt to conceal his lack of enthusiasm. He remained separate from the milling politicians and officials, gloomily staring out windows for much of the time. Sir Robin Butler said to Reynolds: 'We've come a long way from Baldonnel.'

Before the start of the news conference, there was a flurry as someone noted that the Taoiseach had not any prepared opening remarks. Fergus Finlay rapidly drafted a preamble which perfectly suited the occasion. Then, as the Taoiseach was availing of the last-minute ministrations of a make-up artist, Rod Lyne approached him. The Prime Minister, he said, would appreciate if the Taoiseach would agree to his saying *inter alia* that he was a Unionist.

Mansergh and I glanced at each other — this would echo Margaret Thatcher's controversial 'I am a Unionist' remark at the signing of the Anglo–Irish Agreement — and Mansergh whispered to me that it was going to necessitate a change to the Taoiseach's scripted remarks. I think he assumed, like me, that the Taoiseach was going to politely nod agreement. Reynolds looked ahead expressionlessly, appeared to give the suggestion momentary thought, then said levelly: 'No. I don't really think that would be a good idea. Not really.'

In the event, the Prime Minister refrained from such observations but afterwards, as I shook his hand, the thought struck me that he had taken as many risks as Reynolds, Hume and Adams on the way to the accord. It was not that long ago since IRA mortars exploded in the garden we could see from inside No. 10. As Tory leader he was also taking a considerable risk, not just in terms of his reliance on the Unionists in the Commons, but also in terms of the large pro-Unionist element on the Conservative backbenches. However, a British source later told me Major resented Reynolds' rejection of his 'I am a Unionist' affirmation.

Gus O'Donnell, John Foley and I also shook hands as the champagne flowed in the cabinet room and copies of the Declaration were autographed by the signatories and main negotiators. Back in the Irish Embassy, my friend Mike Burns shepherded the Taoiseach and Tanaiste into an upstairs room where they were given a standing ovation by members of the Anglo–Irish Interparliamentary Body. A few hours later, back in Dublin, Reynolds and Spring were given another standing ovation from all sides in the Dáil Chamber.

19 December, 1993

'Albert deified! Even Eamon Dunphy, Shane Ross, Eoghan Harris join the chorus of praise. He sits for a special photo for *The Sunday Tribune* of himself superimposed on pic of Declaration. They actually wanted to use a live dove in the shot. Albert, the Longford Slasher, looking soulfully heavenwards under a snow-white dove of peace! They seemed disappointed when I said "no thanks".'

Sean Duignan and Charlie McCreevy discussing the odds

As I tendered my personal congratulations, Reynolds said to me: 'They're telling me to stand back now and rest on my laurels, when I'm not even going to have a breather before I take even bigger risks.' 'What do you mean?'

'The Declaration is grand if it works. Otherwise, it doesn't amount to a damn thing. I've now got to find out if it will fly — if it can deliver what it was built for — the peace.'

14

'THE PRIEST CHANGES EVERYTHING'

WHAT WAS it about Harry that made Reynolds and Spring face a battle to the political death? What possessed Reynolds to hazard all on Whelehan becoming President of the High Court? And — no less mystifying — why did Spring maintain undeviating resistance to the appointment at such risk to himself?

On the flight to Hong Kong–Australia–New Zealand, on the day of the cabinet crisis (14 Sept. 1994), I tried to draw Reynolds out on the reasoning behind the row. Why did Harry have to get the job? Reynolds maintained he was manifestly the best qualified person offering for the position; Labour had not come up with a name; indeed, he (Reynolds) was not aware of any other candidate; he had told Whelehan he would be recommending him for the job; Labour had never objected to Whelehan being chief law officer of the State, either during the negotiations for government or subsequently; a precedent and a convention existed for the Attorney General to have 'first call' on major judicial appointments and, in particular, Labour had not been able to adequately stand up their contention that Whelehan was unsuitable to be President of the High Court.

'I've repeatedly asked Dick why Harry is not acceptable' he said. 'All he will say is that Harry is "conservative". I ask if being a "conservative" is now a bar to becoming President of the High Court? All Dick says to that is Labour are committed to putting a liberalising stamp on the court.'

What about a compromise appointee? Reynolds maintained it did not arise in the circumstances. Labour had not come up with an alternative. They would have to do a lot better if they were to persuade him of their point of view. When I reminded him that I had talked to Labour before leaving, stressing the vital importance of keeping the cabinet row confidential, Reynolds said: 'Don't fool yourself. . . they'll have it in the "Sundays".'

Three days later, on arrival in Perth, Western Australia, I wrote:

> '. . . Not a line in the Saturday papers. Jesus, maybe it'll be OK. Albert says: "I'll believe it when I don't see it. "We are snowed under in Perth with media attention. Ireland/Peace a big deal. . .'

Within a few hours, I was forced to add:

> 'Mary K. (Mary Kerrigan, FF press secretary) rings to end the blissful illusion. Albert was right. They have it in the "Sundays". Labour leaking like a sieve — full steam/full frontal — to Emily, Olivia, Stephen, Gene Kerrigan *et al.* The story is Labour stopped the Taoiseach railroading/ramroding Harry through in his usual arrogant fashion. Labour, because of their commitment to liberal ethics, could not countenance Harry as President of H.C. when someone like Susan Denham (Ms Justice Denham of the Supreme Court) was available. No way would they allow Taoiseach to force Harry into job, even if it results in an election. . . .'

20 September, 1994

> 'Canberra — we are overwhelmed by the extent of the Labour blitzkrieg. They are going all out. It must be they've decided it's to be an election. We try to fight back, expressing anger at it being brought into the public domain, also at agreement (broken) to wait until the two leaders are back in the country to deal with the appointment. Labour denying they are responsible for spin, but even the papers are commenting on the audacity of the Labour briefings, with little or no attempt to disguise responsibility of Labour sources. Taoiseach tells Denis Coughlan, Michael Ronayne, Annette Blackwell (Irish journalists covering the Taoiseach's tour) it should not be an election issue. But we are losing the propaganda war. . .'

Watching events unfold from Australia, Reynolds was taken aback by the announcement of Susan Denham as the Labour Party choice. Labour were claiming that Spring had informed Reynolds on a number of occasions that she was his 'preferred' candidate. There was also favourable media reaction to such a distinguished liberal female Protestant alternative to Whelehan. I wrote:

> 'Bad to be so far away from action. I saw this happen to Jack Lynch when in America with him in '79. Hard to get a handle on. Labour upset over David Andrews counter-attack in defence of Harry. Still, we detect Nervous Nellie signals from FF ministers. Even Cowen seems "wet". Going on *This Week*, we twice briefed him on tough line with Labour, but he appears hesitant. In the event, his performance is less than rotweilerish. Albert rings him. "I suppose I'm in trouble," says Cowen resignedly. "What are the boys up to at home?"'

Reynolds perused faxed copies of news reports from Ireland. He focused on an *Irish Times* article by Geraldine Kennedy, under a page-wide headline, 'A Question of Who Lays Down the Law'. It began: 'The Taoiseach, Albert Reynolds, and the Tanaiste, Dick Spring, are engaged in such a battle of pride over the naming of the next President of the High Court that one of them, at least, will have to suffer a major political loss if a general election is to be avoided on the most inexplicable of issues. . .' Kennedy's article concluded: 'The breakdown in the relationship between Mr Spring and Mr Reynolds is irreparable.'

It now transpired that Ms Justice Denham had never been in the running. She confirmed not merely that she was not interested in becoming President of the High Court, but that Labour had put forward her name without consulting her. However, if I thought this would force Labour to back off, I was mistaken.

25 September, 1994

> 'The thing that gets to Albert down here (Australia) is that Labour, for the second successive Sunday, return to the attack with even greater gusto, this time attacking Albert personally (briefings to Emily and Olivia) as a "dictator", "High King of Ireland", autocratic, impossible to work with, etc. "That is election stuff" says Albert. "That's the kind of personal invective reserved for when the campaign is actually underway."'

Reynolds now said to me that if Labour had 'fought their corner behind closed doors', a compromise might have been reached, but public threats and insults could not be tolerated. I took notes of how he put it:

> 'They can't send these kind of abusive messages in clear to the other side of the globe, telling the whole world what a bastard the Taoiseach is, as well as telling him what he must do and not do — or else . . . . No Taoiseach can survive having to publicly knuckle under to that kind of blackmail. Apart from anything else, can you imagine how Fianna Fáil will react?. . . I believe Harry is the right man for the job and, besides, there is no other candidate.'

John Foley rang me to say Spring wanted to talk to Reynolds. I noted:

> 'Call comes through at around 1 a.m. I don't hang around. I come in afterwards. Taoiseach is in bad humour. They talked but got nowhere. Dick still adamant Harry not to get job. They agree to meet when back in Ireland together . . . .'

Having been feted by Australian Prime Minister, Paul Keating, and Jim Bolger, Prime Minister of New Zealand, Reynolds returned to Ireland, arriving at Shannon Airport, in time to keep an appointment there with Russian President Boris Yeltsin who was on his way home from the United States. The President's plane duly landed and there followed a bizarre scene as Reynolds and the Irish reception party waited in vain on the tarmac for Yeltsin to disembark.

30 September, 1994

'God's still in his heaven. Long before plane lands, Albert whispers to me Boris is pissed. They circle for an hour presumably while trying to sober him up. Then when he wouldn't or couldn't get off the plane, Deputy Prime Minister Oleg Soskovetz is thrown into the gap. I watch him play a blinder doing the biz with Albert — "President is slightly indisposed, etc." — until he (Reynolds) disingenuously asks would it help if he were to go aboard to meet the President. Oleg nearly has a seizure. His impassive stare suddenly turns to one of naked terror. "Nyet!" — for jaysus sake — "nyet". The mind boggles at what Albert would have beheld if he had been allowed aboard. Fair play to ye, Boris, says Albert. Laugh all the way back to Dublin.'

There was precious little to laugh at upon arrival in Dublin. The Whelehan row was in full spate with Spring adamant that he would not relent on the issue. But the Spring tide was beginning to turn. Newspaper editorial opinion was hardening against any prospect of a general election as a result of the impasse. *The Irish Times* said most who had voted Labour never wanted or envisaged the alliance with Fianna Fáil. 'But, they would now probably say, let Mr Spring and Labour endure their discomfort, and get on with the job they promised to do.'

4 October, 1994

'Albert begins writing, in his spidery scrawl, a statement for me to feed out refuting the Labour briefings or, as he puts it, "setting the record straight on Labour disinformation". He denies trying to railroad Harry through cabinet, points to "unrelenting briefings from certain quarters", and insists the matter must be "resolved" as soon as possible. I tell him Labour will see this as a provocation on the eve of first meeting between Spring and him for almost a month. Labour duly jump up and down . . . .'

5 October, 1994

'Dick meets Albert alone for 45 minutes. No raised voices. According to Albert, he begins: "Look, Dick, this can be a short or a long conversation. From what I see, you want an election." "Where did you get that idea, Albert?" "Because you hit us with a non-stop barrage of anti-Reynolds publicity when our backs were turned Down Under. It was pre-election — no, it was mid-election — stuff."

'Afterwards (after cabinet meeting), they both come into my room. Dick has it written down. Two FF and two Lab ministers (sub-committee) to meet in order to deal with situation. I walk down with Dick and John (Foley) to John's room. Dick uncharacteristically sharp with me. John says: "Albert better believe it. We're going the whole way on this."'

Now, Labour party backbenchers moved to head off an election on the issue. They began publicly accusing Spring's 'Three Wise Men', Fergus Finlay, Greg Sparks and Willie Scally, of wielding disproportionate power as the Tanaiste's 'non-elected' kitchen cabinet, and of having pushed Spring into an unnecessary confrontation. Yet Spring still refused to back off. John Foley and I briefed separately that an election seemed unavoidable.

Bart Cronin marvelled: 'The irresistible force and the immovable object.' 'You're putting pressure on yourselves, John,' I ventured. He responded: 'Albert is insane to be doing all this for Harry. He has got to understand, Dick will not roll over on this one.' I said: 'If Albert's insane, then it behoves Dick to be sane, or the government is gone.' 'The old Henry Kissinger trick' chuckled Joe Joyce of *The Sunday Tribune*. Kissinger, he said, used to go around the globe warning world leaders that Richard Nixon was 'mad', and then he'd add: 'So we'd better put a deal together here. 'But I was no Henry Kissinger.

8 October, 1994

> 'Fianna Fáil guys and dolls getting jumpy. Tom Savage into Taoiseach with messages from Máire Geoghegan Quinn, McCreevy, Willie O'Dea — "You'll lose power, Taoiseach" — and how many more FF "wets" are there out there?'

On the following day's *The Sunday Tribune* published a poll that showed support for the Labour Party had dropped by more than 30 percent since the 1992 general election, while public blame for the Whelehan controversy was allocated equally between Reynolds and Spring.

10 October, 1994

> 'The poll has stripped Dick of the last remnants of Labour backbench support. It has scared the hell out of them and they're admitting it. Eleven of them speak out, eight practically queuing to get on *This Week* to say it's gone far enough; we'll buy Harry rather than have an election; the (Labour) advisers, Fergus *et al*, they say have to be reined in. Nobody backs Dick. John tells me: "Dick has been stabbed in the back by his own followers. "I have never seen John so upset.'

The Irish Times decided: 'It is difficult to see how a solution can be found which does not involve one leader or the other backing off. But there is a national interest which transcends personal sensitivities. If the price is to allow Harry Whelehan to take over as President of the High Court, it is one that Dick Spring should be willing to pay.'

As the early editions of that *Irish Times* issue were coming onto the streets of Dublin, Reynolds and Spring were secretly meeting at Baldonnel Airport. Reynolds came by air from Cork. Spring travelled by road. I wrote:

> 'Baldonnel. *Cúirt an Mhéan Oíche*. John and I arrange that Albert and Dick intersect at Baldonnel at 10.30 p.m. Albert rings me dead on 10.30. "Where are you, Taoiseach?" "I'm at the airport". Wonderful. He's on time for a change. CORK airport, he adds. For jaysus sake. He'll be late for his own funeral. At 11 p.m. Dick rings Colm Butler (Taoiseach's private secretary). I'm WAITING! Albert finally arrives around midnight.'

Reynolds later told me: 'I walked in and said "God, Dick, we must be mad to be in this job, when we have to meet like this, in an airport at all hours of the night; it's no way to live.' Later, I deciphered from shorthand notes what else Reynolds told me:

> 'Taoiseach says he said (to Spring): "Look, we may as well decide, one way or the other, if the story is that, whether we get over this or not, it's just a matter of waiting until you get a better issue to pull the rug, because then we might as well go for an election now, and get it over with. But there is another way if we only look at this with a bit of common-sense. The peace thing is going well; the economy is going well; unemployment is coming down; the Euro billions are beginning to flow. We could almost put this government on auto pilot with the two of us just kicking upcoming problems like Telecom, TSB, or whatever, in front of us all the way to 1997. Then, we — you and I — go to the people on the basis of what we've achieved on the Programme for Government and let the people judge .... We can afford between us to lose 15/17 seats and still come back."'

Reynolds did not tell me how Spring reacted to all of that. He did say that they agreed there would be no general election arising from the row, and that there was a tacit understanding that Harry would get the job in return for key changes in the judicial appointments system — but not yet. Spring needed time, Reynolds said, so the appointment would not be announced until the heads of a new Courts Bill, a major reform package featuring a new judicial appointments board, were approved by government.

I observed disparagingly: 'You mean a smoke-screen. It will be dressed up any way they want, just so long as Harry gets the job.' Reynolds rounded on me furiously: 'I don't want to hear talk like that from you again. This involves unprecedented major reform of the system. There will no rubbing of Dick's nose in this.'

But Reynolds, almost as if he had a premonition, added something else: 'As I was leaving (Baldonnel), I turned around and said: "Just remember, Dick, we can't leave this hanging too long. You know how these things, if they're not wrapped up reasonably quickly, have a way of going wrong."'

The Baldonnel 'deal' was of crucial significance, not just because Reynolds believed it finally disposed of the Whelehan affair, but because Labour subsequently rejected all claims that Spring had conditionally agreed to Whelehan's appointment. My only comment when pressed on this was that Reynolds, the ultimate 'dealer', operating from a position of exceptional strength, was not the sort to present Spring with such a legislative reform package, if he had not first secured his compensatory 'pound of *quid pro quo*'.

Reynolds, however, made an uncharacteristic and ultimately fatal error. The man who had so ruthlessly dispatched the FF old guard failed to press home his advantage on this occasion. Acceding to Spring's plea for 'space' in which to cover his retreat, he withdrew the dagger from his throat at the decisive moment. Denis Coughlan, quoting an unidentified Fianna Fáil source, reported: 'Reynolds is in a less parlous situation than Spring, and that gives him flexibility. He no longer has to be as tough as he was.' But the source then added: 'Dick, on the other hand, is in such a weak position that he will not back off.'

On the following day (12 Oct.) Coughlan wrote: 'On balance, though, Mr Whelehan must be favoured to fill the slot. . . . But time is the great friend of the politician; it blurs memory and creates space for manoeuvre.'

A few days before the Baldonnel meeting, UTV (Ulster Television) transmitted a disturbing *Counterpoint* programme dealing with the depredations of a paedophile priest, Fr Brendan Smyth, who was serving a four-year prison sentence in Northern Ireland for sex offences against young people. Another week went by before Reynolds was warned that there was a legal link between Smyth and the Attorney General's office. He mentioned it to me as a new and irritating development, but not something he regarded as threatening. For a considerable time afterwards, he failed to appreciate its significance in terms of the Whelehan appointment — 'Dick and I have a deal' — but it emerged that Spring and his advisers had understood its potential much sooner. Said John Foley to me: 'The priest changes everything'.

15

'Sinn Féin Will Pay a Price for Going to Capitol Hill'

A FORTNIGHT after the signing of the Downing Street Declaration, an agitated Eoghan Harris rang me at my home. 'Tell him (Reynolds) to stop picking at the Declaration. He is in a win/win situation if he just steps back. He will ruin everything if he keeps going as he is.'

I was not surprised. Unionist spokesmen were already accusing Reynolds of talking the IRA's language. John Bruton had warned him not to make statements that could be construed as trying to alter the Declaration. And John Foley had just told me that Dick Spring was so annoyed by recent Reynolds' utterances that he was going on RTE's *News at One* as part of a damage limitation exercise.

When I relayed these messages to the Taoiseach, he listened intently, then remarked: 'They're talking as if the Declaration were an end in itself, when it's just a stepping stone. So, if they're upset now, they'll be blazing mad before I'm finished, because I'm not going to pull back.'

Reynolds subsequently told me that his strategy was partially influenced by initial Sinn Féin criticism of the Declaration, as well as by British failure to exploit its potential for peace. He constantly used the analogy of the Sinn Féin/IRA 'trout' which had to be expertly played, as it unpredictably darted every which way, before it could be gradually reeled onto the bank.

Initial Sinn Féin reaction was discouraging as Spring announced that the IRA would have to hand over their guns, and Reynolds uncharacteristically spoke of the need for a 'strong security response' if they reverted to violence. Dermot Nally, as he autographed my copy of the Downing Street Declaration, said: 'He (Reynolds) must stop talking of stiffer security measures, or the handing over of guns. They (Sinn Féin/IRA) will walk away if we persevere with that kind of talk.'

23 December, 1993

> 'Provos want "clarification" of Declaration. British say "no way", that the Provos are really seeking re-negotiation. Major said in Belfast he was "casting down the gauntlet of peace" to Sinn Féin. This goes with his "decontamination period" for Sinn Féin, plus "take it or leave it" stuff, etc. Taoiseach, upset by the language and tone, tells me to ring Gus (O'Donnell) to say these guys need "space" to deliberate. Talk to Jonathan Haslam in No. 10, and Gus rings me later from Hillsborough. "They need space, Gus". Later, Mark Hennessy (*The Cork Examiner*) rings that he has been talking to (Martin) McGuinness in Derry. It's not good — "very bleak message" says Mark — I feed out that Hume will act as conduit for clarification.'

As the year ended, a British soldier was shot dead by an IRA sniper in South Armagh, and, on New Year's Day, the IRA launched a firebomb attack on business premises in Belfast, causing millions of pounds worth of damage.

It now transpired that Sinn Féin were questioning British interpretation of 'self-determination' as set out in the Declaration, apparently seeking a single All–Ireland referendum for the island 'as a whole', rather than separate plebiscites, North and South, and also demanding that the British act as 'persuaders' for a united Ireland. In an interview in *The Sunday Business Post*, Martin McGuinness said the Declaration would be 'worthless' if what he called the negative British interpretation prevailed. *The Irish Times* observed: '. . . it would appear to signify the rejection of the Downing Street Declaration, at least as an immediate formula for peace.'

Reynolds, attempting to hook the 'trout', cast a succession of lures. He called for a start to 'demilitarisation' of the Northern situation. He portrayed the British as 'persuaders', if not for a united Ireland *per se*, for a new agreement on the future of the whole island. He promised that he would provide 'continuing clarification' of the Declaration for Sinn Féin, and strongly implied that the British should also do so. In addition, he let it be known that the government intended to lift, after 22 years, the Broadcasting Act (Section 31) ministerial order banning Sinn Féin, the IRA and other named organisations from the national airwaves. John Bruton roundly condemned the move, as did Des O'Malley, Michael McDowell and Garret FitzGerald, but Reynolds, strongly supported by the Minister in charge of broadcasting, Michael D. Higgins, was undeterred.

He was being increasingly attacked for 'pro-Sinn Féin' tendencies — Michael McDowell repeatedly accused him of using 'Provo language' — while Spring was taking a noticeably tougher line with Sinn Féin, warning them that the two governments could proceed without them, and hinting that the broadcasting ban could be re-imposed. *The Irish Times* commented: 'It is likely that more voices will join that of Mr Spring before too long.'

6 January, 1994

> 'Taoiseach tells me to ring Gus to tell him Provos want more than Brit offer of "exploratory talks" if they quit. It is not a question of changing text of Declaration but being screwed by Perfidious Albion after exploratory talks. He (Reynolds) still thinks Provos will come, but he must talk their language to counter Major "decontamination" and "throwing down gauntlet" stuff. They (IRA) need more than "exploratory talks".

> 'I ring Gus who says he might get PM to say he'll try to see how exploratory talks might lead to wider talks involving Sinn Féin with other constitutional parties. Taoiseach tells me this is not enough. PM must say exploratory talks will lead to SF being involved in overall talks process. Gus says OK, he'll try with PM. I tell him Taoiseach believes process still on rails, and that he will warn him (PM) if it starts going awry. Message comes from Provo contact to me for Taoiseach — "They (IRA) are still there and not split."'

After Major publicly agreed to the 'exploratory talks' proposal, Reynolds gave Sinn Féin what I called a 'read my lips' pledge. He pointed out that he had taken it upon himself to give clarification of the Declaration in a succession of speeches and statements, and that the British had never rebutted his interpretation, the implication being that this should satisfy Sinn Féin/IRA.

I asked Reynolds if he worried about being regarded as too 'green'. He replied: 'It just has to be done, despite what your politically correct pals in the media are saying. What they don't notice, which may be just as well, is that I'm also telling Sinn Féin that I won't bend on the simple principle that self-determination by the people of Ireland as a whole cannot be exercised without the agreement and consent of the majority of the people of Northern Ireland. They don't like hearing that there are no buts or maybes, no short cuts, and no way around that.'

As Sinn Féin continued to warn against any 'Unionist veto' on constitutional change, SDLP deputy leader, Seamus Mallon, who was never comfortable with the Hume–Adams relationship, moved to take them up on the issue. Insisting that he knew the contents of the still unpublished Hume–Adams document, he declared that it contained a specific 'consent' proviso indistinguishable from the guarantee in the Joint Declaration. Sinn Féin, interestingly, would only describe that as 'unhelpful'.

None of this prevented Reynolds from using his influence and connections with the US Clinton administration to further facilitate Sinn Féin in the face of powerful British opposition. Gerry Adams, banned from entry to the United States, had applied for a US visa to attend a conference of Northern Ireland leaders in New York. Prominent Irish–American politicians, including Senators Edward Kennedy and Daniel Moynihan, appealed to President Clinton to authorise a visa for Adams in order to facilitate the peace process. The National Security Council, headed by Anthony Lake, recommended to the President that the visa be issued, but the traditionally pro-British State Department, under Secretary of State, Warren Christopher, urged rejection of the application.

31 January, 1994

> 'Albert wins argument, with help of the Irish–American lobby. It's an historic win over the Brits who are shocked and enraged. The Irish coup is recognised by all. Albert tells me the Kennedys, in particular, and not least Jean Kennedy Smith (US Ambassador to Ireland) — "the right woman in the right place"— had just too much White House clout for the Brits. He talks of others, Tony Lake and Nancy Soderberg (US National Security Council), as well as Bruce Morrison, Ray Flynn, Bill Flynn and the heavy hitters of the Irish business scene. We never could have done this a few years back.'

Conor O'Clery, Washington correspondent of *The Irish Times* summed up: 'The dynamics of the Irish-American scene over the past few years have changed. The instigators of the push for a visa were members or close associates of corporate Irish-America . . . "People who think Noraid when they think Irish–America are five years out of date," said one prominent Irish–American . . . . No one can remember the White House ever being so engaged on an Irish issue.'

President Clinton said he supported the 'difficult decision' to grant the Adams visa on the basis that Adams made constructive comments on rejecting violence, and Reynolds said to me: 'John (Major) is very upset now, but the Adams visa will advance the peace. Sinn Féin will pay a price for going to Capitol Hill. A lot of powerful people went out on a limb for Adams. If he doesn't deliver, they'll have him back in the house with the steel shutters (Sinn Féin headquarters, Falls Road, Belfast) so fast his feet won't touch the ground. We're slowly putting the squeeze on them, pulling them in, boxing them in, cutting off their lines of retreat.'

10 February, 1994

> 'Dominick McGlinchey shot dead in Drogheda. Albert says to me: "We'll all wind up like that if we hang around long enough. The odds on survival for anyone in this business are less than on McGlinchey surviving in his business.' That is why a brigand "doer" like Albert is worth more than all these morally indignant wasters put together.'

As the 'clarification' row rumbled on, Reynolds again went to Downing Street where he privately urged the PM to concentrate less on Unionist sensitivities, and to 'just occasionally' address himself to the Nationalists. A week later, Gerry Adams made what was widely interpreted as a hardline 'anti-peace declaration' speech at the annual Sinn Féin Ard Fheis. Although Martin McGuinness subsequently sought to soften that perception, Reynolds told me he was 'puzzled' regarding the IRA's ultimate intentions.

13 March, 1994

> 'New York — More bad news from home. Provos mortar Heathrow (Heathrow Airport, London) for third successive night. Again, nobody killed; mortars either duds or not primed. Nobody sure about the significance of that. British mad and mortified. Albert worried. He keeps saying Provos have "gravely miscalculated", but he can't figure it out. Neither can Hume. Adams makes gung–ho "spectacular" news conference remarks. No embarrassment, very pro-IRA. All media reports say peace initiative "off the rails". What now?'

On the eve of a glittering St Patrick's Day party in the White House, Reynolds needed to show 'peace patron' Bill Clinton that the process was alive and well. From Belfast, Adams obliged by saying the IRA, despite British intransigence, were committed to a peaceful settlement. Clinton, welcoming the Adams statement, said pointedly: 'I still believe the decision we made on the visa was the correct one. We all have to take some chances for peace. I think when he (Adams) came here, he saw that Irish–Americans want peace.'

18 March, 1994: Washington

> 'Astonishing White House bash (17 March). I've been at two Paddy's Day functions here, but nothing like this. The entire upper floor, room after massive room, taken over with eating, drinking, *siamsa* and *craic*.

> 'Food, music, etc. brilliant. Hilary Clinton in her element. Clinton himself in top form. Raw green power, not just shamrockry. What must unionists think of it? Can Sinn Féin resist all of this?'

Reynolds now repeated in public what he had been saying to me in private: 'I know Mr Adams personally wants to deliver on the Joint Declaration for peace. . . I don't know whether he can actually deliver the IRA. . . there will be no split in that organisation.'

Back home, word from Sinn Féin/IRA was that they could not accept the Joint Declaration as it stood. 'It can't be changed,' said the Taoiseach, 'so I've had to find a way around that. I've just told them they don't have to buy it provided they end the (violence) campaign.'

On March 23, he told the Dáil: 'We can have a peace process and a rejection of violence without an (Sinn Féin/IRA) acceptance of the Downing Street Declaration.' Over the next few days, there were indications that the IRA was about to announce a temporary ceasefire lasting perhaps a month, possibly three months. On March 29, my friend Liam Kelly rang me: 'My contacts say there will an Easter ceasefire lasting three days.' 'Three days,' said the Taoiseach, 'he's got to have it wrong.'

30 March, 1994

> 'Taoiseach says "You're friend was right". We're at Garth Brooks concert in Point when confirmation comes through that Provos will start 72–hour "suspension" of military action as from midnight Tuesday (5 April). Albert is totally deflated. Tells reporters it's "one small step", but says to me why did they (IRA) bother. He can't figure their strategy, and speculates on whether Adams is unable to speak for a sufficiently large number of IRA. . . Garth Brooks, about to go on stage and watching me constantly on mobile phone as Albert frets, insists on going to get me a drink because "you've obviously got a very important job". When I don't see him after four or five minutes, I figure "goodbye". Then he arrives back, complete with drink, ice etc. "There you are, sir. Sorry for the delay." Hope Albert notices that some people appreciate me.'

I subsequently learned that the widely dismissive response to the three-day ceasefire had a salutary effect on Sinn Féin. They freely admitted afterwards that they had anticipated favourable political and public reaction, and were shocked at the wave of derision provoked by the announcement. Martin Mansergh told me that Fr Reid also expressed unease at the way I had briefed cross-Channel journalists on the issue.

3 April, 1994

> 'I talk to MM (Martin Mansergh). The priest says "they" are upset by government spokesman talking of a "personal snub" to the Taoiseach. I offer Albert to "soften" the line I laid on foreign corrs. But he says "leave it."

On the following day, I noted:

> 'I ring Taoiseach. He is OK but feels maybe it might be suggested via MM to Blatherwick that Brits could respond in writing (or whatever) to Adams/McGuinness demands, (1) clarification of "textual ambiguities" in Peace Declaration (2) what is the next step after cessation of violence? (3) what are Brits' long term intentions re N.I. (Northern Ireland)?'

In Cork, Reynolds publicly left little doubt as to whom he blamed for the impasse. "While it is a matter for the British government alone," he said, "the peace process can be moved forward if the British agree to clarify the Joint Declaration. . . . Sinn Féin's calls for clarification have been matched by British refusal to do so, and the result is that a deep distrust has built up which is an obstacle to peace.'

At an Ógra Fianna Fáil meeting, Reynolds offered Northern politicians 30 percent of places in an enlarged government, in the event of an All–Ireland settlement, a concept contemptuously rejected by the Unionist parties. Reynolds said to me: 'They pretend they don't want to know. But it's now stitched into the record. Someday, another Taoiseach will be reminded of it — from Belfast!'

As another wave of tit-for-tat sectarian killings now swept the North, long simmering hostility between Spring and Adams surfaced. It was intolerable, said Spring, to have to listen to Adams preaching justice and fairness when he would not condemn 'that sickening and depraved activity'. Adams, who had been privately critical of Spring since he took over at Foreign Affairs, snapped back: 'Mr Spring would be better employed persuading the British government to positively engage in the peace process.'

'Put it in writing,' Reynolds now said to Sinn Féin. He was responding to indications from Sir Patrick Mayhew that clarification of the Declaration might be forthcoming if the British were satisfied that the Sinn Féin questions only required clarification and not re-negotiation. Reynolds advised Sinn Féin to put their questions down on paper. On the eve of our departure for the United States (12 May) he told me Sinn Féin had sent him a list of 'clarification' questions to be passed on to the British. I wrote:

> 'Taoiseach tells me the ones (questions) he is passing on are all "answerable". Says he vetted SF questions, refusing to transmit a number of them, and insisting that his stamp be on the questions before he would pass them on. He has told the Brits not alone to answer these, but to ensure that the "tone" is correct — not "out, out, out" — but, whatever the verdict, at least showing "respect" and "parity of esteem" in their dealings with Sinn Féin.'

While we were in Chicago, Irish Ambassador, Dermot Gallagher, received a message from the White House: 'President Clinton would like to meet with Taoiseach Reynolds in Indianapolis tomorrow.'

The half-hour meeting, arranged with the help of Indiana Democrat, Frank McCloskey, chairman of the Congressional Friends of Ireland group, took place in the tiny robing room of a small red-brick Baptist Church. The Taoiseach assured the President that the clarification impasse would be overcome before he (Clinton) met with John Major in London two weeks later, and that they were still on course for a permanent peace. Clinton told Reynolds of his continuing support for the process.

Conor O'Clery reported: 'The meeting was an audacious coup for the Irish, who now have had five top level meetings with the US President in 14 months. Most other countries, including next door neighbour Canada, have yet to have one.'

On the following day, after Reynolds received an honorary degree and delivered the commencement address at Notre Dame University, I met with Niall O'Dowd, publisher of *The Irish Voice*.

15 May, 1994: South Bend, Indiana

> 'Albert, in full regalia plus mortar board, lays it on 12,500 rich (Catholic?) students. He is a huge hit. I find a bar on the campus where I'm joined by Niall O'Dowd. Fascinating conversation given that I'm told O'Dowd is high "in the loop". The message is that the Provos are going to end the war. "It's on . . . all in train. . . they're coming . . . just be careful".'

16

'THE IRA HAVE NOWHERE ELSE TO RUN'

REYNOLDS NOW began carefully reeling the IRA in.

19 May, 1994

> 'Relief! Brits put out lengthy, serious, helpful list of answers to SF questions. "This removes the clarification roadblock," says Taoiseach and praises Brits. He's jubilant. "We'll box these (Sinn Féin) boys into a corner yet", but he accepts the road ahead could feature more roadblocks.'

The British response, soon hailed by Adams as an important step, sparked angry reaction from loyalist paramilitaries who were again doing more killing than their IRA opponents. Reynolds hastened to support James Molyneaux who was pointing out that both sets of paramilitaries would get equal recognition in the event of a complete cessation of violence. But this failed to prevent an Ulster Volunteer Force attack on a crowded Dublin bar, the Widow Scallan's, in which one man was shot dead, another badly injured, and an 18lb bomb failed to explode.

Once again, in an Oxford Union address, Reynolds pledged that the Irish government would not weaken on the 'consent' guarantee in the Joint Declaration, but he also quoted one of the British answers to Sinn Féin in support of his own most insistent demand: 'To use the language of the British response to Sinn Féin, a reflection of this *(quid pro quo)* understanding would, in my opinion, have implications for key aspects of the Government of Ireland Act, 1920, as well as for the Irish Constitution.'

Around this time, Reynolds and Hume seemed to be the only politicians who still believed peace was on the way. I wrote:

> 'An almost universally despondent mood about the North. The media experts on the ground in Belfast say it is not going to happen. Nobody around here — Ministers included — think otherwise. Only Albert stubbornly insisting to me it will be all right. Is he just incapable of admitting to himself that it is slipping away?'

18 June, 1994: Giant Stadium, NY

'Oh Happy Day! All the crap in this job is worth it for this alone. Republic of Ireland 1; Italy nil. We're in super box, complete with bar, looking down on something I've only dreamed about. Albert, Kathleen, Paddy (Teahon), Donagh (Morgan), Deckers (Declan Ingoldsby), Colm (Butler), Joe (Glennon). Tom Savage comes in. A sea of green all around us. Where are the Eyeties? It doesn't matter. Who put the ball in Ital-ees net? I did, sez Ray Houghton. "One-nil, one-nil, one-nil, one-nil. . ." Go to see Jack (Charlton) and boys in dressing room afterwards. What an experience . . . .'

'Earlier, at hotel, Albert is given a hard luck story by two Dubs. Jaysus, Albert, we've been ripped off. Everything gone, money, the lot. Giz two tickets and we'll never forget you. He gives them two ground tickets. Finally, when we get through all the security at Giant Stadium to the Taoiseach's private box, two heavies on the door insist on checking with the "occupiers" of the box, who turn out to be the two Dubs. "Aw, fair play. There y'are Albert. He's all right. Let him in." Afterwards, we're still around stadium, talking to fans, when word comes through of UDA/UVF (?) killing 5/6 people watching the game in Catholic bar in Co. Down. Albert is upset. . . .'

Loyalist gunmen, choosing a moment midway through the second half of the World Cup game, caught customers by surprise as they watched television pictures from Giant Stadium. Six Catholics, ranging in ages from 34 to 87, were killed, and five others injured, as the bar was raked by automatic fire. Reynolds, on arrival back in Ireland, told the Dáil: 'I cannot for the life of me understand how the shooting dead of an 87-year-old man, whose only crime was to watch a football match, can serve any cause. It beats me.'

A month later, Sinn Féin held a national delegate conference in Letterkenny, Co. Donegal, to consider their response to the Joint Declaration. Resolutions endorsed by the delegates were predominantly critical of key elements of the Declaration, including definitions and parameters of self-determination, persuasion and consent.

25 July, 1994

'Shinners say NO! Universal Irish/British reaction that SF effectively rejected the Declaration. The terms of the DSD (Downing Street Declaration) motions — negatives swamping positives — cannot be otherwise interpreted. *IT (The Irish Times)* says they're not going to come now. Spring saying the same thing. Bruton, Harney, de Rossa as well. Mallon ditto. Hume in France, cannot be contacted. Albert says: "You think it's gone too, Diggy. "I say nothing, shrug. He says: "So, I'm in a minority of one."'

145

Reynolds kept insisting to me that Sinn Féin had simply got it 'arseways'. He told me he had read a copy of Adams speech before it was delivered and considered it acceptable, if somewhat ambiguous. The problem, he said, was that he (Reynolds) had not got advance notice of the hardline motions which were passed by the delegates at Letterkenny. Sinn Féin, he told me, had not anticipated that the media would concentrate on these clear-cut decisions rather than on the generalities of the Adams address.

Through July and August, the IRA targeted key loyalist paramilitaries, first murdering Ulster Defence Association (UDA) activist Ray Smallwoods, and then Raymond Elder and Joe Bratty, also of the UDA. "Unfinished business," I was told.

Adams said in London that peace was in sight, and former Sinn Féin publicity officer, Danny Morrison, who originally committed Sinn Féin/IRA to an 'Armalite and ballot box' strategy, said it was important that republicans should now develop an 'unarmed' strategy. Reynolds, on the eve of departing for a holiday in Mexico, said to me: 'It's coming, but nothing will happen while I'm out of the country. They will not do business with Dick Spring."

Aboard the luxury yacht of his Mexican friend Romulo O'Farrill, off the Mexican coast, Reynolds kept in regular telephone contact with me. When I reminded him that Marie and I were shortly going on holiday to Thailand, he asked when I would be back in Ireland. I replied that it would be in early September, and he said: 'I may need you before that.'

12 August, 1994

> 'I ring Albert, or he rings me every day from yacht. He's absolutely convinced that we are on the verge of an end to it all. Keeps asking me when I'll be back from Thailand. I can already feel he doesn't like the idea that it'll be Sept. 3/4. He is like someone who knows the day and the hour. "Wouldn't it be funny if they did it on the day of the Beef Tribunal (Dáil) debate, Taoiseach?" "Don't rule it out!" his response. It's a strange waiting period. Albert says: "They (IRA) have nowhere to go. I've stripped away all their excuses, one by one. They have nowhere else to run." Martin M. (Mansergh) talks a lot to me. Since Letterkenny, he has been puzzled by Provos but never despairing; just not sure about their thought processes. . . . I know in my bones the Thai holiday thing is going to go off the rails by end August.'

Just before Marie and I left for Bangkok in mid-August, Sinn Féin sources convinced their journalistic contacts in Belfast, Dublin and London that a ceasefire was imminent, but predictions were that it would be 'indefinite' and 'conditional' rather than permanent. As I travelled between Bangkok, Chiang Mai and the island of Ko Samui, I got telephone calls from the Taoiseach and John Foley keeping me abreast of developments.

The British had finally offered to amend Section 75 of the Government of Ireland Act, 1920, which enshrined its claim to sovereignty over Northern Ireland, in return for changes to Articles 2 and 3 of the Constitution.

Former US Congressman Bruce Morrison, leader of a six-member US group heading for Belfast, first visited Reynolds and Spring in Dublin where he was given a blunt message for Adams. There would have to be a permanent cessation of violence. That was the only basis on which Sinn Féin could become involved in the political process.

Reynolds told me the IRA signalled that they wanted to declare that they reserved the right to defend nationalist communities against future aggression, and that he then spelled out his position in even blunter terms: 'I've told them if they don't do this right, they can shag off; I don't want to hear anything about a six-month or six-year ceasefire; no temporary, indefinite or conditional stuff; no defending or retaliating against anyone; just that it's over. . . period. . . full stop. Otherwise, I'll walk away. I'll go off down that three-strand talks/framework document road with John Major, and they can detour away for another 25 years of killing and being killed — for what? Because, at the end of that 25 years, they'll be back where they are right now, with damn all to show for it, except thousands more dead, and all for nothing. So, they do it now, in the name of God, and be done with it, or goodbye.'

He also told me John Major did not believe the IRA had any intention of ending the violence permanently. 'But,' he said, 'he's going to get peace, and he deserves it, because he did more than any other British Prime Minister to bring it about.'

28 August, 1994: Ko Samui

> 'This is it! 8 a.m. Marie's birthday. Declan (Ingoldsby) rings me. "He wants you back. It's on. You're booked out of Bangkok. Just get there somehow or another." Kiss Marie "happy birthday" and start hustling. It takes baksheesh to get aboard 40-seater plane. I pull it off as other passengers protest. Now in Zurich for three hours until we get flight to Dublin. . . .'

'Welcome back, Diggy', said the Taoiseach as I entered his office, 'You saw it start in '69. I figured you might as well see it finish . . . . It's tomorrow, but say nothing yet. It's still all or nothing, no conditions.'

He told me that it hung in the balance until a few hours before my arrival home, right up to the moment President Bill Clinton personally authorised a US visa for former Provisional IRA leader, Joe Cahill, to enable Cahill to explain to republican supporters in the United States the strategy behind what was about to happen.

This seemed like a minor detail to me, in the context of an historic event, but I was told it had actually provoked a Dublin–Washington 'five minutes to midnight' confrontation. The Army Council of the IRA was adamant that there would be no peace announcement until Cahill entered the United States. US Attorney General Janet Reno was equally adamant that Cahill should not be allowed into the country. The US Justice Department had pointed out that there was a glaring difference between granting a visa to Adams and affording the same facility to Cahill. Adams had not got a serious criminal record; Cahill had been sentenced to hang for the murder of an RUC man in 1942 — he was subsequently reprieved — and had convictions for gun-running and being an IRA member. Granting him a US visa would be in contravention of a rigid regulatory code and would establish a potentially catastrophic precedent.

Reynolds told me he had spent most of the previous night on the telephone between the "priest" and Nancy Soderberg who, as staff director of the US National Security Council, had exerted a powerful influence on the decision to grant Adams a US visa. He (Reynolds) said he eventually became so tired that he grew irritable with Fr Reid who was trying to convey the urgency of the issue — '(IRA) Army Council preparing to meet in emergency session; nothing happens unless Cahill gets in' — while Nancy Soderberg confirmed that the British Embassy in Washington was strongly opposing the application, and seeking to have the decision at least delayed until after any IRA announcement.

As Soderberg repeatedly emphasised the distinction between Adams and Cahill, and the latter's high criminality rating, Reynolds again became exasperated. 'Dammit, Nancy, I never claimed we were dealing with saints.'

Only President Clinton could break the logjam, she said, and, yes, she would put it to him. Reynolds said to her: 'If his inclination is to say "No", please ask him not to announce that without contacting me first.'

I was told he eventually spoke to Clinton and gave him his personal assurance that a visa for Cahill would remove the final impediment to a permanent ceasefire. Finally, the word came back: 'The President has personally authorised a US visa for Mr Cahill.'

1 September, 1994

'IT'S OVER! (31 August). I can't believe it. I saw it start in Derry and Belfast and I've lived to see it finish. Albert has it for past two days, reads it out to me. A complete cessation of military operations. No qualifications, no strings attached. The word "permanent" not used, says T, because they (IRA) will not — cannot — speak for future generations. He says he is still trying to reel in the loyalists (paramilitaries). "Listen for the Angelus bell, o'er the Liffey swell, ring out on the foggy dew" is the Provo message. In other words, they meant it to be first broadcast on the 12.01 headlines (RTE), after the Angelus. They give it to Charlie Bird on tape, and on scrap of paper, at 11.15 a.m. On that basis, Charlie, of course, has it out live on air within minutes. . . . Clinton rings. "It couldn't have been done without you, Mr President." Major rings, cautious and even sceptical, and T. tells him: "We did it together." — "John (Major) doesn't really believe it's for real," says Albert afterwards He also talks on phone to Hume. They are curiously cool and careful with each other. Is it vanity, rivalry, jealousy? "Posterity" says Bart. "They're already jostling for their place in the history books."

'Champagne with Dick who is generous with praise; he (Spring) made his contribution. I hope Albert and Hume stick together. Hume is my hero, the man who started the movement, but Albert took the ball and ran with it. Albert tells me to ring Vinnie Doyle (Editor, the *Irish Independent*). "What the hell is he giving out about now?" says Vinnie. "Howya, Vinnie," says Albert. "Remember that (election) night in November, '92. You, Joe Hayes and myself. Me going down the tubes. Any regrets, Albert? Only one. I had something going on the North which I think would have worked. I just rang to remind you, and to say, Vinnie, it worked — and it's done." The tribunal (Dáil) debate has started. Some timing! Some stroke? Poor Kevin O'Kelly (former RTE colleague) dead. He saw it start too. And he died just as it finished. . . .'

A few days later, Reynolds had an awkward meeting with an SDLP delegation led by Hume. Apart from tensions between Reynolds and Hume, the SDLP leader and his deputy, Seamus Mallon, were having one of their periodic disagreements. Reynolds was finding it difficult to persuade Hume to be present at the much heralded first meeting between him and Adams. Hume was effectively telling the Taoiseach to meet Adams on his own, that he (Hume) had to go to Vienna, and that he wouldn't be back in time.

I knew Reynolds felt he required the presence of Hume for this controversial exercise which he was pledged to fulfil. Spring had already told him that he did not wish to be present — a visit to Germany would explain the Tanaiste's absence — so it was felt that Hume's presence was essential. It seemed clear to me, however, that Hume was still smarting from what he regarded as earlier rebuffs from Reynolds and Major. However, on the evening of 5 September, Reynolds told me: 'It's sorted out. Adams comes in tomorrow morning.'

6 September, 1994

'*An Bean Rua* (Rita O'Hare, press officer, Sinn Féin) rings: "I'm your opposite number. Where will we go? How will we recognise the building?" Albert enjoys it. "She knows damn well where we are. They cased the joint often enough." Shades of James Dillon (former Fine Gael leader) describing FF (Fianna Fáil) first arriving in the Dáil: "They came in, their pockets bulging with revolvers. . . ." I ask O'Hare if they will be driven in. "No, we're going to walk through those gates." Good thinking — good press officer. Huge media crush around the fountain. Adams, carrying filo fax as distinct from bulging revolver, walks towards me. I shake his hand — Adams is as important as Hume, Albert, or Major, in achieving this — and he, Jim Gibney, O'Hare and SF minders pass through as the Special Branch lads glare at them and the Shinners look impassively back. Afterwards, Albert says to me: "He's (Adams) a cool one." Before we go out to face media, Adams and O'Hare insist on group photograph, even producing a camera. Albert winks at me, then says: "You take it, Philip." (Philip Grant, Garda Special Branch.) Philip doesn't turn a hair, bangs it off and hands the camera to Adams, who says: "That's the first time you boys ever took a picture of us, and then handed us the camera." Outside, a security man tries to push Rita aside. She's onto me like a flash. "That day is over!" Questions fast and furious, but it's all about the pic. Finally someone, Matt Kavanagh I think, gets it. They are about to turn around and go, when Hume and Adams reach across to again shake hands, and the Taoiseach's hands descend on theirs — click — the Triple Crown or the pan–Nationalist mafia, take your pick.'

Six weeks later, telephone contact was established between Reynolds and the legendary UVF veteran Gusty Spence whose shooting dead of a Catholic barman, off the Shankill Road, Belfast, in 1966, was regarded by many Northern Ireland analysts as a contributory factor to the 1969 outbreak of the Troubles.

12 October, 1994

'"I've just had a chat with Gusty Spence," says T. From Malvern Street to Merrion Street! He (Spence) was in at start. Will he be in at finish? Spence says David Irvine, himself, and one other, would like to come down to see Taoiseach. Will he see them on the same basis as Adams *et al*? "Absolutely," says Albert, "if you're going to make the right decision re present speculation that a loyalist ceasefire is on the cards." OK. "In Dublin?" asks T. "Yes" says

Spence. "Private?" "OK." "Is this wise, Taoiseach?" I say. 'It's OK,' he says: 'I gather Fergus (Finlay) has already met them, so Labour will have to wear it.

'Also, the Brits have been bending the rules. John Major approved the recent meeting in the Maze of loyalist paramilitary leaders and loyalist prisoners there.'"

On the following day, I noted:

'Gusty ends it from loyalist side. At CLMC (Combined Loyalist Military Command) news conference, he says they "universally cease all operational hostilities." And he apologises to all who suffered as a result of the Troubles. I believe Spence — that's it; it's over — even though the Brits still won't accept it.'

14 October, 1994

'Major addresses Tory conference in Bournemouth. Albert and he talk for ten minutes by phone pre-speech. Albert tells me that he again presses M. (Major) on basis that he is not up to scratch, either because he doesn't know or isn't told. Shades of "The IRA have better intelligence than your (British) intelligence". Albert demands: "Why are paras going into Belfast? Why are Marines screwing up people in S. Armagh? Come on. John!" He (Reynolds) tells me he believes some of the loyalists will meet him tomorrow in Dublin.'

15 October, 1994

'I talk to Taoiseach in afternoon. He tells me loyalist heavies (he doesn't name them) met with him for two hours this morning. They discuss all aspects, including Articles 2 and 3 etc. They agree they don't matter very much, and that 2 is of no consequence. Any change should be to 3. Also that DUP (Democratic Unionist Party) doesn't speak for them. They say on radio that they may make submission to Forum (Forum for Peace and Reconciliation), but that, at moment, they won't send reps. It may be that Gusty and (David) Irvine were among the guys that met Reynolds.'

Several weeks later, I noted in my diary:

'... Nobody sussed the Albert/Gusty meeting...'

Around this time, Adams led another Sinn Féin delegation to meet Reynolds in his office. On this occasion, Dick Spring attended. Afterwards, he and the Taoiseach told me Martin McGuinness spoke frankly about the need to dispose of armaments. I took a note of what they quoted McGuinness as saying: 'We know the guns will have to be banjaxed.'

A few days after the loyalist ceasefire, while discussing what had been achieved, I said to Reynolds: 'Don't expect compliments. The politically correct liberals despise this peace. If it were to last a thousand years, and not a single other life were to be lost, it would still be hated by those types as a fascist formula, and if it were to collapse, they would celebrate with a chorus of "We told you so". Reynolds merely grinned at me, 'Don't be cynical, Diggy. It doesn't become you.'

About the same time, Mary Holland wrote in *The Irish Times:* '. . . If the pundits are right, and trust between the Coalition partners has been so irreversibly damaged that an early election is virtually inevitable, then it does seem worth noting the particular characteristics which Mr Reynolds has brought to dealing with the North, and how they have contributed to bringing us this far along the road to peace. These qualities are all the more interesting because they are, in many ways, the aspects of his style which, in other areas, have attracted the most violent distaste and angry criticism.

'It has been precisely the skills of a huckster, well, successful entrepreneur — his readiness to take a risk, cut corners, drive a hard deal and, crucially, to back an instinctive hunch with the necessary action — which not only wrested the much longed for "complete cessation" of violence from the IRA, but has since provided, almost single-handed, the momentum to keep the peace process on course. . . .

'Looking back over the past 25 years, it is impossible to imagine any other Taoiseach capable of pulling off this outrageous *coup de théâtre*.'

17

'I AM PRESIDENT OF THE HIGH COURT, I.E. GOODBYEEE'

LONG BEFORE Mary Holland put forward her Reynolds analysis, Bart Cronin and I had arrived at an analogous conclusion. The characteristics which made him such a powerful proponent of the peace process were the same as antagonised such as O'Malley and Spring. Bart echoed Kathleen Reynolds: 'That's Albert. He is what he is. He won't change now.'

24 October, 1994

> 'Chequers —TROUBLE. Nothing to do with talks here. It's Albert, Dick and Harry again. Labour bad mouthing Harry over his office keeping the extradition application from NI, for paedophile priest Smyth, for 7 months until the bastard went back voluntarily to the North. Albert tells me something wrong with Harry's whole AG office operation . . .
>
> 'John F. (Foley) says the deal on Harry is not OK. Harry shouldn't be appointed dog catcher; should be sent to Europe, anywhere but preside over High Court. Fergus talking the same way on flight over. I tell them to stop putting pressure on themselves. They should know Albert by now. A deal is a deal. Harry gets the job. End of story. But I have this recurrent nightmare. Albert appoints Harry; Labour pull the plug; Harry waves a cheery goodbye, "nice to have known you", as we all — barring Harry — head out the gate . . . .'

A few days earlier, after lunching with Harry, I had told the Taoiseach that Harry believed there should be no undue delay in appointing him. Reynolds, although furious about the mishandling of the Smyth case in the Attorney General's office, subsequently told me the 'heads' of the Courts Reform Bill promised to Spring at Baldonnel had been agreed by government almost a fortnight earlier, and that Spring had now been given ample time to deliver on the deal. Harry, he said, had been instructed to give a full explanation of the Smyth affair to the next cabinet meeting on 10 November. Once that was satisfactorily delivered, he said, the appointment could proceed forthwith.

On 6 November, an opinion poll in the *Sunday Independent* showed 55 percent of the public opposed to the Whelehan appointment and only 20 per cent in favour. On the morning of the cabinet meeting, the voters in two Cork city constituencies cast by-election ballots which were to result in opposition victories and a significant slump in Labour preferences.

A post office worker was shot dead during a raid in Newry — republican paramilitaries were responsible — and Justice Minister Geoghegan Quinn announced cancellation of the planned release of nine Provisional IRA prisoners. In the event, the cabinet meeting was largely devoted to consideration of the implications of the Newry murder, and the AG/Smyth issue was adjourned until the following day.

10 November, 1994

'. . . Cabinet 5 p.m., and just as I'm beginning to relax around 7 p.m., comes the wallop. John Foley rings me: "Come down, I've something to tell you." I go down. "We can't buy Harry." He says the decision is off until tomorrow but "we have been overtaken by events on the priest." Baldonnel deal is off. He says Dick and his ministers will not come into tomorrow's (cabinet) meeting if Harry is to be appointed. . . I meet with Taoiseach, Dempsey, Mansergh in Martin's room. I tell them the story from John. Albert looks at me and says: "You know, I'm not sure they will come in. But we'll go ahead with appointment with or without them. Are you worried, Diggy?" We say nothing to pol corrs. They suspect nothing.'

I could not believe this was happening; first of all, that Labour were upping the ante yet again; and, then, that the Taoiseach was not just calling — their bluff (?) but betting all he had that they would ultimately fold. Still, I told myself, crafty operators like Bertie, Quinn, McCreevy, Howlin, Cowen, and others, would not let it get to that. And, yet, I had a feeling that things were finally spiralling out of control. I kept recalling the strangely excited, almost challenging, look in Reynolds' eyes as he said: 'Are you worried, Diggy?'

11 November, 1994

'We LOST. I thought it was OK when Labour said they would go in (to cabinet). I become more confident as the hours go by. Surely they can't stay in there that long (five hours) without working out something. I'm touched by John (Foley) leaving envelope on my desk from Una's (Una Foley, wife of John) mother for my mother's birthday party tomorrow. Dempsey rings me: "Harry has been appointed, also Eoghan Fitzsimons." Brilliant — Labour finally agreed. "No," he says, "they walked out before the decision." Jesus Christ! Albert gambled and lost. We finally got caught. They (Labour ministers) said Harry's explanation not acceptable, and Dempsey says they (FF ministers) just went ahead and appointed him after Labour walked out. Jesus.

'Albert has that excited look in his eye. The same as when we went down the tubes in November '92. He is engaged, involved, but somehow removed from it all. I ask what I tell the pol corrs. He picks up phone and rings Dick. "What'll we tell the press? Is it over, or what?" Just like that. Can't hear Dick, but Albert says Dick says he's got to discuss it with Labour ministers. We dash for Áras (Áras an Uachtaráin) 5.30-ish — rushing over the cliff? — for Harry and Eoghan Fitzsimons appointments.'

'Eerie. We cut across a dark rush-hour city with sirens, etc. I think of Nora Connolly being brought across Dublin to see her father in Kilmainham before he was shot. Áras only needs tapers and guttering torches to resemble some Hollywood horror set. Midnight in the crematorium, matched by her (President Robinson) smile — "like moonlight on a tombstone". Eoghan (Fitzsimons) also with rictus smile. Máire Geoghegan Quinn like Vesuvius before eruption. Harry, of course, beaming. Jiggy Diggy twitching in the middle. "Extraordinary haste," says Bride Rosney. The nightmare coming true. He's President of the H.C. and we're all off to the boneyard. . . . At Áras, Albert talks to Dick by phone. Albert says to me: "No Taoiseach ever sacrificed so much for an Attorney General." Now, that's for fucking sure!'

Back in his office, Reynolds told me he thought Labour might not necessarily be pulling out of government. They might have decided to absent themselves from cabinet as a tactical gesture while the appointment was being made. He gave me to understand that he based this on his telephone conversation from Áras with Spring.

13 November, 1994

'On way to Galway for my mother's (90th) birthday party. Marie driving; me reading the Sundays. They are a disaster. Editorials flay Albert, and Labour are back on ethical pedestal. Harry quoted as saying priest was not thought likely to offend again! A priest found lying dead in gay club abandoned by his cleric pals! We're on a total loser. "Turn the car, Marie. I can't leave him in this shit". She agrees, and brings me home, then off to Galway on her own. "What about your mother?" says Albert. "She'll understand."

'A day of depressing phone calls — 5/6 with Taoiseach — as he rails against unfairness of it all. He insists Harry didn't know about the priest; that Labour accepted that; that a deal was made between four wise men, and Labour cannot deny it; that Labour accepted it would be dealt with Thursday, then Friday; that it is wrong of Labour to say there was no Harry deal. The deal, the deal, the deal — and the pound of flesh. . . .'

On that Sunday, a marathon Labour parliamentary party meeting gave Dick Spring a unanimous mandate to decide whether to stay in or resign from government once the Taoiseach gave his account of the Smyth affair to the Dáil on the coming Tuesday. On the following day, *The Irish Times* editorialised: 'The die is cast. The appointment is made and cannot be unmade. The former Attorney General is now the President of the High Court and cannot, even if he wanted to, add or amplify his account of events. He could, of course, if he were so minded, resign and thus defuse the immediate crisis. . . .'

14 November, 1994

> 'An extraordinary day. An emergency meeting of FF ministers in a.m. with Albert tensely presiding . . . (Seamus) Brennan comes over with talk of having contacted R. (Ruairi) Quinn and that the Taoiseach must come up with specific responses in Dáil tomorrow. He must apologise to Irish people for paedophile priest being on loose for seven months; must not offer defence of AG's office; agree totally changed system in AG's office; tribute to Spring/Labour in government plus regrets to Spring at hurt caused. I meet John Foley who makes similar points. He says: "We don't want an election." Extraordinary late night (2.30 a.m.). session of FF ministers as Máire Geoghegan Quinn, Michael Smith and Tom Savage direct operations. Too many cooks? Albert balks at word "apologise". He tells me in the jacks that other stuff is emerging re AG's office dealing with sexual abuse; that he sent message to him that he should consider his position and at least postpone his swearing in; that Harry responded: "I am President of the High Court." i.e. goodbyeee! He (Reynolds) tells me his gut instinct is that Labour want an election, that they engineered Friday with that in mind. His speech for tomorrow, according to Maire Geoghegan Quinn/Smith, is brilliant. But Albert hyper. His instinct is the game is up . . .'

When I arrived in my office on the following morning (15 November), I was told FF Ministers including Geoghegan Quinn, McCreevy and Cowen, with Mansergh and Savage, had worked on the speech until 5 a.m.; that the word "apologise" would not be used; "regret" was considered sufficient; that, otherwise, the "five points" demanded by Labour were included. When the Taoiseach arrived, he said to me: 'My belly tells me it's not on. They want to get rid of me.'

I noticed as Geoghegan Quinn, Smith and Brennan grew more confident that the problem was going to be resolved, that the Taoiseach, untypically, became increasingly apprehensive and despondent. It was as if he had suddenly awakened to find himself inextricably enmeshed in a terrifying snare. It was summed up in a phrase he used repeatedly over the next forty-eight hours: 'I am being led to my execution.'

15 November, 1994

'. . . Harry first puts it up to the lot of us. Goes ahead and is sworn in. . . Goodbyeee . . . Optimistic messages flow back and forth. Quinn, Howlin, Mervyn, Michael D. all reported as ready to accept "5" points. Brennan up and down with messages. "Quinn says delivery on all five will fix it." "Has anyone confirmed that he is speaking on behalf of Tánaiste?" "Well, no." "My belly," says Albert, "tells me they set this up last Thursday. . . ."

'We depart T's office at 2.25 heading for Dáil. Albert like boxer flanked by handlers, filing down the long corridor to the arena; words of encouragement, Noel Treacy at his shoulder, McCreevy whispering in his ear. Just before we reach Dáil door, Albert mutters something about everyone being under pressure. "Not really," says McCreevy. "Pressure, Taoiseach, as you once told me, is driving home on a filthy Friday night in winter, knowing that you're bollixed unless you have a £14,000 cheque for the bank manager by 10 a.m. Monday morning. That's pressure."

'Albert does the business in Dáil, Says he's sorry to Irish people, to Dick Spring *et al*. Almost immediately, word comes back: "It's not enough." Greg Sparks comes over and says to me in corridor: "It's not enough." I say automatically: "General election?" He pauses, eyes momentarily glazing, then says: "Prob-ab-ly." Jesus. Probably my arse. Suddenly, it's clear. They're going to go for it. Gambling just like Albert. The trick is no election. Shaft Albert but stick with Fianna Fáil? Albert may have walked into a trap. . .'

When I voiced my suspicions about Labour's calculations to the Taoiseach, he didn't disagree but neither did he dwell on it. He told me that when he returned to his office from the Dáil chamber, there was a letter waiting for him from Eoghan Fitzsimons. It confirmed, contrary to what Harry reported to government, that the Smyth case was not the first considered under the 1987 Extradition Act, that there had been one involving a monk named Duggan, in 1992, and that it was a precedent for the Smyth case.

When I reminded Reynolds that he had mentioned something of that nature to me on the previous day, he agreed Fitzsimons had already informed him and his ministers of the Duggan case, but that he also reported conflicting views about its significance; that he (Reynolds) then told Fitzsimons that they required better than 'on the one hand, on the other hand' advice, and asked him to provide them with a definitive opinion in writing. Said Reynolds: 'It came too late. I was on my way to the House. Declan (Ingoldsby) rushed it down, but it was never handed to me.' McCreevy shrugged resignedly. 'I suppose we'd better find out what Labour mean by "not enough."'

Bart Cronin, Sean Duignan and Albert Reynolds thinking it over

18

'I AM WHAT I AM . . . A RISK TAKER'

THE NEXT 48 hours were so turbulent and traumatic that three days elapsed before I sought to synopsise the sequence of events.

My first shock, on the afternoon of 15 November, was when the Taoiseach said to me that he now felt betrayed by Harry. Even his Dáil speech that morning, expressing his regrets about the Smyth affair and criticising the way it was handled by the Attorney General's office, had failed to prepare me for this *volte-face*. I still believed that he was merely expressing a private opinion, and that it would remain private, until he added: 'Harry could become the first senior member of the judiciary in the history of the State to be impeached.'

Even at this late stage, Reynolds was still talking of a general election — "They (Labour) must want an election" — despite my earlier voiced suspicion that Labour was calculating whether they could bring down the coalition, and become part of a new government, without having to face the electorate.

Talking separately with Smith, Cowen and Dempsey, I realised that barring some extraordinary development the government was going to collapse. They all expressed anger and frustration that Harry Whelehan was still hanging tough — they talked openly of 'messages' having been sent to Harry to save the government by stepping down — but what left the biggest impression on me was their unconcealable fear.

15 November, 1994 (cont.)

> 'Late night, Albert calls me to his office. Cowen, McCreevy, Woods, Smith others later maybe — and they're all agog. McCreevy has been talking to his Labour pals. And Howlin has rung Dempsey to say all is not lost. If — wait for it — if Taoiseach goes into Dáil tomorrow, in no confidence debate, and says, if he knew then what he knows now, he would never have appointed Harry, and that Dick was right all along, and he was wrong, it'll be OK.

'I can't believe it. Albert notices. "What's wrong, Diggy? Say what you think." I blurt out: "They'll say we're grovelling just to survive." Albert says simply: "I don't care about that." I say something like: "Why go out this way? If we stick with Harry, you at least go out with your head high." Albert's face hardens: "It has to be done." *Nuair is cruaidh do'n cailleach, caithfhidh sí rith.* I plough on. "Can you trust Labour?" Yes, says Charlie (McCreevy), he's been in touch with Pat Magner or Howlin — one or the other — and then I ask does he (Magner/Howlin) speak for Spring. That will be verified, says Charlie.

'Much later, maybe an hour later, something strikes me. "What about knowing it on Monday?" Albert stares at me. "What about Eoghan Fitzsimons telling you all about the Duggan case?" "We couldn't take it in then," says Albert. "Fitzsimons couldn't make up his mind about its actual significance and effect. I told him to go away and study it in detail, then give me a full written report."

'The others seem to think I'm introducing not so much an irrelevancy as an unnecessary distraction from the central issue. i.e. framing a statement for the no confidence debate which should meet Spring's requirements. They're so human. They're just scared. And it shows. I don't care, not the way they do. "I'm only the devil's advocate," I say.

'Cowen the only one to pick up on it. His legal brain grappling with the possible implications and pitfalls. He begins pacing up and down listing the risks, i.e. if we say this, what about that? Albert seeming not to hear. "You get a formula to deal with that," he says to Dempsey who is drafting something with Woods, I think, in nearby meeting room. At some stage, back in my office, I say to Paddy Teahon: "Spring is on for the treble. He gets rid of Harry; he gets rid of Albert and gets into bed with Bertie without any election."

'Back in T's office, they're still talking. "What about the new AG?", I ask. "Have you checked him out on this?" Now about 1 a.m. but Albert immediately says: "Get him in here. Get him out of bed, if necessary." Again, I say if we go ahead Dick could win game, set and match. I am convinced we are making the wrong move, but I can't think it out, can't articulate it out. Just an instinct. Taoiseach, stick with Harry and, if we go down, so be it.

'Brenda (Brenda Boylan, Taoiseach's private office) comes in and says the AG is outside — 1.30 a.m.? — and I immediately say to Albert: "Look, I shouldn't be here when he comes in." He says OK. Just tired and wanting to go to bed, but I also didn't want to embarrass Fitzsimons. He entered the room with the air of one entering a lion's cage. I simply shook his hand and walked straight out. Did I make a mistake? Could I have helped if I hung around? Probably not.'

On my way home, it struck me that none of the Ministers present mentioned the implications for the Taoiseach of saying one thing about Harry to the Dáil on the Tuesday and then returning to the House to effectively contradict himself on the following day. It seemed to me, that, even if this ensured his survival, he would become a lame duck Taoiseach in perpetual thrall to Labour.

On arrival home, (Wed. 2.15 a.m.) I checked shorthand notes of my brief conversation with the Taoiseach after the Tuesday speech. He had again said his every instinct was that Labour were setting him up. I replied that I didn't believe such as Quinn, Howlin and Taylor were as machiavellian as that. He said he believed the culprits were closer to Spring, advisers such as Finlay, Rogers and Sparks who were now dictating the play. He maintained that if the Fr Smyth case had not materialised, they would have come up with another excuse to bring him down. He added: 'In fact, if Harry had never been a problem, they would have found some other issue.'

When I demurred, he said that, at one stage, he confonted Spring in an effort to get him to say precisely what Labour found so objectionable about Harry, apart from their claim that he was a conservative. He maintained Spring, pacing up and down, kept saying that he couldn't tell him, and that when he (Reynolds) continued to press him. Spring would only say: 'All I can say, Albert, is I can't take him.'

16 November, 1994

> 'It's GONE. I oversleep — "could you not watch that one hour with me?" — and Grace tells me FF ministers wound up, after Eoghan (Fitzsimons) session, at around 5.15 a.m. and were back in again around 7.30. I miss the most astonishing bit of all. By the time I get to Dempsey, ashen faced, they have run the whole gamut from snatching victory from the jaws of defeat to the exact opposite. Either Dempsey or McCreevy got onto Howlin to tell him of this decision to do Spring's bidding, that it was wrong to appoint Harry etc. McCreevy and Dempsey go across and get Spring to sign deal ("On the basis of the statement, prepared by me, being incorporated in the Taoiseach's statement, I will lead my ministerial colleagues back into Government, to complete the Programme for Government. Signed Dick Spring 10.22 a.m, 16.11.94"), and Dick then comes across to confirm. Handshakes, backslaps, relief all round. I missed it. Everyone saying it was OK now; it wouldn't happen again. Three-quarters of an hour later, all tragically changed.
>
> 'It seems Dick, upon his return, is phoned by some guy — who he? — to check out AG on when he told Albert and Co. about the new (Duggan) case.
>
> 'He apparently called AG in and asked him one question, "When?" Eoghan said he told Albert on Monday. Dick then came straight back with Quinn, Howlin, Mervyn, walked into Albert, told him what he had learned, that Albert had misled him and the House, that he knew about Duggan and never told

them, and the deal was off. They pleaded with him (Spring) to go back to AG to fully understand the special circumstances. He said he would not. Raised voices, panic, pleading. Ruairi says they've come for a head, Albert's or Harry's, and it doesn't look as if they will get Harry's. Albert putting his hand on Dick's shoulder and saying: "All right, if that's the way you want it, Dick." Jesus. I miss all that.

'I arrive to see Spring and Howlin — they seemed to be arguing — walking off down the corridor. Then I meet Dempsey who is almost speechless, suddenly aged for such a young guy, and he tells me what happened. It's just unbelievable. Máire Geoghegan Quinn like I've never seen her before, utterly shattered; Smith as if he has been hit between the eyes with a hammer. All standing around Albert, beating their breasts, saying: "We let you down." Albert occasionally taking out the sheet of paper (the note signed by Spring) and looking at it bemusedly. A dud cheque. . . .'

The Reynolds camp now launched a succession of 'stay of execution' attempts while simultaneously making frantic efforts to renew contact with Labour. I noted afterwards:

16 November, 1994 (cont.)

'Death watch. We got three Dáil postponements to try to delay execution. Wild rumour that Cardinal Daly had tried to intervene. Daly was publicly denying it. Surely, the Labour lads would be back with a suggestion on how to get over the problem. Surely, it couldn't end like this? But, from Dick's area, there was this deadly silence. Again and again, the ominous word from Bertie, Dempsey, McCreevy, Brennan, and all the rest — no joy, can't raise anyone, they've put up the shutters . . . .'

By early afternoon, I could see that the Taoiseach was resigned to his fate. When I hesitantly inquired precisely why he changed his mind about Harry, he said that once he finally received the written advice of Eoghan Fitzsimons he had no other choice, as it showed that Harry has misled the government and the Dáil. I had not the courage to say what I believed that, despite the totally unacceptable handling of the Smyth case by his office staff Harry would never deliberately mislead either him, the cabinet or the House.

He compulsively recapitulated the see-sawing events of the previous twenty-four hours, railing not merely at perceived Labour perfidy but hinting also at betrayal from within his own bailiwick. Who timed the revelation of the link between the paedophile priest and the AG's office to spike the Baldonnel deal? Why was he not given the Fitzsimons letter when it went from hand to hand amongst those sitting closest to him in the Dáil, through Declan Ingoldsby, Paddy Teahon, Frank Murray, Noel

Dempsey, Bertie Ahern and yet never got to him. Who rang Dick Spring after a deal was finally signed, sealed and delivered at 10.22 a.m.? Who were the cunning assassins who lured him to his destruction?

Finally, it was time for the Taoiseach to go to the House. I perfunctorily wished him well, aware that he was about to deliver a speech which was effectively a Labour diktat and that his reward would almost certainly be summary Labour execution. I had no conception of how to advise him, and merely asked if he still intended to disown Harry and apologise to Spring. He said: 'I have to play the hand I've been dealt.'

16 November, 1994 (cont).

> 'He (Reynolds) finally delivered the speech in a robot-like monotone, apologising to Dick, saying he would not have appointed Harry if he knew then what he knew now, saying his statement yesterday (15 Nov.) did not refer to Duggan because AG's letter emphasising importance of Duggan arrived late, etc. Then he had to watch Dick with the air of a condemned man staring at the executioner's hand on the switch. We live by the sword, we die by the sword, but this is cruel and unnecessary punishment. No stay of execution, no commutation, no clemency, no mercy.
>
> 'Dick did his thing, prolonging the agony — will he, won't he? — then threw the switch. "Albert never told me... so we will be pulling out of government... etc." Pandemonium in the House. Albert slowly walks the long corridor back. "They intended to do me down all along, Diggy." I don't know. I think they just got lucky. They picked up great cards. The priest was the wild card!'

The Reynolds wake, as after the 1992 election, began almost immediately. But, now, there was no prospect of resurrection. Tea and sympathy were dispensed in the Taoiseach's dining room, which took on the appearance of an executive funeral parlour as Kathleen Reynolds and her daughters Cathy, Leone, Emer and Andrea patiently listened to the condolences of a long line of friends of the *famiglia*. I met Spring and Taylor, surrounded by ministerial and party officials, coming through a corridor leading from the House. We all shook hands and passed on. Interestingly, I had no sense of this being a cynical or insincere gesture. Politicians are gladiators and only the victors can be sure of emerging from the arena.

The drink flowed in my office through the night, a maudlin and curiously celebratory occasion — as with all good funerals — with Cowen temporarily taking his leave to put on a pugnacious pro-Reynolds performance on *Prime Time* and then bursting into tears upon his return.

Smith, McCreevy and Sean Doherty, alternately downcast and side-splitting, dominated the proceedings. McCreevy, in between a merry dissertation on the twin impostors, triumph and disaster, kept saying: 'Albert Reynolds is being hung for the wrong offence.' Cowen, self-accusatory yet defiant, did hilarious impersonations of the dramatis personae including 'Jiggy Diggy'. Doherty, in oracular mode, kept intoning significantly that 'it' was not over yet. A steady flow of casual sympathisers kept the glasses clinking until close to dawn.

After a few hours sleep, I was awakened by a phone call from Grace Fagan, who was warning me not to miss the Taoiseach's resignation speech. Stumbling from bed to shower to taxi, I made the office just as the Dáil bells, like funeral knells, began to sound. I was concerned that he should not make an over-emotional speech. I said to Grace: "He dished it out often enough in his time. He's got to be able to take it now." I needn't have worried. Reynolds parting remarks to a packed chamber were largely unscripted, colloquial but dignified.

'There is only one message I want to get across; that I am what I am, and I don't pretend to be something that I am not. Yes, we all have human failings, but. . . . that's me, that's what I have been, that's what I always will be. . . Above all, throughout my life in politics and in business, I have been delighted to be a risk taker. . . . because I believe, if you are not a risk taker, you will achieve nothing. . . . the easiest way of life is not to be a risk taker. . . . I am quite happy that, having taken the risks, the successes have far outweighed the failures. . . .'

17 November, 1994

'Once you're safely dead, it's bygones be bygones. The opposition leaders, even Dick Spring, pay tributes. . . I wait outside chamber for him. But he wants to be chief mourner as well as the deceased. He planks himself in front of his seat and receives them all, as they file by, handshakes for everyone, a word here, an embrace there, a particular word for Neal (Blaney), (Austin) Deasy — *aithníonn ciaróg ciaróg eile* — Treacy totally downcast, and his pal Eddie Bohan near to tears. Then, looking up at the boys and girls in the press gallery he says: "I'm no use to you now. I never kept a diary" adding — literally famous last words of Albert Reynolds as Taoiseach in the Dáil — "It's amazing. You cross the big hurdles, and when you get to the small ones, you get tripped." He then walks out of the chamber, and says to me: "Did I do it all right, Diggy?"

'To Áras to tender his resignation. I think of Pat Lindsay's tale of a similar occasion. 'I now know why we're going in this direction today. . .' President, so forbidding on the last occasion, is quite pleasant. Michael Ronayne (RTE) wants an interview, but Bride Rosney and I arrange he simply addresses cameras with "and now the time has come to face the final curtain" stuff.

> 'Back, and he notices the (Garda) outriders suddenly peeling away. Because he's no longer Taoiseach? As the man (Enoch Powell) said, all political lives, unless they are cut off in midstream at a happy juncture, end in failure, because that is the nature of politics and of human affairs. . . .'

Shortly afterwards, at an FF parliamentary party meeting, Reynolds loyalists desperately sought to launch a last ditch counter attack. First, Reynolds read out a letter he had received from John Major recording that they had both worked together '. . . in a way in which no two holders of our offices have done in the 70 years or more since Ireland divided.' News then arrived that Harry Whelehan had resigned as President of the High Court regretting that he had not recalled the Duggan case when setting out the facts of the Smyth case for the Taoiseach. The meeting adjourned to assess the implications. I noted:

> 'I'm standing in corridor as they sweep back. "It's not over yet," says Treacy fiercely. "It's not over yet," says Bertie too. They've lost the run of themselves, clutching at straws, they must know that. Everyone talking about "What if Harry had done this earlier?" But he didn't. Albert telling me fellas telling him to hang on and not to resign as leader of FF. But he admits to me that he had, before Harry's resignation news, told the meeting that he would resign "at the wishes of the party." Yet the remnants keep urging him on. This is bunker fever. Where is Wenck? Where is the Ninth Army? Total fantasy. I feel I'm watching from a distance. Stupefying.'

There was widespread confusion. Radio and television reports indicated that Reynolds had resigned at the meeting and that the parliamentary party would meet again two days later (Saturday, 19 November) to choose his successor as leader of Fianna Fáil. Reynolds immediately said to me: 'That's not so. I did not resign. A meeting was not agreed for Saturday.'

Shortly afterwards, during a tense briefing session, the pol corrs put it strongly to me that Reynolds was trying to cling to power, or at least to the leadership of Fianna Fáil. It was the only time I felt overwrought during the entire crisis period. I had no doubt that Reynolds would be universally savaged if that remained the media perception. I desperately tried to convince the pol corrs that he was stepping down, but they remained highly suspicious.

17 November, 1994

'I follow Albert down to Dublin Castle reception for Archbishop of Canterbury. I warn him that tomorrow's newspapers will be full of "Reynolds Clings to Leadership" stories — Return of the Beast From 10,000 Fathoms — "As a martyr ex-Taoiseach, you'll get praise; as Lazarus trying to get back up out of the grave, they'll destroy you all over again, even worse." He says he's not trying to hang on. We've got to get that across, Taoiseach. He asks me how to deal with it. I tell him Tom Ruddy of the Indo (the *Irish Independent*) is out on the Battle-axe landing. "Tell him to ask me if I'm still in the race?" Within minutes, he is telling Ruddy "I'm not in the race. . . and I don't think there should be an election. . . it would endanger the peace process." I immediately ring around to make sure everyone knows.

'I'm drained — it's getting to me — I see Albert to his car, then go over to Greg and Eileen Collins and we drink and chat to all and sundry. As the man said: "They think it's all over. . . . It is now!"'

High-flying advice

19

BRUTON FINALLY BANJAXED... BRUTON TO BE TAOISEACH

IT CERTAINLY seemed over and done with. *The Irish Times* editorialised: 'It is all over now bar some detail. Fianna Fáil and Labour, will form another loveless — though mutually pleasurable union...'

Dick Spring was moving sure-footedly to complete the treble. The underpinning was being carefully checked. Bertie Ahern had been unanimously elected leader of Fianna Fáil after Máire Geoghegan Quinn withdrew a half-hearted challenge. Opinion polls in the *Sunday Independent* and *The Sunday Tribune* clearly indicated, not just that the Irish were overwhelmingly opposed to a general election, but that they strongly favoured continuation of the FF–Lab government under Ahern and Spring. Indeed, for the first time, Labour enjoyed greater national support than Fine Gael, and only 13 percent of respondents favoured John Bruton for Taoiseach — a *Sunday Press* poll estimated he was actually on 10 percent.

The Irish Times led with a story headlined 'Fine Gael May Accept Rainbow Coalition Led by Spring'. A senior Fine Gael figure disconsolately told me that a rotating Taoiseach arrangement between Bruton and Spring was being considered. 'Otherwise, if he fails to form the rainbow, they'll take him (Bruton) out by January at the latest.' I observed to Bart Cronin that Spring might do better than the treble, going for a jackpot which would actually deliver him the Taoiseach's job.

In fact, soon afterwards, Labour upped the ante. Once again, as after the 1992 general election, they appeared intent on humiliating John Bruton. They briefed media contacts that the rotating Taoiseach option was no longer relevant, and that they would be demanding the top job for the full term of any 'rainbow' coalition. Significantly, Fine Gael sources were evasive on the issue and would not specifically rule out such a possibility.

However, Reynolds observed to me that it was a case of Labour again angling for a deal with Fianna Fáil and making Bruton an offer he couldn't accept. And that seemed to be borne out by the 36-point Labour position paper sent to Bertie Ahern as a prelude to the opening formal negotiations for a new FF–Lab government deal. We noted that there was no reference in the document to the implications of Eoghan Fitzsimons' disccussions with Fianna Fáil ministers re the Duggan case on 14 November.

Bruton, as always, was refusing to acknowledge defeat, but few seemed interested. Nevertheless, he persisted: 'Labour withdrew from government on the basis that Albert Reynolds misled the Dáil, but his ministers knew precisely what he knew, when he knew. Labour can't go back in with these people.'

Garret FitzGerald took up the same theme: 'What fails to be considered this week is why the likely outcome of this crisis is the return of Labour to a new coalition with Fianna Fáil under the leadership of one of those principally involved in this (misleading) process.'

The Irish Times columnist Vincent Browne accused Fianna Fáil ministers of originally sweeping the Duggan case under the carpet and then, when it suited their purpose suddenly pretending to find it of enormous significance. The real outrage, he said, was that Dick Spring had all the proof he needed that Fianna Fáil ministers knew fully the significance of the Duggan case (such as that significance was) 20 days before he pulled out of negotiations on the re-formation of the FF–Lab coalition.

This reasoning was widely presented as self-serving and unhelpful. After all, the punishment had been seen to fit the crime. The Taoiseach had paid the ultimate penalty. The President of the High Court had also to resign. The polls showed the public thirst for retribution had been sated. It was time to put the Reynolds–Spring mismatch to rest and move forward — "in the national interest."

But Fianna Fáil nerves were close to breaking point. A demoralised front bench, like drowning men, clung to one last ray of hope, that Ahern and Spring would somehow put the show back on the road. McCreevy stoutly insisted that Fianna Fáil was not for sale, but everyone knew the imperative was to placate Labour in order to survive. The problem was that a caretaker Taoiseach and the new FF party leader were restlessly prowling around each other.

Reynolds still seemed to many to be setting the agenda. He told the FF parliamentary party that Labour had accepted his contention that there could be no legislation on the substantive abortion issue in the lifetime of the government. I then briefed the pol corrs on the "agreed" running of the Spending Estimates for 1995, a move which infuriated Labour. And when Fianna Fáil insinuated that the Estimates decision was Reynolds' responsibility, he forced Ahern to publicly accept that he had asked for his (Reynolds) help to sort out the Estimates.

At one stage, on the eve of publication of Eoghan Fitzsimons' full report on the Fr Smyth file, I leaked that eight more Extradition Act cases, including several dealing with sex abuse, had been discovered in the Attorney General's office. In the Seanad, Reynolds was taxed with having authorised the leak of a highly sensitive document before it was even considered at cabinet. I noted:

1 December, 1994

> I briefed pol corrs on AG's report on the other sex abuse extradition applications in Harry's time. Albert tells the Seanad that he never authorised any media briefing on the contents of the report. Oh, dear. Well, Diggy, if you can't stand the heat, stay out of the kitchen!'

FF general secretary Pat Farrell, and Paddy Duffy, chief adviser to Bertie Ahern, separately rang me with similar messages. The 'boys' felt Albert was becoming something of a loose cannon and should be asked to 'pull back' while the delicate FF–Lab negotiations were being concluded. I replied, somewhat tetchily, that I was not a party member and that any such approach should come from his parliamentary colleagues. However, as we prepared to depart for a Conference on Security Cooperation in Europe meeting in Budapest, an Ahern/Spring power-sharing deal seemed inevitable.

4 December, 1994

> 'Budapest (CSCE meeting) — John Bruton finally puts the kibosh on it on *This Week* with Mark Lane. I hear some of it before going to Baldonnel. He sounded as if he was coming from a home for the bewildered. He wound up accusing the AG of being implicated in a conspiracy to cover up the Duggan case. Fitzsimons rings demanding withdrawal or he'll take legal proceedings — they're still on air — and John makes a kind of half-assed retraction. A complete and absolute fuck up. That's John finally banjaxed. At any rate, it's all over bar the shouting. Albert tells me: "Pay no attention to talk about a few things still to be decided. The (Ahern/Spring) deal is done. It's all over"...'

On the following morning, I glanced through press clippings faxed from Dublin by the Department of Foreign Affairs. They included a front page story in *The Irish Times* by Geraldine Kennedy. She wrote: '. . . The correct sequence of events, revealing the knowledge of Fianna Fáil members of the cabinet about the Duggan case on November 14th, contradicts the information given by Fianna Fáil ministers to *The Irish Times* two weeks ago. *The Irish Times* then reported that Mr Fitzsimons personally conveyed two messages to Mr Whelehan on November 14th and 15th, first, on the threat to the peace process, and second, on misleading the cabinet, in efforts to get him to resign. *The Irish Times* is now satisfied that the messages were conveyed in reverse order, indicating that the Fianna Fáil members of government had full knowledge of the significance of the Duggan case on November 14th.'

The newspaper's inside editorial summed up: 'It is now apparent that virtually all of Mr Reynolds' cabinet colleagues were up to their necks in the misleading of the Dáil. It is beyond credulity that Dick Spring will take their sins upon his own head and carry them back into office . . . .'

The timing of the Kennedy story was critical for Fianna Fáil. Reynolds, trying to stem the tide from Budapest, immediately encountered communications and other problems in his attempts to evaluate the rapidly deteriorating situation in Dublin. To make matters worse, Bertie Ahern, overseer of the practically concluded FF–Lab pact, was attending a EU finance ministers, meeting in Brussels. Amidst the confusion, Labour moved to suspend negotiations with Fianna Fáil until the 'serious issues' raised by Kennedy were investigated by Fitzsimons.

To the consternation of Irish officials, the security co-operation priorities of our delegation to the Budapest conference were now swept aside in face of the sensational developments at home. I watched as Reynolds and Mansergh began a series of telephone conversations with such as Eoghan Fitzsimons in Dublin and Bertie Ahern in Brussels. Throughout that day and into the night, their increasingly desperate attempts at long range damage limitation continued. By 11 p.m., when we boarded the government jet to return to Dublin, I could see the FF–Lab negotiations hung by a thread. By 3 a.m. on the following morning, I realised they had irretrievably collapsed.

6 *December, 1994*

> 'Budapest — John Bruton to be Taoiseach! He went down the tubes yesterday. Today, he's going to form the next government. I really think it's time I got out of this business . . .'

I continued:

'Albert first affected to brush it (Kennedy story) off but I have become used to that kind of initial reaction by him. "Get Eoghan (Fitzsimons) on the phone," he finally said to Martin (Mansergh). The moment Martin began talking to Fitzsimons, I knew we were in deep trouble. Martin is a genius but picking up on human vibes is not his strongest suit. "No, we're not trying to contradict you. . ." And, when the conversation ended, Martin said in a puzzled way: "He is in a very prickly defensive mood."

'Albert is now fully engaged. He decides to miss lunch with other heads of State — consternation among officials — and Martin has another even pricklier conversation with Eoghan. It seems he (Fitzsimons) tells him he will, if necessary, have his story to tell, and nothing will stop him. Jaysus! Albert then phones Eoghan upon which I shag off out of the room. A long and obviously unsatisfactory conversation from Albert's point of view. The (Fitzsimons) message is that he knows exactly what happened that Monday/Tuesday (14/15 Nov.) and he's not going to change his story.

'He accuses Taoiseach of having sent someone — me! — to Vincent Browne telling him two draft copies had gone to him of Taoiseach's Tuesday speech, and that he had approved them when he had not. Albert says he'll ring him back on that, hangs up and grills me. I explain what happened. Albert phones him back to confirm it was me who told Vincent that they were sent to him (Fitzsimons) for approval, but that I never claimed he did approve them. Then comes news of Dick's (Spring) announcement that, on foot of the Geraldine (Kennedy) story, he has suspended negotiations with FF on the formation of the government.

'Unbelievable. Theatre of the Absurd stuff. We're going around in ever decreasing concentric circles. Eoghan faxes us his report of conversations with Harry and it goes to the Forum Hotel, then to Novotel, is finally tracked down too late to get to Albert before he goes to address the conference — *déjà vu!* — and, meantime, Bertie's people, now back in Dublin, are screaming for it. On way to conference, Tommie Gorman (RTE) and Seamus Martin *(The Irish Times)* doorstep Albert in hotel lobby. We're so hell bent on getting away from them that I lead Albert into the hotel kitchens — like a scene from a Marx Brothers movie — absolutely manic stuff. All we say is Geraldine's story is "inaccurate".

'After speech, Albert goes through the (Fitzsimons) report line by line before finally sending it to Bertie. It confirms details of the Geraldine story, but I keep saying to Albert that Labour knew Eoghan told Harry about Duggan before they went into negotiations with Bertie, that Máire Geoghegan Quinn said it all in the Dáil, also that it was in his (Reynolds') speech for Wednesday the 16th which McCreevy and Dempsey showed Spring before Spring signed the famous dud cheque. But Cathy (Cathy Reynolds, Taoiseach's daughter) sums it

> up when she arrives back from city tour and is told the whole crazy saga. She says to her father: "In the present climate, who'll believe us against the new man (AG) on the white horse?" Back in Dublin, although it's after 1 a.m., Taoiseach goes to Government Buildings, I think, and I go to bed. The phone wakes me sometime before 3 a.m. Liam O'Neill *(The Cork Examiner)*. I am quite testy as he goes on about Dick's announcement, and I keep saying we've no more to say about it. Gradually, it sinks in that Liam is not talking about Dick's earlier announcement suspending the talks with FF. He (Spring) has just issued another statement saying the talks have now been "abandoned". Say good night, Dick, Bertie, Diggy and all. . . .'

On arrival at my office that morning, I remarked to Grace Fagan that it was eerily quiet. The new Fianna Fáil ministers who passed by my open door seemed almost literally speechless. Even the departmental officials appeared lost for words. Albert Reynolds, when I spoke to him, returned to the conspiracy theory. Someone had rung Geraldine Kennedy 'on her day off' in order to sabotage the FF–Lab deal. Finlay, Sparks, Rogers and Scally were high on his list of suspects.

7 December, 1994

> 'The wheel of fortune has finally stopped turning, and the little ball rests at last on the blue Bruton spot. The no hoper will form the rainbow on his own terms — no rotation or anything else with Dick — and good luck to him. I'm sorry for Bertie. Dick will be well satisfied. No election, still in government, with a better deal than with Albert, and another two years in power with excellent prospects for the economy etc. He has only a small price to pay — knocking on that office door every morning, being told to come in, and then having to say to John: "Good morning, Taoiseach."

A week later, remnants of the disintegrating Reynolds forces launched a final desperate attempt to disrupt the emerging rainbow coalition. I was instructed to brief that on Wednesday, 16 November, the day Labour pulled out of government, Spring had been told by Fianna Fáil ministers that the Fitzsimons' approaches to Whelehan on the Monday and Tuesday (14/15 Nov) had included a request for Whelehan to 'consider his position or at least postpone his swearing in on the basis of the Duggan case', i.e. that Spring knew all of this in advance of the Geraldine Kennedy 'revelations'.

There followed a *This Week* (11 Dec.) interview performance by Spring which he himself later agreed was 'uncertain'. At one point, under questioning by Mark Lane, he seemed to accept that he had been told by Fianna Fáil ministers, on 16 November, about the Monday approach to Whelehan on the basis of the Duggan case, but he subsequently issued a statement categorically denying that. It all proved a non-issue due to a distinct lack of public interest, especially since most analysts, including Geraldine Kennedy, came down in favour of Spring, on the basis of what they maintained were striking inconsistencies in the Fianna Fáil version of events.

12 December, 1994

> 'Back from Essen. Appropriate (EU Summit) grey industrial setting for *Night of the Living Dead* farewell performance. Having said goodbye to Albert in Budapest, the other leaders are somewhat taken aback when we pop up again. Forgotten but not gone. Still, Albert gets ovation, so too John Major, and Kohl pays them brilliant tribute saying the achievement of T. and Major not just unprecedented in the history of the two islands, but also in terms of the European experience....

> 'Bertie doesn't stay long, goes back to Dublin. He talks to me about the "mistake" of appointing Harry on the Friday instead of waiting until after the Tuesday debate. Albert already saying he now sees the Duggan case had no relevance to the Smyth case, and that he wouldn't have criticised Harry if he had known that. For the love of Jesus. I now know why we're going in this direction today... The Spring thing sputtered and fizzled. Thus ends our forlorn "Ardennes" counter offensive. We retreat on the bunker to await the end.'

Gerry Ryan, talking to me on his TV show, marvelled that a Taoiseach with so much going for him — the peace, a vibrant economy, the largest majority in the history of the State, etc. — could have allowed his government to go down the plughole so rapidly. How did I feel watching it happen?

I said I felt like the parrot on the great ocean liner, watching the ship's magician perform a disappearing trick. Just as he cried 'abracadabra', the liner hit an iceberg, turned turtle almost instantly slid under the waves, leaving nothing but a few bits of flotsam, onto which the parrot fluttered, looked around and said: 'Fantastic, How the fuck did he do that?' David Curtin, public relations officer of An Post, faxed me: 'What happened to the parrot?'

16 December, 1994

> 'Yesterday (15 Dec.), anniversary of the signing of the Downing Street Declaration, John Bruton became Taoiseach as Donal Carey wept with joy. Proinsias de Rossa gets Social Welfare.

> 'John gives hostage to fortune straight away, saying government must always be seen as operating behind a pane of glass. That'll be the day. Playing to the

gallery. Will they never learn? Still, fair play to him, everyone wishes him luck. I say goodbye to all I can get around to in the Department, Paddy Teahon, Brian McCarthy, Colm Butler, Declan Ingoldbsy, Brenda Boylan, so many others. Frank Murray not there, but he rings me. So too Bart (Cronin). Padraig O hUiginn walks in off the street and hands me a bottle of vintage Californian wine from the famous Concannon (originally Aran Islander emigrants) vineyards, the same as we shared in California. I'll miss a lot of this, I suppose.

'Fascinating to watch the way it's done. Like as if the North Vietnamese Army were advancing up the long corridor. Packing and shredding going on everywhere — I'm provided with a big cardboard box — is that the crackle of small arms fire coming from the bottom of the corridor? Pat Moran (Commdt. Pat Moran, Taoiseach's aide de camps) will try to cover our retreat.

'Also goodbye to Grace, John and Martin, Donal Cronin, and the Branch boys, Terry, Philip, Kevin, Peter, Martin, Joe, and the rest. Albert, in his stripped down room, waiting to receive John (Bruton). I just say: "*Chonaic muid an dá lá*. It was a privilege. Good Luck." He thanks me. We shake hands. I'm on my way. Grace asks do I want a taxi. No, I want to walk out. The last thing I do is write a quick note to Harry (Whelehan). What can I say? Good luck. No hard feelings. You're some tulip. Going down the stairs, I bump into John Murray, the office mail man. "Good luck, John." "Will you be all right, Sean?" "Oh, I'll be fine, John." "Well, don't be stuck whatever you do." And he pulls out a copy of a cheque he got that morning for £722,000. "Do you know something, I just went and won the Lotto." I start laughing. Then John starts laughing — the last laugh? — and I say I'm going to have to write a book about all of this.

'Out into a beautiful December day. Down past the fountain. Through the main gate. Picking up speed. Onto Merrion Row. Across the top of the (St Stephen's) Green, Grafton Street, Wicklow Street, Temple Bar — no mobile phone, nobody ringing me, nobody for me to ring — cutting down by Anna Livia "where the seagulls fought and played." Into Ireland International (news agency on Wellington Quay) to Liam (Kelly), Tom McPhail, Dermot McDermott and Mary Carolan. "I'll be across in the Oliver St John Gogarty if anyone wants a drink." A tall stool and a tall glass — "here's to the top and I wish the bottom were a mile away" — and a tall story according to some of the sceptical clientele.

'OK, so where did we go wrong? Do you want to hear this or do you not? Just let me tell you the story. . . ." "Entitled," says the man opposite. 'All right. Now, would you believe, it began with Harry and it ended with Harry . . . .'

INDEX

A

Adams, Gerry 26, 31, 97, 98, 102, 104–7, 118, 120, 123, 138–42, 144, 146–48, 150
Ahern, Bertie 18, 46, 54, 58, 62, 70, 71, 73, 74, 78, 83, 87, 91, 92, 110, 154, 162, 165, 167–72
Ahern, Dermot 7, 24
Ahern, Miriam 18
Allen, Lorcan 60
Allende, Salvador 11
Andrews, Annette 74
Andrews, David 17, 54, 70, 74, 83, 130
Arnold, Bruce 5

B

Balladur, Minister 109
Barnes, Eamon 20
Barrington, Ted 74
Barry, Gerry 52, 53, 124
Bean, Peter 38
Bird, Charlie 55, 56, 63, 65, 93, 149
Blackwell, Annette 130
Blaney, Neal 164
Blatherwick, David 119, 120, 142
Bohan, Eddie 16, 164
Bolger, Jim 131
Boylan, Brenda 16, 160, 174
Brady, Conor 42
Brady, Vincent 7, 24, 70
Bratty, Joe 146
Breathnach, Niamh 81, 83, 113
Brennan, Seamus 23, 37, 47, 54, 69, 75, 83, 156, 162
Briscoe, Ben 70, 71
Brooke, Peter 98, 103
Brooks, Garth 141
Brown, Dr Godfrey 97
Browne, John 59
Browne, Vincent 171
Bruton, John 15, 26, 27, 53, 56, 58, 60, 62, 64, 68, 70, 72, 77–79, 87, 88, 116, 136, 137, 145, 167–70, 172, 173
Buckley, Tara 43
Burke, Ray 5, 7, 37, 44, 47, 51, 54, 69
Burns, Mike 127
Burton, Eithne 112
Burton, Joan 112
Bush, George 30
Butler, Colm 16, 134, 145, 174
Butler, Sir Robert 105
Butler, Sir Robin 103, 120, 122, 127
Byrne, Eric 70, 71
Byrne, Hugh 60

C

Cahill, Joe 148
Calleary, Sean 24
Canterbury, Archbishop of 166

Carey, Donal 173
Carolan, Mary 174
Carroll, Joe 43
Casey, Eamonn 25
Cassidy, Donie 64
Cassidy, Joe 25
Castro, Fidel 30
Ceauçescu, Nicolae 11, 22
Charlton, Jack 28, 145
Christopher, Warren 139
Claffey, Una 43
Clarity, James 22
Clinton, Bill 30, 31, 102, 120, 139, 140, 143, 148, 149
Clinton, Hilary 141
Clouseau, Inspector 116
Colley, George 9
Collins, Eileen 166
Collins, Gerry 7, 24, 69, 79, 91
Collins, Stephen 65, 78
Comiskey, Brendan 25
Connell, Dr 62
Connolly, Nora 155
Cooney, John 43
Cosgrave, Liam 97
Cosgrave, WT 99
Coughlan, Denis 43, 89, 130, 135
Cowen, Brian 16, 17, 31, 49, 66, 78, 83, 94, 95, 130, 154, 159, 163, 164
Cox, Pat 45, 73
Cromien, Sean 74
Cronin, Anthony 13
Cronin, Bart 11, 33–35, 37, 45, 48-50, 53, 58, 69, 96, 97, 109, 125, 133, 149, 153, 167, 174
Cronin, Donal 35, 113, 174
Crotty, Raymond 40, 41
Cullen, Martin 45
Culligan, PJ 82
Cullimore, Seamus 24, 60
Culliton 45
Currie, Austin 68
Curtin, David 173
Cushnahan, John 73

D

Daly, Cahal 25
Daly, Cardinal Brendan 7, 162
Danaher, Gerry 33, 81–83
Davern, Noel 7, 63, 80
de Rossa, Proinsías 31, 69, 145, 173
de Valera, Síle 95
Deasy, Austin 164
Delors, Jacques 28-30, 73, 79, 109–111
Dempsey, Noel 16, 23, 29, 70, 75, 78, 86, 87, 154, 159–62, 171
Denham, Ms Justice Susan 130, 131
Desmond, Barry 71, 91
Desmond, Dermot 92
Dillon, James 150
Doherty, Mickey 65
Doherty, Sean 5, 164
Dougal, Jim 122
Dowling, Brian 43
Doyle, Anne 1, 2
Doyle, Vinnie 66

Duffy, Joseph Dr 25
Duffy, Paddy 169
Duggan, Fr 157, 161, 163, 165, 168, 170
Duignan, Marie 3, 5, 53, 76, 146, 147, 155
Duignan, Sean 60, 155
Dukes, Alan 68
Dunlop, Frank 2, 59
Dunne, Eileen 2
Dunphy, Eamon 77, 127

E

Eames, Robin 101
Elder, Raymond 146

F

Fagan, Grace 109, 161, 164, 172, 174
Fallon, Sean 16, 49
Farrell, Pat 54, 59, 63, 169
Farrelly, John 68
Finlay, Fergus 75–77, 82, 85, 88, 113, 114, 117, 118, 120, 121, 127, 133, 151, 161, 172
FitzGerald, Dame Eithne 16, 90, 112
FitzGerald, Garret 14, 25, 40, 97, 137, 168
Fitzsimons, Eoghan 154, 155, 157, 160–62, 168–71
Flynn, Bill 139
Flynn, Padraig 16, 20, 31, 32, 49, 57, 60, 63, 65, 69, 70, 75–78, 89
Flynn, Ray 139

Foley, John 85, 86, 88, 91, 94, 111, 113, 123, 124, 127, 131–36, 147, 153, 154, 156
Foley, Una 154

G

Gallagher, Dermot 143
Geoghegan Quinn, Máire 1, 16, 17, 31, 49, 75, 83, 126, 133, 154–56, 162, 167, 171
Geraghty, Des 69
Gibney, Jim 101, 150
Glennon, Chris 43, 54, 58
Glennon, Joe 145
Gonzalez, 30
Goodman, Larry 12, 33, 50, 115
Gorman, Tommie 111, 171
Grant, Philip 150

H

Hamilton, Justice Liam 36, 44, 51, 71, 112, 115, 116
Hand, Michael 65
Hardiman, Adrian 51, 81, 82
Harney, Mary 23, 45–47, 53, 78, 145
Harris, Eoghan 127, 136
Haslam, Jonathan 38, 137
Haughey, Charles 2, 4, 5, 9, 10, 12, 14, 16, 19, 21, 32, 33, 37, 40, 47, 63, 84, 86, 98
Hayes, Joe 66
Heath, Edward 97

Hendron, Joe 31
Hennessy, Mark 43, 137
Hickey, Henry 44, 113
Higgins, Michael D. 83, 87, 88, 137, 157
Higgins, PJ 79
Hilliard, Colm 24
Hilton, Stephen 59, 63
Hogan, Dick 55, 56
Holland, Mary 152, 153
Hone, Evie 10
Houghton, Ray 145
Hourican, Liam 2
Houston, Whitney 119
Howlin, Brendan 83, 85, 154, 157, 159–62
Hume, John 97, 98, 102, 104-6, 118, 123, 138, 144, 145, 149, 150
Humphreys, John 119
Hurd, Douglas 124, 126

I

Ingoldsby, Declan 16, 145, 147, 157, 162, 174
Irvine, David 151

J

Jacob, Joe 16
Joyce, Joe 133

K

Kavanagh, Denise 55
Keating, Paul 30, 131
Kelly, Donal 43, 64, 68
Kelly, Liam 3, 141, 174
Kennedy, Edward 139
Kennedy, Geraldine 5, 116, 130, 131, 170–72
Kennedy, Jean 139
Kenny, Shane 61
Kerrigan, Gene 34, 130
Kerrigan, Mary 130
Kerwick, Lavinia 29
Killeen, Tony 95
Kinnock, Neil 31
Kirk, Seamus 69
Kirwan, Wally 5
Kissinger, Henry 133
Kitt, Michael 24
Kitt, Tom 74
Kohl, Helmut 30

L

Lake, Anthony 139
Lane, Mark 169, 172
Lenihan, Brian 32, 64
Lenya, Lotte 6
Leyden, Terry 24
Lindsay, Pat 164
Liston, Eoin 56
Little, Joe 60
Lord, Miriam 55, 65
Lydon, Don 24
Lynch, Jack 130
Lyne, Rod 123, 124, 127
Lyons, Denis 24

M

Mac Aonghusa, Proinsias 26
MacCoille, Cathal 34
MacGiolla, Tomas 31, 71
Magee, Rev. Dr Roy 101, 103, 126

Magner, Pat 85, 160
Maguire, Conor 113
Major, John 30, 31, 38, 96, 99, 100, 102–5, 118, 119, 122, 124–26, 137–39, 143, 147, 149–51, 165, 173
Mallon, Seamus 138, 145, 149
Manning, Maurice 68
Mansergh, Martin 14, 15, 66, 72, 75, 98, 101, 102, 104, 118, 119, 121–123, 125, 127, 141, 146, 154, 156, 170, 171
Mara, PJ 1, 2, 12, 23, 114
Martin, Seamus 171
Mayhew, Sir Patrick 104, 124, 126, 142
McCarthy, Brian 174
McCloskey, Frank 143
McCreevy, Charlie 1, 10, 16, 17, 26, 37, 49, 66, 68, 70, 83, 154, 156, 157, 159–62, 164, 168, 171
McDaid, Jim 32, 69
McDermott, Dermot 174
McDowell, Michael 45, 68, 82, 93, 137
McEllistrim, Tom 24
McGlinchey, Dominick 140
McGuinness, Diarmuid 82
McGuinness, Martin 123, 137, 140, 142
McKenna, Gene 43
McKernan, Paddy 74, 110
McLoughlin, Marie 124
McMahon, Brendan 106

McPhail, Tom 174
McSharry, Ray 31, 45, 47, 64, 74, 79, 111
Mengel, Dr 15
Millan, Bruce 110
Mills, Michael 43
Milotte, Mike 34
Mitterand, François 30
Molloy, Bobby 46, 53, 100
Molyneaux, James 103, 121, 144
Moran, Pat 174
Morgan, Dermot 3, 16
Morgan, Donagh 8, 16, 145
Morrison, Bruce 104, 139, 147
Morrison, Danny 146
Moses 114
Mother Teresa 50
Moynihan, Daniel 139
Mulhall, Dan 110
Murphy, Annie 26
Murphy, John 41
Murphy, Mike 5
Murray, Frank 108, 112, 113, 162, 174
Murray, John 174

N

Nally, Dermot 14, 74, 118, 124, 136
Newman, Jeremiah 25
Nixon, Richard 3, 133
Noonan, Michael J. 24, 69

O

O Cuiv, Eamon 24

O hUiginn, Padraig 6, 13, 14, 74, 79, 109, 174
O Huiginn, Sean 118, 125
O'Byrnes, Stephen 12, 51, 86
O'Clery, Conor 139, 143
O'Connell, John 83
O'Connell, Maurice 74, 79
O'Connor, Sinead 23
O'Donnell, Gus 38, 121–25, 127, 137, 138
O'Donoghue, John 7, 24, 69
O'Dowd, Niall 143
O'Farrill, Romulo 146
O'Hanlon, Rory 7, 24, 26, 44
O'Hare, Rita 42, 150
O'Keeffe, Ned 69
O'Kelly, Kevin 149
O'Kennedy, Michael 7, 24, 37, 47
O'Leary, John 24
O'Leary, Olivia 77
O'Leary, Sean 64
O'Mahony, TP 119
O'Malley, Desmond 9, 12, 23, 29, 31–34, 36, 44–45, 47, 49–54, 67, 68, 78, 79, 81, 137, 153
O'Malley, Pat 32
O'Neill, Liam 51, 172
O'Reilly, Emily 43, 108, 111, 112, 121, 130, 131
O'Rourke, Mary 7, 62
O'Rourke, Sean 65, 125
O'Toole, Fintan 4, 34, 51, 61

P

Paisley, Ian 121

Parkinson, Cecil 17
Powell, Enoch 165
Prendergast, Peter 2
Prince Charles 74
Princess Diana 74
Prone, Terry 17, 54, 59, 61

Q

Queen Elizabeth 74
Quinn, Ruairi 66, 74, 78, 83, 85, 90, 94, 95, 116, 156, 157, 161, 162

R

Rabbitte, Pat 71
Rasmussen 103, 109
Reid, Fr Alex 98, 101, 141, 148
Reno, Janet 148
Reynolds, Albert 1–8, 12, 14, 16–18, 21, 23–33, 36–41, 43–47, 49, 50, 52–54, 56, 57–59, 61, 62–73, 75–77, 79–87, 89–102, 104, 106, 107, 108–22, 124–130, 131–42, 144–48, 150, 151, 153, 155, 157, 162, 163, 165, 166, 172, 173
Reynolds, Albert Jnr 4
Reynolds, Andrea 4, 163
Reynolds, Cathy 4, 163, 171
Reynolds, Emer 4, 163
Reynolds, Gerry 98
Reynolds, Kathleen 4, 60, 61, 111, 116, 125, 145, 153, 163
Reynolds, Leone 4, 163

Reynolds, Miriam 4
Reynolds, Philip 4
Robinson, Mary 1, 4, 50, 107, 155
Robinson, Peter 107
Rock, Jean 11
Rogers, John 85, 172
Ronayne, Michael 130, 164
Rosney, Bride 155, 165
Ross, Shane 127
Ruddy, Tom 166
Ryan, Gerry 173
Ryan, Tim 43, 119

S

Savage, Tom 2, 3, 6, 13, 17, 33, 54, 55, 59, 80, 113, 145, 156
Scally, Willie 85, 112, 113, 133, 172
Schacht, Chris 22
Seamus, Brennan 65
Sherwin, Sean 54
Smallwoods, Ray 146
Smith, Dr Michael 16, 17, 23, 24, 46, 49, 83, 156, 159, 162, 164
Smurfit, Michael 92
Smyth, Fr Brendan 135, 153, 155, 157, 159, 165, 169, 173
Soderberg, Nancy 139, 148
Soskovetz, Oleg 132
Sparks, Greg 85, 91, 112, 113, 133, 157, 166, 172
Spence, Gusty 150, 151
Spring, Dick 23, 28, 33, 66–73, 76–78, 81–83, 86, 89, 90, 92, 94, 97, 100, 102, 103, 105, 107, 108, 110, 112, 114, 116–18, 120, 121, 126, 127, 129, 131–34, 136, 138, 142, 145–47, 149, 153–157, 159, 160, 163, 164, 168, 170–172
Stagg, Emmet 92
Strangelove, Dr 15
Sullivan, Sinead 11

T

Taylor, John 121
Taylor, Mervyn 83, 85, 157, 161, 163
Teahon, Paddy 109, 110, 113, 145, 160, 162, 174
Thatcher, Margaret 17, 97, 127
Treacy, Noel 16, 21, 157, 165
Turner, Martyn 18
Tutty, Michael 74
Tynan, Maol Muire 27, 43

W

Wallace, Mary 24, 69
Walsh, Joe 37, 83
Walshe, Dick 43, 58
Weir, Jack Dr 97
Whelehan, Harry 1, 18–21, 26, 27, 36, 44, 78, 82, 116, 129, 133–35, 154, 155, 157, 159, 160, 162, 163, 169, 170, 173, 174
Wilson, John 83

Wilson, Senator Gordon 101
Woods, Mary Rose 3
Woods, Michael 18, 54, 60, 75, 83, 84, 159, 160

Y

Yeltsin, Boris 131, 132